T0162684

Showroom

The Saga of a Family,
a Car Business and
the Seven Deadly Sins

Sam Markley

iUniverse, Inc.
Bloomington

Showroom
The Saga of a Family, a Car Business and the Seven Deadly Sins

iUniverse books may be ordered through booksellers or by contacting:

iUniverse
1663 Liberty Drive
Bloomington, IN 47403
www.iuniverse.com
1-800-Authors (1-800-288-4677)

ISBN: 978-1-4620-0768-4 (sc)
ISBN: 978-1-4620-0770-7 (dj)
ISBN: 978-1-4620-0769-1 (ebk)

Printed in the United States of America

iUniverse rev. date: 5/12/2011

Dedication:

To Ephraim "Frenchy" Gagnon
Rest in Peace

Acknowledgements

I would like to thank Paula Panteleakos and Ronald P. Coderre for their invaluable assistance in the editing of this book

Chapter One

The Way It Was

"They paved paradise and put up a parking lot"
The Counting Crows

2009

Curiosity made me take Exit 89 off the turnpike. A fire was burning within my gut to see for myself what seemed not very long ago to be impossible. Ward Chevrolet, a 25-year rival that at times posed severe competitive problems, and at times provided a valuable ally in our joint war on corporate elimination, was gone. The signs that once illuminated the night were black; the showroom and service departments that once were the center of activity in a growing, busy car dealership were empty–the showroom windows uncluttered with only the outdated sale of a week gone by providing a glimpse into the suddenness of the closing. The streets of the downtown parking lot that had once been lined with new cars and trucks were vacant with weeds growing from the unoccupied asphalt. An eerie silence pervaded the air, a silence that punctuated the awful realization that Ward Chevrolet was, indeed, closed.

It wasn't long ago that Ward was a capable and viable combatant in our mutual war for customers. Geographically, there was too little distance between us. Anybody who was searching for a new car within a twenty-mile radius would go to both stores to compare prices, facilities, the color of the salesman's tie, the cleanliness of the rest rooms–whatever button needed to be pushed to provide the incentive to buy from one dealership versus the other. Many times these decisions left one of us upset. Most of the time what we considered the wrong decision by a customer to go to our competitor left us bitter with disappointment and a determination to get the "next one." These everyday disagreements and business defeats went on for twenty-five years, but somehow, through it all, Pete Ward and I became friends. Our battle was a border war, not a personal one. There were no vendettas. Our families got to know each other and our wives became close. Somewhere along our very similar paths, we had found a common ground. I respected Pete Ward a great deal. He could be pompous and arrogant, sometimes too filled with himself, but he was a solid family guy and a good businessman. We enjoyed our times together—an occasional lunch, a mutual road trip to a dealer conference, or a meeting at one of our sons' games also competing against each other at two rival area high schools. Someone once said, "you should keep your enemies close." That wasn't necessary in our case. I always thought it was more of a pleasure to be in competition with Pete Ward because I knew that no matter what went on in the sales situation, the customer would be treated honorably. We weren't at odds in integrity. For that virtue, we shared a strong commitment. The recession and the mismanagement of corporate America left Pete with little choice but to abandon his investment and move on to more meaningful pursuits. I wished him well.

When I made the decision to sell my dealership due to family problems and stress-related health issues three years ago, it was Pete Ward who called to see if everything was all right. Now our dealerships were both deleted from the business directory of the local scene. Some critics, unknowing of the good things the two of us did for our respective communities, probably relished the fact that we were no longer in business, but as the words from a popular song said it best, "…you don't know what you've got 'til it's gone."

The road off of exit 89 on the turnpike led to the downtown area of Miller Falls, Connecticut. There were once restaurants and diners and banks and a car dealership that occupied the better part of the center of town. Those were the good old days.

Chapter Two

As Time Goes By

"Grow old along with me!
The best is yet to be . . ."
Robert Browning

I can remember clearly the first day I walked into the showroom at Cassidy Motors. Everything was new and shiny, ready for the grand opening. It was 1974. I was brimming with confidence and enthusiasm for my new position, but, at the same time, I was harboring doubts about whether this chapter of my life would have a successful outcome. I wondered if I had made the right decision to give up my life in Boston to undertake this new adventure. Time would tell, but I was going to give it my best shot. I owed that much to my father for giving me this opportunity and for entrusting me with the responsibility of bringing success to the new dealership. This was a huge gamble for my father. He was putting his faith in the hands of his inexperienced younger son. I vowed to make his decision one that he would not regret. The road would be long and the path would be sometimes littered with obstacles, but I was comfortable in knowing that I had made my choice and I believed I was where I was suppose to be.

Spring 2006

How much of life can be attributed to fate? How much of the outcome of our lives do we really have a say in? Is free will a tool we are given to influence the direction our lives take, or are the twists and turns of fortune, the unexplained luck of the draw, or the unfortunate bounce of the ball totally out of our control?

There are many unanswered questions as to why our lives turn out the way they do. Certainly, we have a modicum of control over the end product, but, for the most part, life goes speeding by without many chances to influence the direction we are headed. It often appears that we are just along for the ride. Is this a controversial view? Probably, but this is what I truly believe. For instance, I believe that I was meant to go through life with Katie at my side. As many times as I have found ways to screw up that relationship, she has brought it back together. Had I married someone with the same personality flaws as I have, the relationship wouldn't work. She doesn't have the vindictive gene, or the wandering eye disease, or the irrational temper syndrome. She doesn't possess the big ego, or the competitive fervor, or the unforgiving persona. I believe relationships fail when the two parties possess irreconcilable similarities. There has to be an ebb and flow, a Yin and a Yang, a Punch and a Judy. How many times has the 'couple that has everything' ended up in divorce court?

Katie can look at a pile of weeds and see roses. She can bring an inner light to a darkened room. Her patience astounds me, not only with our kids and our grandchildren, but with people she deals with every day who deserve a lot worse, and with me, her irrational, argumentative, grumpy old husband. Any discussion of the outcome of my life–where I worked, who I influenced both positively and negatively, how I related to friends, relatives, customers, perceived enemies, pets, etc.,–has to include the influence Katie had in mitigating my combative nature. As the song goes, she's the "wind beneath my wings." Without Katie, I very well could have been an Irish drunk or a character out of a John Updike novel, sitting in a bar living my life over and over again in a dream world of exaggerated athletic prowess.

I owe my life to Katie. So when she voiced her concern over the direction our lives were heading, I was wise to listen. I had already had one heart episode, in the late fall of 2000. Five blocked arteries, three stents, and a total change of diet and lifestyle were my Christmas presents that year. Now I was back, almost one hundred percent. Mortality can smack you in the face, leaving you with more humility and a clearer view of your own importance. Nobody is irreplaceable–if they were, Winston Churchill would still be alive.

It was March of 2006. Six years had gone by since my episode. Business sucked. The bills were mounting. Income was down. The economy was showing signs of going in the tank. Katie was detecting familiar signs of stress in my face and in my mannerisms. It was time to sell. We had discussed selling the business before, but I kept thinking of the legacy of sixty-five years as a dealership that my father had left me to be the steward of. I had stubbornly hung in there, hoping that the times would get better. But times didn't get better. I looked around at the dedicated employees that had shared my last days in the car business and I grieved for them for I knew how difficult the sale of the dealership would be for most of them. I thought about their families and recalled the glorious moments we all shared when one of them got married or had children or fell in love. We were a close-knit family of people who shared a passion for selling cars and taking care of our customers. They made coming to work enjoyable, at least until the last days when the inevitable had everyone on pins and needles. I knew that I could never thank them properly for all the many years of loyalty to Cassidy Motors. Memories of so many good times were overtaking my mind as I thought back to when we began in the business, the trials and tribulations, the glaring mistakes, and the glorious triumphs. It would be difficult to leave these people and move on to another place in another time, but the fond remembrances would stay with me forever for it was here that we spent a large portion of our lives. This place had become the home of our extended family. My thoughts turned to the people who had passed on–my father, my mother, my brother Chip, Francois, Henry, Maurice, Buzz, Mark, Benny. I shut out the lights for the last time and stopped briefly to look back. Sadness filled my soul. I took some solace in knowing that our spirit and the spirits of the many people who worked for us through the years would forever live in this showroom.

Chapter Three

From The Ground Up

"Mighty things from small beginnings grow."
John Dryden

Spring 1976

I was happy that my first year and a half in the car business was complete. We had dug out from another brutal New England winter and were looking optimistically to the spring selling season. All my early troubles with personnel were in the past, my relationship with my father was going unexpectedly well–except for salary negotiations, and the mood in the dealership was decidedly better. Everything was in place to truly make my mark in this business that I had once sworn I would never get into. Other than Francois, who had been with the dealership since before I was born, the sales staff was all new–three young guys whom I believed would eventually be good, but they definitely had a ways to go. Their lack of experience was frustrating.

"You take them. I have to make an important phone call."

"I can't take them. I'm expecting my customer from Saturday. They said they'd be here in half an hour. I guess that leaves you, Tory."

"Who made you the boss? You can see by the way they're dressed that they don't have any money, and it's obvious they're here to kick tires. I don't want to get stuck with them and miss out on a real customer."

Unfortunately for my three new rookies, I heard their conversation from my corner office. I recognized the couple that was roaming the lot unattended and immediately paged Francois to go out and see what the Greenbaums were interested in. Francois had successfully concealed his secret for years of not being able to read or write. In spite of his shortcomings, he was an outstanding salesman that people naturally gravitated to. My father had written his deals for him since he came to work at Cassidy's at the end of World War II. That duty had now been passed on to me.

The Greenbaums were chicken farmers who were too busy with their farm to shower and dress appropriately when they were in the market for a car. Francois greeted the old Jewish couple with a friendly, "Bon Jour!" He then disappeared with the two farmers outside into the yard to look at new cars. I waited for a few minutes to react and then exploded at the befuddled rookie salesmen.

"You three get in here, NOW!"

I slammed the door behind me as the three entered my office. My Irish temper was showing visibly on my red face as I collectively berated them for the callous way they were approaching their new jobs. I reminded them that the number one responsibility they had as a salesman at Cassidy Motors was to meet and greet every customer, regardless of whatever preconceived evaluation they had made on that person's looks, or status, or ability to buy a vehicle. They were there to represent me in a professional and respectful manner and, if they weren't able to do that in the technique I demanded, they had no business working for me.

My anger quickly subsided and so did my rapid-fire rhetoric. I began to quietly reiterate that pre-judging a customer is one of the fatal flaws of the business. I told the whipped threesome to "treat everyone the same. Never assume anyone is beneath you or not worthy of your time."

I was about to finish the meeting when there was a knock on the door. It was Francois. The Greenbaums had decided on a brand new Impala, the most expensive car we had on the lot. They wanted to pay in cash and Francois wanted me to count the money before he turned it into the office. I made the three new guys sit and watch as I counted the cash. The money smelled of chicken manure because it had been in Mr. Greenbaum's dirty pocket in the pants he was wearing when he had cleaned the chicken coop hours before. I assured the new guys that the money was still green and still worth the government currency it represented.

The next day the Greenbaums came to pick up their new car and each salesman went out of their way to greet them. One of the novices changed the license plates from the trade-in and never mentioned the stench that seemed to last for hours on his hands. Francois, in his wise old French manner, thanked the young man for his help but reminded him that any stench that came from the Greenbaums also came with a nice commission. Francois and I laughed at his remark and I hoped that there had been a permanent lesson learned. In the car business, you should never judge a book by its cover because that "book" could be a best seller.

Francois Gaston was indeed an institution at Cassidy Motors. Like so many of his fellow French compatriots who came down from Canada to work in the various mills in Danville, he was nicknamed, "Frenchy." Francois really liked women. He would flirt with every woman who came near the dealership. With some, he was successful and therefore carried a reputation as a womanizer. His French wife of many years knew of his transgressions, but was content in her tolerance because of their advancing ages. She was a feisty woman who wasn't afraid to put Francois in his place. She once threatened to stick a fork in his groin at a Christmas party if he wouldn't stop flirting with the waitress. In spite of his weakness for the opposite sex, he and his wife seemed to be perfect for each other.

I had known Francois since I was a small boy growing up. Whenever I visited the dealership to see my father, he would always make a big deal of my being there. When I took over the management of Cassidy Motors, I was initially worried how he would react to my being in charge. I soon grew to love the man and counted on him for almost everything. Although you would think he was limited by his illiteracy, he was simply the cleverest man I ever knew. When Katie and I first moved into our house, I came to rely heavily on Francois to help me with the many handyman jobs that had to be done. One day, after hours attempting to put together a swing set in the backyard, Katie called Francois and asked him to come over and save me from myself. She knew how frustrated I got attempting to make sense out of directions that I claimed were written by some sadistic bastard. Francois came over and while I was attempting to read the directions to him, assembled the whole thing without looking at one diagram. He never ceased to amaze me.

Francois was one of those characters in your life that forever hold a place in your heart. He bore a striking resemblance to Bob Hope, was rarely without his ever-present cigar, and loved gin and tonics. He was a proud member of the Old Hickory Regiment of the Army that was part of the attack force that stormed Omaha Beach on D-Day. He later fought in the Battle of the Bulge. He was proud of his participation in the war, but as he got older, his mind became a trap for memories that were increasingly more vivid of fallen comrades and the other atrocities he had witnessed during the war. He would often cry when he talked about World War II. The longer he lived, the more he talked and the more he cried.

As an employee of Cassidy Motors, Francois was well known and extremely well liked, especially by his fellow French-Canadians. He would do almost anything for any of his customers, including getting up in the middle of the night to help someone who was stranded. My father thought the world of him, but I often wished that he would someday tell him that. I think the fear that Francois would ask for more money kept my father from telling him what he truly thought of him. The two of them worked together their entire adult lives and, in spite of rumors to the contrary, shared a great bond of respect and admiration. Although he had his faults and at times could try our patience with his antics, in my mind, and I know in my father's mind as well, Francois was invaluable.

Chapter Four

Roots

"Be thou the rainbow in the storms of life."

Lord Byron

February 1978

Our new life in Danville afforded Katie and me a chance to settle into marriage and establish our careers. Through the recommendation of one of my father's friends who was the president of the local bank, Katie was able to secure a nursing job at the local hospital, in Cargill Falls, just ten miles from where we lived. The administration and the doctors at the hospital welcomed her arrival for it was a rare occasion when they had the opportunity to hire someone with her background as a big city emergency room nurse. She was good. Her new salary was more than double what I was being paid so it helped in the management of our budget. Our combined income was enough to purchase the cute little cape on Beverly Avenue in the Forest Park section of town that we loved from the moment we saw it. The house reminded us of a gingerbread house in a fairy tale. We were soon busy saving money to buy furniture one room at a time. We shared a very basic philosophy that worked well for us as newlyweds of not buying anything we couldn't pay for with cash. Other than our mortgage payment and related monthly bills, we wisely avoided any debt. We were often ridiculed by our friends and some of our neighbors for the empty rooms and the windows without curtains, but we were determined to stay the course in our own very conservative and wise manner. In due time, the house was complete. Life was good and our careers were in full bloom. Of course nothing lasts forever.

The end of 1977 and the beginning of 1978 brought a couple of huge surprises that would profoundly affect our lives. The first surprise was the result of a lot of hard work with a great deal of early disappointment. For Katie, her announcement in November that she was pregnant was the culmination of many months of trying. I was beginning to think I was the problem for we tried everything. I would get calls in the middle of the day with instructions to get home as soon as I could because her temperature was just right and her eggs were at their most fertile. When that didn't work, she had me change from briefs to boxer shorts. My old roommate from Boston, Baxter, stopped by one day and was laughing at me when I told him everything she was putting me through. I was so frustrated at one point that I told her to ask Baxter to come over and give it a try. I took a pretty good slap for that suggestion.

Baxter and I had been buddies since high school. We moved to Boston in 1970 to experience the city life and to reap some wild oats. Baxter was short in stature but big in charm and swagger. He believed that with his dark hair, good looks and perpetual tan, he could get any girl that was on his radar. For the most part, that was true. In contrast, I was more the "Richie Cunningham" type, taller, but decidedly less experienced with women. My "Aw Shucks" approach was effective but not nearly as successful. Along with my faithful dog, Sam, Baxter was my best friend. The two of them shared a penchant for chasing any female stray they came across.

When I first met Katie in Boston, the dynamic changed in our apartment. We all became more civil, including the dog. Months later Katie and I decided to get married and move back to Danville; it wasn't long before Baxter followed. I was glad to see Baxter because I needed someone to vent to. This whole trying to get pregnant thing was draining me in more ways than one. The biggest problem for me was I felt like some old warhorse that was put out to pasture and brought into the barn whenever the young filly needed some loving. This was hardly the stuff of romance novels.

All who knew us, especially my father who more than once asked the people at work where I was and was told I was breeding, welcomed her gleeful birth announcement. Katie was delighted and immediately went into the nesting mode. Every word out of her mouth was about getting the house ready for the baby. It's safe to say there was probably never anyone who was ever more excited about having a baby than she was. I can categorically state that fact because I had to live with her constant state of euphoria until I thought my brain was going to freeze.

With all the excitement that was generated by her announcement, it was easy to forget the miserable state of the economy that was sucking the life out of our business. Sky high interest rates were a major deterrent to potential buyers who were being hammered from all sides by the double digit inflation and the double digit unemployment that were the legacy of the Jimmy Carter presidency.

In January of 1978, the weather seemed to be adding more hurdles to our misery. Four weeks in a row we had a measureable snowfall. In the northeastern part of the country, there is nothing that affects the car business like a significant snowstorm. In anticipation of a storm, all the cars have to be moved to allow the snowplow access to the yard. After the snowfall, plowing would take most of the night to complete, a job that somehow I ended up with. The next day all the cars had to be cleaned off, many jumped when the batteries would go dead, then moved back into position. It was an exhausting job that took the entire sales staff many hours of non-productive work to complete. Snow removal days were generally considered a loss for all concerned. In particular, the dealer would take the biggest hit because very little was being done in terms of generating income, yet the workers would still get paid. Long hours and little income! We were all looking forward to February.

The first couple of days of February were beautiful. The sun was out and thoughts were turning to spring, which certainly couldn't be far away. On February 3rd, an innocuous weather forecast outlined the possibility of a significant storm developing along the Virginia coast. It was predicted the storm would hit the New England region early

Monday, February 6th. When no storm arrived in the morning, many people across New England went to work as usual. Around three o'clock in the afternoon, it began to snow significantly. After moving all the cars in preparation, we sent the employees home early as a precaution. I stayed at the dealership until five o'clock to finish some work. The phone rang like it was in a panic mood. It was Katie.

"Sean, when are you coming home? The weatherman is saying the roads are nearly impassable."

"It's a good thing you called, Katie. I guess I wasn't paying attention. I didn't expect this much snow in such a short period of time. I'll be coming home as soon as possible. Don't panic! I'll be there shortly.

I looked out my office window and was alarmed to see the fast mounting snow swirling and blowing. After bringing the plow inside the service area so it would be ready for what looked like a long night of plowing, I immediately locked up. I hopped into my car and started home only to be nearly blown away by the wind. There were no cars on the road, not even plows. Visibility was almost zero. It was eerie, like I was driving into an abyss. With both hands, I battled the wind until I reached my street. Katie was five months pregnant and her hormones were raging with worry wondering if I was going to make it home. She was obviously relieved when I drove into the driveway and entered the house through the side door with the howling wind and gusts of heavy thick snow as my companions. By the way she was holding her stomach bulge, it appeared she was trying to protect our unborn child from the storm. We settled in front of the television, thrilled that we hadn't lost our power, to watch the emergency broadcast. The news wasn't good. Blizzard conditions were predicted for the rest of the night and possibly beyond. By ten o'clock I called my father and we mutually decided it would be better if I just stayed home until the storm was over. Neither of us knew at that time that the storm would last until late the next day. Katie and I were startled as we looked out the window and noticed the snow was up to the steps on the front porch… then the landing… then the top of the railing. I soon lost sight of the mailbox at the edge of our front yard. The wind felt like it was going to blow the roof off the house. We decided to go to bed and pray that we would be able to get out of the house in the morning. I was restless all night wondering if I had a big enough plow at the dealership.

We awoke the next morning and were shocked at what we saw outside the house. A huge snowdrift had blown almost up to our window on the second floor. I hurried down stairs knowing I would have to let the dogs out and opened the garage door to find a wall of snow covering the opening. I quickly went to the back door to get a shovel and was pleasantly surprised to see that there was a bare spot that ran the entire length of the house. The dogs and I went out to find very little snow near the house but huge drifts beyond. I guessed God was providing for his pets. The front of the house was impassable. We were stranded, but we weren't alone. The whole street was untouched by the town plows and there appeared to be several feet of thick drifting snow on the road. We weren't going anywhere anytime soon. I began to shovel the driveway in case we would later be able to get to the main road. Slowly, as my arms and back began to ache, I realized that one man shoveling this much snow was going to take a long time. You had to shovel in layers starting with snow that was over my head. Nevertheless, I felt I had to do something so I stubbornly continued. After about an hour, I had only cleared about three feet across. Katie called me in for hot soup. We watched the morning's emergency newscast and only then did we realize the enormity of this storm. This was a monster. Parts of New England were paralyzed. Providence was at a standstill and the mayor had declared a state of emergency. Other cities throughout the northeast corridor were buried and would remain so for days. Route 128 that surrounds Boston was a disaster with hundreds of stranded vehicles and no way to get to them. The storm would last for thirty-three hours in some areas of New England and drop up to four feet of snow.

The drift in front of my house had to be over ten feet, the result of hurricane force winds which gusted to above a hundred miles an hour in some places. It would be three days before a town plow came down our road and four days before I would get to the dealership. When I was finally able to get there, I was shocked to find that one side of the dealership was entirely under snow with cars completely buried. We had to hire a private trucking firm to dig us out. Hardy New Englanders were indeed tested by this monstrous storm, but with the help of a lot of friends, we survived. Someday we would brag to our kids that we lived through the biggest blizzard to ever hit New England. The calm after the storm was welcomed and as the enormous snow piles slowly melted away, it reminded us that there were better days ahead.

Chapter Five

Sir Galahad Arrives

"If you build it, he will come"
–Field of Dreams

Although we had made great strides in improving the personnel at the dealership and were slowly becoming an efficient and cohesive operation, I still felt we had to improve our sales force. To use a baseball analogy, we had a bunch of singles hitters. We needed a cleanup hitter to complete our lineup, someone who could carry the team in good times and bad. Sure, we had Francois, but he was most effective with the customers he had dealt with for years. I was looking for Babe Ruth. With that in mind I thought I had found my man and asked him to come in for an interview.

"Is Sean Cassidy here? My name is Pierre LeCoeur. I'm here to apply for the salesman's job?"

From my office, I could hear very clearly this young man's remarks. It was evident by the volume of his voice that he was brimming with confidence. I immediately looked up from my desk to see if the person matched the voice. Indeed, it did. Pierre was a strapping presence who stood well over six feet tall, rugged, and handsome. The girls in the office beeped me with their approval before I even talked to him. Pierre knew enough about the dealership that he had to first make an impression on our elder statesman, Francois, the man who was a vital part of the dealership for many years.

"You must be Francois," he said as he walked over to his desk. "I've heard a great deal about you. Sean told me on the phone that you were indispensible. I'm Pierre. If things go well in this interview, you and I will make a hell of a team."

Francois was immediately struck by the friendly smile of this new guy. In the two years I had been in charge, Francois had seen many changes, some personnel moves that he never expected. You could tell that this latest potential move didn't faze him.

"Comment ca va." Francois addressed Pierre in French to see if he was a true French-Canadian.

"Tres`bien, merci!" Pierre replied. A friendship had begun.

The other three salesman seemed befuddled by the scene that was unfolding in front of them. They hadn't heard that I was looking for another salesman. Certainly, business wasn't good enough to add somebody else to the payroll. They wondered if this meant that one of them was going to be let go. Their concern was evident on their faces, although they were all acting like they were busy. Pierre was hard to ignore and harder not to acknowledge. He went over to each of them with his big hand extended and introduced himself. If only the three incumbents had mastered that basic sales technique, there probably wouldn't be an interview going on this morning. It was the fall of 1977 and the economy was showing signs of going in the tank. The dealership needed a spark. I was confident that Pierre might be the one to light up this sales staff.

I paged my father prior to meeting with Pierre. I told him I had a new candidate for the sales team that I thought he should meet. Dad hadn't involved himself in the hiring and firing of personnel for some time, so he was curious why I wanted his opinion now. We both sat down in my office and I told Francois to get Pierre. After the usual introductions, I asked Pierre if I had ever met him before. He was from the neighboring town of Cargill Falls so our crossing paths was to be expected. He said he thought we played against each other in the big Thanksgiving football game between our schools. My curiosity was aroused.

"What number did you wear?" I asked.

"I was a lineman-offensive and defensive tackle. I wore number 74."

"I thought I recognized you. The last time I saw you your face was in the mud and I was jumping over you for a big gain. It's funny how certain numbers stick in your memory."

I thought Pierre was going to explode but he laughed off the remark. I was testing his sense of humor and his confidence and he passed the test with flying colors. The rest of the interview went smoothly. Pierre's demeanor won my father's approval. He insisted that I hire him as soon as I could work it out. It was the beginning of a great relationship between the two of them. Of all the people that came and went over the years at the dealership, Pierre was always my father's favorite.

Chapter Six

The Wholesalers

"I like making deals, ... That's how I get my kicks."
-Donald Trump

My indoctrination into the car business wouldn't have been complete without an introduction into the art of wholesaling. I use the word 'art' to describe the process because it is truly an acquired gift learned from the wounds of your mistakes. Not only is its importance inherent to the success of a profitable used car operation, but it is also predicated on the knowledge that negotiation is directly related to your ability to appraise the vehicles you are dealing with and the people to whom you want to sell them. In every case, where I was concerned, I was immediately behind the eight ball (a cool billiard reference) because these potential buyers were schooled in the art from an early age and their credentials, for the most part, were based on years of experience. I was the rookie, but I couldn't afford to be clueless. It was baptism by fire and St. John The Baptist was nowhere to be seen.

New car dealers generate their own used cars and trucks in the form of trade-ins. Some of the trades are in such good condition that all you have to do is clean them up and park them on the front line of your used car lot. Most, however, require some kind of reconditioning–cosmetic repairs that could include: minor body work, a tune-up, tires, an alignment, new wiper blades, upholstery cleaning, etc. The more repairs, the more money has to be added to your bottom line. A sharp sales manager can save the dealership hundreds of dollars in reconditioning costs with the proper appraisal of the trade. On the other hand, if a mistake is made and the repairs escalate beyond a reasonable amount, that car has to be disposed of–hopefully not at a loss. This is where the wholesalers come in. Some are looking for high-end vehicles without many problems and others are looking to make a quick buck at an auction with a junk that they can sell cheap. High or low, the wholesalers are looking to get the best of you.

Wholesalers are generally referred to as 'used car jockeys.' Most of them have small used car operations that are typically far enough away from your dealership to be non-competitive. With our location on the eastern border of Connecticut, many of our wholesalers came out of Rhode Island, specifically the Providence/Cranston area. Because of the demographics of that area, most of the wholesalers were Italian. It didn't take much imagination to wonder if some of them were connected.

My father pulled me aside when I first came into the dealership and alerted me to the dangers of dealing with the wrong wholesalers. The advice was close to the same warning he gave me before I moved to Boston.

"Don't trust anybody. Don't lend anyone money. Don't owe anything to anybody!"

"I know, Dad." I replied arrogantly. "Neither a borrower nor a lender be. And to thine own self be true." I knew my reference to Hamlet would elicit a positive response.

"Well, thank God," he responded, "those four years of tuition I thought I wasted on you were not in vain. Just keep in mind that the education these guys get on the street is at least the equivalent of your college degree. They've gone to the 'school of hard knocks' and their degrees are in street smarts. Don't underestimate any of them, and…"–he hesitated quite a while–"be careful."

I knew where he was coming from, but I also knew that dealing with wholesalers was an essential part of a successful operation. Besides, some of these guys were quite likeable and some were definitely not "connected" to any family. The mix of characters was almost entertaining–almost.

One day in the spring of my first year on the job, my father came searching for me.

"Sean, I have somebody here that I want you to meet. This is Tony from Providence. You want to know anything about wholesaling, you ask Tony. I'll leave you two alone to get to know each other. I'm going to read a chapter from Hamlet."

I thought it was pretty clever the way my father had alerted me. Having been forewarned, I introduced myself.

"I feel like I already know you, Sean. Your dad gave you quite a buildup. I'm glad you're here. I didn't trust that other guy your father had in charge. I think you and I are going to get along just fine. I'll tell you what. If we can get together on a few cars today, I promise I'll take you with me to see SIN-A-TRA."

Tony had a way of pronouncing the name of Sinatra that almost seemed like he was speaking in slow motion, a real emphasis on the syllables.

"He's in Atlantic City this weekend and I've got two tickets in the front. Tell your wife you're going with Tony from Providence and by the time we get back, you won't remember her name."

As great as that all sounded, I thought maybe I ought to get to know Tony a little better before I slipped off with him to Atlantic City. I was sure Katie–or what's her name–wouldn't appreciate my going off for a weekend with some Italian stud from Providence.

"I appreciate the offer Tony, but my wife and I already made plans for this weekend. Nothing as exciting as Sinatra, who I love by the way, but newlywed things–we're shopping for furniture."

"Oh, Sean, I remember when I was a newlywed with my first wife. We were like RAB-BITS, Sean. On my mother's grave, I miss those days. It wears off so fast, especially in this business. I'm never home. Always out making a buck. When the heat wears off, let me know. Then we'll go to SIN-A-TRA."

Tony had a way about him that made you feel like you were an old friend. I took my new, old friend out in the yard and showed him all the cars that we wanted to wholesale. He said he would check them out and be back inside in a few minutes. I went inside where my father was waiting for me.

"Well, did you give away the store?"

"Not yet," I laughingly replied, "but I'm working on it. He's quite a character, Dad."

"I've known Tony for a few years. He's very sharp, Sean. Be prepared to negotiate, because no matter what you ask for a price, he'll counter it."

After several minutes, Tony came bouncing in with a list of the cars he wanted. He slipped into my office and began to whisper.

"Let's put a package together, Sean. Here's a couple of Ben Franklins to help you sharpen your pencil."

He was testing me. If I took the Franklins, he owned me and I would forever be selling cars to him at the price he wanted. This was precisely what my father had warned me about. For a moment, I wondered if my father was also testing me. I answered quickly and decisively.

"I don't need any money, Tony, but thanks for the offer. It's just not my style. Let's keep these negotiations on top of the table." The testing was over.

Tony said he understood and that the offer was an attempt to see what kind of guy I was. He claimed he was happy to find out that I was honest because he liked my father a great deal and he wanted to continue coming to Cassidy Motors without all the drama that he got at other places.

Now that we understood each other, I gave Tony the prices on his list of cars.

After feigning a heart attack, he settled on four of the cars. My father was impressed that I got as much as I did. I came away from the experience having learned a valuable lesson. There were snakes on the paths that should be avoided if you didn't want to be bitten. I also made a new friend in the car business, one that I would do a great deal of business with in the future. Tony never stopped trying to get me to go to Atlantic City. I never went, but I often wondered how much fun I would have had seeing SIN-A-TRA.

Chapter Seven

Fatherhood

"Father!–To God himself we cannot give a holier name."

William Wordsworth.

Baxter stopped by the dealership one day in early June. He had been working as a bartender at the dog track in Sterling. He decided to quit there when he started to fall into the old habits that he had tried to get away from in Boston. He was about to start a new job at an aerospace factory, his first steady, legitimate job in years. Apparently, his new wife was having a positive effect on him. He knew Katie was ready to pop with our first baby so he had stopped by to offer his encouragement as only Baxter could.

"You ready for this?" he said as he settled onto the couch in my office.

"You know, Bax. That's the same question you asked me when we were approaching Boston on the way to our great adventure. I guess you're going to ask the same question every time something big happens in my life."

"Well my overworked buddy, this is something big. Can you believe you are about to be a father? If I hadn't dragged you to Boston in the first place, you never would have met Katie. Once again, I'm the reason you're so happy."

"The best thing you did for me in Boston was not being around the weekend I met my bride. Somehow, you would have screwed that up. It was better that she was introduced to our sordid lifestyle without the devil at home. It gave me a chance to make a positive impression."

"Don't kid yourself. Some day she'll figure you out and realize there was more than one devil living in our apartment."

Conversations with Baxter were never dull. It was good to see him because I knew when the baby was born, my life would never again be so carefree. I looked forward with some trepidation to the birth of our first child. Katie's due date had already gone by and we were still waiting for the baby to come out and join us. By choice, we decided not to know the sex, and I was consistently saying that it didn't make a difference, but deep down I had a preference. The closer the big day came, the more I was doubtful that I was prepared.

"I don't know if I am ready for this. You know, girls spend their whole lives getting ready for the birth of their first baby. As toddlers, they play with dolls and learn how to hold them and feed them. They read books and magazines on parenting that glamorize the whole process. They have baby showers and go shopping months ahead to prepare the nest for the baby bird. Men don't have the same advantages. We're ignorant. I don't have a clue how to hold a baby or change a diaper. It's going to be on-the-job training and there is more than a good possibility that I might be horrible at it. I've got to say, I'm more than a little worried that I won't be much help–especially with the stinky diapers."

"You'll be fine," Baxter said interrupting my panic attack. "Just imagine that you're carrying a football. Just don't fumble it like you did in the Stonington game."

"Nobody remembers that except you. At least I didn't throw up an air ball from the foul line against Saint Bernard's. That miss cost us the game and an undefeated season."

Our conversations always ended up with a discussion of sports. Sports were such a big deal in our lives that I could only hope that my unborn child was athletic, whichever sex it turned out to be.

"Well, I have to run. Good luck to you and Katie. Tell Katie, I'll be thinking about her–as always."

"Thanks, Bax. I'll call the minute we know something."

A few days later, two weeks after her due date, Katie was induced. After many hours of labor, she gave birth to an eight pound, nine ounce baby. It was a boy! We named him after Jim Rice of the Boston Red Sox–James Edward Cassidy.

Chapter Eight

Trick or Treat

"You can't handle the truth!"
–A Few Good Men

My first experience with Tony from Providence turned out to be entertaining and profitable. I looked forward to his next visit and knew that as I got to know him better, the entertainment part would be more interesting.

"Dad, do you really think Tony is connected–you know–to the 'Family'?"

My father was thoughtful in his reply, careful, I guess, not to mislead me or give me a false sense of security. His answer was elusive.

"Everybody belongs to something. If they're lucky enough to call that a family, then I guess you could say yes."

Was that an answer? Was I suppose to believe that Tony was connected and was therefore someone to be concerned about, or was I being initiated into some weird kind of father-son fraternity that answered all direct questions with riddles? And why wasn't I getting a direct answer?

"What are we playing here? What's My Line? I'm going to have to deal with these guys and maybe a little background info would be helpful."

"Just remember your quote from Hamlet and you'll be fine. Shakespeare possessed a great deal of wisdom. In the car business, ethics are the mother of understanding."

"Riddles, again. I feel more like Batman than Hamlet."

Dad stiffened to make one last statement on the subject.

"Never forget. A word to the wise is sufficient."

I surmised from his last quote that if I possessed wisdom, then a brief warning was all I needed. I laughed to show him that I understood his cloaked meaning. I also pardoned my father for engaging in one of his favorite pastimes–verbal sparring. Realizing that his expertise in bantering was something he always enjoyed, I accepted his answer as a maybe. All that was missing was a quote from one of his favorite Irish poets. There was great relief that I didn't have to decipher one of those.

The rest of the day was typical of the car business–customers would come and go; some would just come to the showroom to have a place to hang around. When it got slow as it often did in the early hours of the afternoon, Pierre and Francois got involved in one of their daily practical jokes. They would take turns pulling pranks on each other, some more imaginative than the others. Today's prank was the reaction of Francois trying to get even with Pierre for putting black grease on Francois' phone. As a result, he walked around much of that day with black grease all over his ear and face. Francois was seeking revenge of a more sinister nature. He put 'Ex-lax' in some chocolate brownies that Pierre had brought from home. Pierre was a breath of fresh air in the showroom. His good nature and commanding personality kept the atmosphere loose. Francois' practical joke had the added result of keeping Pierre loose as he began to show signs of discomfort early in the afternoon, spending much of his shift moving back and forth to the men's room.

Francois sat off to the side with mischief written all over his face. His ever-present cigar was moving rapidly up and down as he chuckled to himself. Pierre was grumbling about his stomach pain and called his wife to ask what she had put in the chocolate brownies. It didn't take Pierre very long to realize that the impish look on Francois' face was tantamount to a confession. He had been the victim of a return practical joke, and even though he thought it was funny, he vowed his own revenge.

For the next two weeks, Pierre brought a 'donut' tube to sit on because he said he had a severe case of hemorrhoids that developed from the excessive use of laxatives in his brownies. To his credit, he didn't miss any work and even used his malady for a couple of sympathy sales.

Francois had gotten a good laugh from his little evil prank, but he knew from that moment on, he would have to watch his back. There was no way Pierre would let this go without plans for a more elaborate retaliation. At some point, there would be hell to pay.

From my perspective, I found the whole conflict amusing. I knew the two liked each other a great deal and were enjoying their little battle of wits. I drew the line at physical harm and although the laxative caper came close to going over that line, I chose to ignore it. For the first time since I had been reluctantly drawn into this business, I was enjoying going to work in the morning. Surely, there remained the negatives of the business–the disgruntled employees, the irate customers, the everyday money worries and the diverse group of wholesalers with their own personal agendas–but I was learning that a pleasant work environment was healthy for everyone. I was happy with the direction the dealership was headed, and, I believed, so was my father–riddles or no riddles.

Chapter Nine

Settling In

"Adults are obsolete children"
–Dr. Seuss

I had no idea. There is absolutely no way to prepare for the arrival of a little one in your house. Throw the routines away; throw away the freedom to move around without jumping over baby gates or navigating hidden toys on wheels waiting to attack you as you walk in the dark to make sure the baby is safe and sound in his bed. Alas, throw away sleep! Prepare yourself for strange noises emanating from a baby monitor in the middle of the night. Prepare yourself to be a provider, a feeder, an entertainer, a rocker, a storyteller, and, of course, a diaper changer. Prepare yourself to be at the mercy of the new boss in the house. And lastly, prepare yourself to lose your heart for the outcome is out of your control. Once the baby looks at you with those trusting eyes and laughs at your feeble attempts to be funny, you're hooked. There is nothing you can do about it except stand by their bed when they are tucked in for the night and just look at what you and your wife have created. It's as close as you're ever going to come to your creator while you are on this earth. The bond between a parent and a child begins the first time you hold them and lasts a lifetime. I had no idea!

Katie was exuberant when she finally came home with the baby. She had endured a difficult birth. The baby was almost one tenth of her weight and was two weeks overdue. She struggled mightily with the size of the baby and ultimately needed the assist of forceps to guide the head of the baby down the birth canal. The pressure of the procedure broke her coccyx bone. Thankfully, her mother was able to come live with us until Katie was again up and around. I did what I could, but I was definitely out of my comfort zone. The baby was too cute to blame for his mother's troubles. He was very flirtatious and disarming to anyone who approached him. I was probably biased, but I never saw a happier baby. My mother-in-law left after a couple of weeks when Katie was able to take over. Thank God for mothers-in-law because I would have been up the creek without her. With the three of us together as a family unit for the first time, Katie, little Jimmy and I began our new lives together.

When Katie was able to go back to work, she did so on a part-time basis. She was very much in demand at the hospital, settling into a schedule that would allow her to be with the baby most of the time. Her three to eleven shift in the emergency room included alternate weekends and meant that there would be times when I would be with the baby by myself. The thought terrified me. Luckily for us, we had a very loveable and reliable young lady living next door that was available to fill in some of the time. She was a Godsend. My alone time with Jimmy was usually after I came home from work at eight o'clock when he was generally asleep. After a tough, long day at work, it would have been difficult summoning the energy to properly care for an infant. For the time being, everything was working out, but I knew once he started crawling around, my tranquility would be challenged.

Sundays were my day with Jimmy. We spent the whole afternoon and evening together. We played together, we rolled on the floor, we watched TV together, we went for walks in the stroller, we tossed a ball, we giggled, and we read together. His unnatural powers of concentration were evident whenever you would read a nursery rhyme to him. He listened intently and loved every minute of it. I have to say; I enjoyed some of the books myself because being the youngest of five very active kids, rarely was I ever read to. I could sense how much he was enjoying it and I think he could sense I was enjoying it also. I was still cringing every time I had to change a diaper, but other than that, we were bonding just fine.

Jimmy was about four months old when Pierre showed up on a Sunday with a custom made pipe about twelve feet long with a backboard and a basket to attach to it. Knowing I probably wouldn't have any tools, he brought his own including a shovel. I bundled Jimmy up and put him in his stroller so he could watch Pierre and me dig the hole, drink a few beers, laugh our heads off, and finally raise the basket in a prominent spot at the edge of the driveway. Pierre then lifted Jimmy out of his stroller, put a basketball in his hands for the first time and helped him shoot the ball at the basket. We could tell by his reaction that Jimmy was thrilled. Pierre had no way of knowing on that Sunday, but his assisted dunk was the first of thousands of shots that Jimmy would shoot at that basket. He was four months old and with the help of Pierre, Jimmy Ed Cassidy had launched his basketball career.

Chapter Ten

My First Crisis

"The sharp employ the sharp."
–Douglas William Jerrold

As time progressed, Pierre's role in the company expanded. He was easily our best salesman every month and volunteered to help the remaining two inexperienced rookies in closing their deals. During the daily downtime that is routine in a car dealership, he would hang around the office where Josette and her girls worked, offering his assistance whenever they needed it, but mostly just entertaining them with his wealth of stories. Josette was very fond of Pierre, not only because of their shared French-Canadian heritage, but also because he was a good guy and a good family man. Josette's strong sense of values included an affinity for men who were loyal to their spouses and their families. Pierre very much fit the image of the type of man that she most admired. It didn't hurt that he was also a strappingly handsome young man. There was little doubt that in just a short time working at Cassidy Motors, Pierre had carved a secure niche in the organization. He was confident, gregarious, and affable. With Pierre as the cornerstone of the business, we were building what appeared to be a strong sales future. I was responsible for the sales staff, and having Pierre as my right hand man was the beginning of structuring a solid, capable sales team.

"Sean, could I talk to you in your office? I have to ask you something that's very important to me and my wife."

Sometimes you can just sense when trouble is brewing. I had an immediate bad vibe about Pierre's request.

"Sure," I said. "Let's talk right now before it gets busy."

"Here's my problem in a nut shell. I don't know where I fit in here. I don't know where I'm going."

"I didn't realize there was a problem."

"Don't get me wrong. I appreciate everything you've done for me. I know you believe I'm doing a good job. You said as much at this morning's sales meeting. I love your father and you and I have become good friends, but I've got a wife that expects me to be the main provider in my family and two very talented little girls at home that will be going to college before you know it. I know your father is tight with his money. We've certainly talked enough about that, but I just can't imagine making enough here to accomplish what I want to do for my family."

"Are you leaving us?" I said sheepishly.

"I don't want to. I love it here, but…"

"Say no more, Pierre. Let me talk to my father and we'll get back to you by the end of the week. Quite honestly, I wouldn't want to lose you, and I know my father feels the same way. Don't do anything rash until we get back to you. OK?"

"I'll wait to hear from you."

It never fails. As soon as you become comfortable in a situation, somebody or something has you sailing against the tide. Pierre was more than just a competent employee; he had become a friend to everyone at the dealership. His loss would be like trading Babe Ruth to the Yankees. I had to convince my father to loosen up his purse strings–something I couldn't get him to do for my own salary–to attempt to hold onto our most valuable asset.

Dad wasn't going to be thrilled with this latest development. He was already complaining about too much payroll. The economy was rough, but he was still living in the past, still paying the same type of wages that he had at the old dealership. It was like he never moved emotionally from his old facility with the one car showroom and the two-car service area, where his weekly payroll was so small that he paid everyone in cash, counting each employees earnings by hand and stuffing their money into small payroll envelopes. Life was changing too fast for my father. He had to adapt to the new facility, with the larger overhead, the new management team headed by his aggressive son, and a sales staff that was generating numbers that he could have only dreamed of in the old days.

My father was in his sixties when he undertook this new venture and I think the enormity of the change in his business was almost too much for him. His daily routine had gone from simple to complicated at a time in his life when he probably just wanted to work in his garden. Keeping all this in mind, I hesitated for some time before I brought up the issue of Pierre. On Thursday, one day before we had to give Pierre an answer, Dad showed up at work in a good mood. How much I was going to ruin that mood was up to him, but for all concerned, I was hoping for the best. With some anxiety, I approached my father as soon as I spotted him.

"Dad, we need to talk."

"What about?" he replied casually. "I haven't had my morning muffin over at Berris's yet. Do you want to join me?"

He must have been in a good mood. This was the first time he had ever invited me to join him for his morning muffin, a daily ritual that had begun long before I had joined the company. I accepted the invitation and off we went, father and son, for our first ever muffin together.

"Order whatever you want," he boasted like he must have done years before when he'd blow all his money at the Elks club in one of his drunken stupors. To his credit, he had stopped drinking years ago when he had his cancer scare. Sometimes life itself has a way of sobering us up.

"Just a coffee for me. I've already had breakfast."

"Are you sure, Sean? The muffins are homemade and they'll warm them up for you if you want."

"No, thanks, Dad. Listen, we've got a problem with Pierre."

"Pierre's doing a great job. I can't imagine he's a problem."

"He's not … I mean … Here's the deal. Pierre approached me on Monday and said he would be leaving if he couldn't make more money. He said he's worried about having enough money to pay for his girls' college in the future."

"What did you tell him?"

"I told him I would talk to you and we would get back to him."

"Is he bluffing?"

"I would guess no. He seemed very concerned that we would be upset."

"Well, I guess he was right about that. I would hate to lose Pierre. I think he's good for the dealership and he's someone you can trust. I know the girls in the office would stage a mutiny. How much is he looking for?"

"He never said, but I think we might be able to get him to stay if we could offer him incentives based on sales performance that's comparable to what he would get at another dealer. Pierre's no fool. I'm sure he has already inquired about other dealer's pay plans. I know you don't like commissions, but it's a way of rewarding him for what he does and not paying him a higher salary for just showing up. He'd have to earn his incentives. It should be a win-win situation for us because the more he makes, the more we would make."

"OK, OK, you've convinced me. Put something together when we get back. If it makes sense and he agrees to it, we'll all be happy."

I left my father to enjoy his muffin and went back to my office. Before I put a proposal together, I anonymously called several local dealers. Acting like a job applicant, I inquired about their pay plans. The sales managers were very forthcoming with their plans and their information provided me with the ammunition I needed to put together a competitive proposal. When my father returned, I showed the plan to him and he reluctantly approved it. The next day, I called Pierre into my office and laid my cards out on the table. I told him how much my father thought of him and how much effort it took to get him to go along with this plan. Pierre studied the payment figures for several minutes and then seemed to withdraw into deep thought. I was about to explode from the silence, when Pierre looked up, stuck out his big hand and said, "It looks like you've got yourself a salesman. There is one thing, however. I want to do more–be more of a help to you."

"Not a problem," I answered. "You can start by emptying my waste paper basket."

We both had a good laugh and shook hands. For the time being, anyway, the best salesman that had ever worked at Cassidy Motors was staying.

Chapter Eleven

Inexplicable Reasons

"Cruel is the strife of brothers"
–Aristotle

"Hey, kid. How's your little boy doing? I haven't seen him since he was born."

My relationship with my older brother, Chip, had deteriorated over my first few years at Cassidy Motors. It was never a perfect bond between us, and the revelation that I was coming into the business ostensibly to take over the company when our father retired must have been a hard pill for him to swallow. I could understand his bitterness toward me. It was a reflection of his disdain for my father. How they had co-existed in the business for so many years was almost unfathomable. From my point of view, I wished things were different. It bothered me so much that I had many conversations with Josette about it. She said that I was doing my best in a bad situation and all I could do was treat Chip fairly and take care of him whenever he needed help. His irrational behavior towards his co-workers led to many near conflicts that could have easily turned physical. He would yell at mechanics for no reason and refuse to get them the parts they needed when they interrupted one of his countless breaks. I was not only my brother's keeper; there were many times I was my brother's savior.

"Little Jimmy's great," I replied. "He's just starting to crawl so we're busy putting up barricades everywhere to keep him from getting hurt. It's a full time job. Why don't you come over and see him sometime. It's about time he met his Uncle Chip."

"Maybe I will. His uncle could probably teach him a few things– just like I did with his father." He laughed and went back to his parts room–his refuge from the clamor of our busy service department. Knowing that he probably wouldn't come over any time soon, I went about my business back in the sales area. Before long, our other parts guy, Denny, came running into the showroom.

"Sean! Come quick. Chip's about to get his ass kicked."

Sure enough, the inevitable had happened. Chip had taken a swing at one of the mechanics whose only offense was ordering a part while Chip was eating a donut. He was in the middle of spewing irrational statements at the mechanic when I approached.

"Do you know whose name is on the signs out front?" Chip asked the disgruntled young man who had only worked for us for several weeks. His mechanical ability was raw but he seemed to be a good worker and was willing to learn. He also seemed to be very fit. Certainly, he would be a physical mismatch for Chip whose only exercise was getting up from his chair to get another donut.

"I know what the sign reads," he said, "but it doesn't mention 'crazy son' anywhere."

"That's enough," I said with urgency trying to defuse the mess my brother had gotten into. "Both of you calm down. This is a place of business and certainly there is no room for this type of behavior. I don't really care who started what, but I'm going to finish it. This is over. Chip, why don't you take the afternoon off. Go home and cool off."

I took the mechanic aside and explained to him that my brother can be irrational at times, and I was sorry for that but he is part of the family that owns this business.

"Look," I said. "You're doing a good job. The rest of the guys like you. Just forget this ugly little episode ever happened and let's go on from here. I'll talk to Chip to make sure it doesn't happen again."

"Thanks for understanding, Sean. I know I'm new here and I want to do well. But, I've got to say, it's a good thing the punch missed."

The incident was over, for now. I was beginning to feel more like a peacekeeper than a car dealer. Part of that responsibility would be to keep this incident from my father who would have reacted in anger with Chip and precipitated another ugly scene between the two of them. I was quickly learning that running a family business is far more involved than just opening and closing the doors. It was apparent that my job included family counseling with an emphasis on crisis management. I needed a break, too. I welcomed the opportunity to go home and watch my son as Katie went off to her afternoon shift at the hospital.

Things started off very quietly as Jimmy was still napping when I got home. New fathers with solo duty taking care of their infants are fond of the afternoon nap. It gave me time to unwind from the problems at work and relax until Jimmy decided to open his big blue eyes and join his father in all the fun activities we usually engaged in. It wasn't long before I heard him up in his room and went to get him. He was excited to see me. His little hands were reaching up signaling to me to free him from his crib. I picked him up and gave him a huge hug. He giggled. I bounced him up and down until I realized his diaper was radiating a smell that had to be dealt with before the dogs got sick. Katie was usually around to change the really smelly diapers. I thought long and hard about leaving the diaper on until she got home, but then I realized that would be a horrible thing to do to my beautiful little boy–and to the dogs. It was a task I tackled out of necessity, but it was still one that I gagged on. Katie had set up a changing area in the downstairs bathroom which included a shelf that ran the length of the wall and was equipped with everything I would need including: clean diapers, handi-wipes, a diaper pail, talcum powder, and a changing pad. I took a deep breath and went into the bathroom with old stinky pants. Everything was going smoothly when I suddenly dropped the new diaper bag on the floor. Jimmy, who was five months old, thought it was hilarious. I stood Jimmy up and balanced him on the changing table with one hand on his waist as I reached down behind me to retrieve the bag of diapers. Just as I grabbed the bag, Jimmy wiggled unexpectedly and fell from the table head first onto the tile floor. A terrible feeling ripped through my heart as I thought I had permanently maimed my son. Luckily I caught him on the first bounce, but his horrific crying alerted me to his pain. Panic set in quickly. What was I to do? I held him tightly but he was crying hysterically. I called the hospital but Katie was busy, so I had to leave a disjointed message. I thought for a minute and decided to call Katie's gynecologist, Dr. Behar. I got his office receptionist, Liz, on the phone and told her what happened. She was very calm and comforting and told me to look for certain signs of distress. When Jimmy seemed to be OK, she gave me some advice that I would never forget for the rest of my life.

"Sean," she said. "Most babies are father proof."

I thanked her for her understanding and her help, but I was still overwhelmed with worry. Katie came home early after getting the message at work and reassured me that Jimmy was going to be fine. I was never happier I had married a nurse because I was borderline useless at that point. I decided to go back to work to keep my mind busy. As I approached the showroom, Pierre came out to greet me. It seemed the news had travelled fast because Pierre knew all about what had happened.

"Let's go for walk," he said.

We walked outside among the cars and he attempted to console my broken spirit. Before long, the unfortunate incident that had just happened caught up to me, and my eyes filled with tears. Pierre was very understanding and put his arm around my shoulder.

"There will never be a doubt, Sean, that you love that little guy. He'll never doubt it; Katie will never doubt it; and certainly you'll never doubt it. Maybe God puts us through these trials so we can realize just how much we care for our kids. You are going to be a great father."

After closing that night, I left the showroom and sat in my car pondering the events of the day. In one afternoon, I had intervened on behalf of my brother and had been fortunate to avert a serious accident to my infant son. In many ways, the incidents were ominously related for it pointed out to me that my carefree days of self-involvement were over. I was now responsible for many branches of my family tree. One lesson stood out. I learned that you could never love your family enough, no matter how difficult that might sometimes be.

"He Ain't Heavy, He's My Brother"

The road is long
With many a winding turn
...but I'm strong enough to carry him
He ain't heavy, he's my brother.
The Hollies

Chapter Twelve

Cement Shoes

"I'm going to make him an offer he can't refuse."
Marlon Brando-*the Godfather*

I knew cleaning the waste paper baskets wouldn't keep Pierre's attention very long. His comforting remarks to me during my diaper-changing crisis proved that he was someone who I could count on to uphold the goals and the integrity of Cassidy Motors. I began to expand his duties in several areas while attempting to utilize his strongest asset, his charisma. One of the areas that I thought Pierre would be most helpful would be dealing with some of our other wholesalers. The experience would sharpen his knowledge of the used car market and his outgoing personality seemed to be perfect to handle the carnival atmosphere that many of these wholesalers brought with them to the dealership. Some of these guys came with an entourage of characters that would hang around obtrusively while waiting to perform their sole purpose of driving any purchased vehicles back to their used car lots. Depending on the area they were from, the personalities of the entourage reflected the degree to which you could trust these guys. If the drivers were boisterous and irreverent, chances are the wholesaler was someone to be leery of. It was very much like a "birds of the feather" philosophy, and unless you were born with a tomato for a brain, you were wise to notice these things.

I decided to break Pierre in slowly by letting him deal exclusively with two of our regular wholesalers. The first was my favorite local dealer and 'bon vivant,' Pat Letters. Pat was a harmless sort who was short in stature but big in personality and warmth. He stood only about five feet five inches tall but had a stout build. His entourage was a group of old timers, none younger than sixty years old, who were all shorter than Pat. When Pat and his boys wobbled into the dealership, it looked like the seven dwarfs were coming for a visit. Pat only bought cheap cars that he could sell quickly at a local auction for a twenty-five or fifty dollar profit. He always paid with cash and never asked for any paperwork or a receipt. He would pull one hundred dollar bills out of every pocket like he was performing a magic show. They would come from his sport jacket that somehow had enough material to reach around his rotund figure, from his baggy pants that looked to have some abnormal measurement like a forty-five inch waist and a twenty-eight inch leg, and from his shirt pocket that was well worn and ripped from frequent use. In the course of paying for a car, he would often drop several bills on the floor without noticing. The dealers that I knew locally generally took good care of him, picking up any money he dropped and giving it back. He wasn't the most conscientious person I ever dealt with, but he may have been the most pleasant and engaging.

Pat liked to tell the story of how the IRS once made a visit to his used car operation to audit his books. After three days of trying to figure out his outlandishly cluttered office, and his illogical bookkeeping records, the IRS auditor threw up his arms in the air and gave up. He was never audited again. On Christmas week, Pat's travelling circus would always show up with a present for all the salesmen and all the girls in the office. None of us ever used the fake leather gloves that were his annual gift, but we loved the fact that he thought of us. Indeed, Pat was a unique individual with a big heart, and he and the 'dwarfs' were always welcomed at Cassidy Motors. I knew Pierre would have a great deal of fun negotiating with Pat. It was an indoctrination that included the benefit of laughter. Pierre's personality was a perfect fit.

The second wholesaler was on the opposite end of the spectrum from Pat. His name was Ralph or 'Ralphie' and he represented A and

G motors, a big used car operation in Warwick, Rhode Island. The location and size of A and G and the demeanor of its employee, Ralph, would make one guess that the family connection that we all worried about was a distinct possibility. Ralph was a big man with a crippled arm who only dealt in high-end, more expensive used cars. He was slick and obviously very sharp when it came to used car values. I had personally dealt with Ralph for over a year and never had a problem with him. I did, however, make sure that all my prices were crystal clear and that there was no "bushing" going on. Bushing was a practice of quoting a price and then raising it when the other party showed interest. I never did it with customers and I, most certainly, never did it with Ralph.

Ralph's last name started with a "D" and had a lot of syllables. Every time I talked to him I expected to hear the theme music from THE GODFATHER. To his credit, he never "bushed" me either. On the contrary, just dealing with Ralph taught me a great deal about salesmanship and how to set up the close on a sale. He would often ask a question to get a response to his advantage. For example, he would ask, "Would you sell this car for five thousand dollars?" You would have to answer yes or no. If you answered yes, the deal was done. If you answered no, the next question was, "How much would you sell it for?"

The question once again begged an answer, and each answer eventually led to the conclusion he was after. It was salesmanship 101.

Although I'm sure Ralph knew very little about subordinate clauses in the English language, he masterfully used them to get to his price. For instance, he would ask about a couple of cars. "If I gave you ten thousand dollars, could I buy these two cars?" Again the answered response was a yes or no and the original pattern would repeat itself. The whole approach was used to get to his price as quickly as possible–a very clever and effective way to manipulate the sale. Ralph was indeed a professional and definitely a graduate of that school of hard knocks my father had talked about. With the proper warning from me, I believed Pierre could handle Ralph and subsequently learn a great deal from him.

Sometimes our best intentions go awry. I introduced Pierre to Ralph and I could immediately sense a problem. Ralph liked to deal with me. He was noticeably miffed that I had turned him over to Pierre, who did his best to be accommodating and gracious. Ralph snapped at Pierre right away and was ordering him around as if he was some sort of dog to be whipped and trained. I could tell Pierre's blood pressure was boiling, but he maintained his calm. I figured everything would straighten itself out so I left the office to take care of a minor problem that Josette needed help with. I occasionally looked out into the yard to see if the negotiating was going smoothly, and things seemed to settle down. I was confident that Pierre would win Ralph over and everybody would be happy with the new arrangement. One warning I had given to Pierre before he met Ralph was to be careful not to quote any wholesale prices out in the yard. The bottom line prices of our used cars were listed on his wholesale sheet in code. It would be too easy to make a mistake trying to decipher a code outside the building with all the distractions of a busy dealership and the presence of an aggressive wholesaler. Pierre must have been rattled because he quoted prices that were too low. When I went back to my office, Ralph had his checkbook out and was beginning to write a check for the incorrect figures. Pierre told me what he had quoted and I told him that wasn't enough. We were a thousand dollars off. Pierre immediately apologized to Ralph and said he had made an honest mistake. Ralph didn't think his mistake was honest. He suddenly became 'Ralphie' and flipped out. With his good arm, he slammed the door to the office. He then began to scream at Pierre and called him every name in the book.

"You little punk! You tried to bush me! Do you know who you're dealing with?"

Pierre told him to calm down, but 'Ralphie' was just beginning. He threw a chair across the room slamming it into the wall of my office. When I walked into the fracas to try to mediate, 'Ralphie' tipped over a desk showing remarkable strength in his good arm. He then attempted to break a window. I was able to get his attention and tried to settle him down.

"Ralph, what's the problem? Calm down, my friend, before you kill somebody."

"That's exactly what I plan to do," he screamed. "I'll put this little punk in cement shoes."

"Ralph, I'm going to call the police. Perhaps, you should just leave."

"I'm leaving, Sean, but I hope this punk doesn't attempt to sleep soundly tonight."

With his final threat delivered, Ralph left the premises. Pierre, who was more than capable of handling himself in a fight, was noticeably shaken. I tried to relieve the tension by saying to Pierre that there was no way a one armed man was going to beat him up.

Pierre remained silent for quite awhile as things quieted. His life had never been threatened before. He asked if he could go home for the rest of the day. Realizing that he was definitely shook up by his brush with the "family," I told him to go ahead. I wondered, as he left through the showroom door, if he would ever come back.

Chapter Thirteen

The Lost Decade

> "The older generation are leading this
> country to galloping ruin."
>
> \- John Lennon

The pride that every American feels for their country was severely tested in 1979. We were becoming the laughing stock of the world. We had a weak president who had a hard time rallying the populace behind his unpopular programs. The Federal Reserve raised their prime loan rate to banks to 14.5%, crippling the finance market. Motorists were idling their cars in long lines at filling stations for only a few gallons of gas at a time. The Shiite Muslim leader of Iran, the Ayatollah Khomeini, ousted the Shah from control of the country and his terrorist forces stormed the US embassy and took sixty-six Americans hostage. As the hostage saga dragged out for weeks, the morale of the country was at an all-time low. It was in this environment that Cassidy Motors attempted to stay out of debt and continue in business. With literally no financing available, only customers with cash were able to purchase a new car or truck. Sales were down and Chevrolet was pushing its least desirable inventory on dealers with the caveat that we play ball or we don't get any of the good stuff. The scenario was dismal. There we were with no customers, no way to finance, and a lot full of undesirable product. When we got our first five, rear wheel drive, diesel Impalas in the middle of winter, I knew we were in for a bumpy ride. I needed to relieve some stress.

Like the commissioner in the comic book *Batman* waiting for the "Bat signal," Baxter appeared seemingly knowing that I was in need of a diversion.

"Hey, my sorry looking friend, you can't be too happy with the lines of cars stretching from the gas station to the front of the dealership. I had a hard time getting into the driveway. President Carter's a trip isn't he? Promises–promises -promises! It's a good thing we've got tennis. What do you think? Do you want to join that new indoor club in Essex? I hear the girls there are unbelievable."

Baxter and I had learned to play tennis while we were in Boston. We actually thought we were pretty good until we entered into the doubles competition last spring during Danville's annual festival. We played a father-son team who were considered the best in the field. We did a whole lot of trash talking before the match about how we should be the favorites and were promptly skunked, 6-0, 6-0. Tennis people called that a double bagel. We called it an ass kicking. To add insult to our injury, the father of the victors told us we could have the balls after the match, a gesture laced with sardonic exultation. It was a lesson learned, but it didn't dampen our enthusiasm for the game. We played a great deal over the summer and were getting better and better. I couldn't forget the cocky faces of our springtime conquerors and used that image for motivation to improve. I was psyched up for the opportunity to play all winter indoors at a beautiful new facility.

"You think they're ready for us in Essex? You think they're ready for the Boston boys? Let's go up there right now and sign up. I might just as well. There's nothing to do here except watch people pump gas next door at the gas station."

My father had been very specific about my playing sports when I first came back from Boston. He said I was too aggressive and too argumentative. He didn't think it was a good idea for me to go around "pissing" everyone off with the way I played baseball, or basketball, or even touch football in the various leagues around town. He thought I would be costing us customers in the long run. He, himself, had been a tennis player and viewed it as a 'gentleman's game.' He didn't think even I could provoke an argument that would cost us a customer while playing tennis. With some trepidation, he was in favor of my joining the Essex Racket Club. I guess he had never seen John McEnroe play.

Baxter was all excited about joining the club. It was a way for him to get out of the house on a weeknight. He still harbored the mischievous gene and it was evident he was anxious to see all the girls in short tennis attire parading around the indoor courts and lounge. Tennis was huge in 1979. It was the age of Connors and McEnroe, Borg and Nastase, Guillermo Vilas, Chris Evert, Billy Jean King, and Martina Navratilova. The public courts at most locations were constantly in use and it was very difficult to find an outside court to play on. Joining an indoor facility insured us a reserved court and perfect conditions. Essex is one of those picturesque New England towns that are the subject of many postcards. It was exhilarating just going there. The fact that it was winter, and we were able to exercise and play a game we were addicted to was gravy. Tennis was the medicine I needed to forget the problems confronting me at work.

"Did you see that girl behind the desk? She definitely was giving me the eye. I'm going to love this place. It's better than the strip joints in Boston. The girls are hot!"

"Baxter, Baxter, Baxter! This is why you can never beat me anymore. You never keep your eyes on the ball. You're too busy checking out the babes."

"Just remember, that's why I joined. I could care less about beating you. Girls like it when you're gracious on the court."

"Show me a good loser, and I'll show you a loser," I retorted.

"It doesn't matter. I love tennis. Not only are the girls gorgeous, they're in great shape. You know I'm a leg man."

"Well, I didn't know that. I pretty much thought you liked all the parts of the girls."

"Right again, my overworked buddy. But legs are my favorites."

Tennis night was a big deal for both of us for obviously different reasons. Baxter was there for the scenery and I was there to actually play the game. Eventually we got some of our friends to also join the club and each week we had round robin matches, always playing a different opponent. It was a night to look forward to at a time when getting up in the morning meant going to work to face another depressing day. Tennis was a break from the tedium of everyday life. I had to keep reminding Baxter that the word love in tennis was meant for scoring. His idea of scoring included a different kind of love.

Chapter Fourteen

End of an Era

> "Politicians are like diapers. They both need changing regularly and for the same reason."
>
> –Anonymous

Pierre came back after a long weekend and seemed to have put the incident with Ralph aside. He was joking with the girls in the office and was planning his retribution on Francois for the ex-lax caper. He was full of energy and mischief. It was a relief to me that he had seemingly gotten over the Ralph incident so quickly. Francois was going to be the target of Pierre's wrath today. He was going to use his guile to perpetrate his revenge. Francois had been seeing a woman secretly for some time. Pierre described her as a forty-footer. From forty feet away, she didn't look too badly. She was in her sixties and always wore a blond wig to appear younger. She would call Francois at all times of the day and he would go running like a trained dog. He obviously liked what he was getting from this woman for just the mention of her name would lead to his turning beet red. He had recently been on pins and needles waiting for her to call, but she had been silent for a couple of weeks. When he confided to Pierre that he was going crazy waiting for her to call, he opened up a whole new scenario for Pierre to explore. Pierre waited for mid-afternoon, when business usually slowed down and Francois was at his most impatient, to make the phone call.

"Frenchy," he started in an exaggerated high-pitched voice. "I can't stand it any longer." Pierre could hardly restrain himself from bursting into laughter. "I'm parked behind the service area. Can you come out and we can spend the afternoon together."

Francois was so excited to hear from his playmate that he failed to notice that Pierre was hiding in the closing office and talking on the phone in his best, fake female voice. The other salesmen, who were in on the prank, were literally in tears at their desks trying not to give away the ruse. Francois couldn't get out the door fast enough, only to return minutes later disappointed that no one was there. One of the salesmen told him he saw a blonde driving out of the dealership on the opposite side from which he went out. Francois was distraught. He was pacing the floor when the girls in the office, who were also included in the prank, paged him for another phone call.

"Frenchy, I'm so sorry I had to leave. Mr. Cassidy drove in and spotted me and I didn't want to get you in trouble. Can you come over? I promise I will make it up to you."

Pierre suddenly popped out of the office and Francois said to him he had to go help a customer. Pierre continued the charade and somehow managed not to burst out laughing.

"Oh, Frenchman," he said. "Did you hear from your honey? Was that her on the phone?"

Francois still didn't catch on because he wanted to believe that this was his big moment. His face was red and his unlit cigar was moving nervously up and down.

"Don't tell Sean. I'll be back after I take care of business."

Pierre told him to take his time and enjoy himself. We would all be waiting for him and his inevitable stories. Francois was gone for just a short time when he returned, obviously disappointed.

"She wasn't there," he said to Pierre. "Something must have spooked her."

Pierre was relentless. He continued making phone calls in a fake, sultry voice for the rest of the week. He had Francois talking to himself. Finally, he couldn't contain his laughter any longer and admitted to Francois that he was the woman on the phone. Round two had gone into the books. It seemed the score was even–one to one. Both practical jokers would be a little bit more skeptical in believing the other in the future.

…………………

Though it seemed like we were having a good time at work, it was evident from the faces of the sales staff on payday that 1979 was one of the worst years in the car business.

Thankfully, the final year of Jimmy Carter's presidency would soon be over and the hope was that a new voice and a new direction would spur the economy and ignite a firestorm of car sales. The economists spoke of a great deal of pent-up consumer demand that would surface at some point. Our hope was that it would be sooner than later. My father had dipped into his personal finances on a number of occasions to free up enough capital to meet the payroll and pay the bills. I knew that process had to be painful for him because of how much he cared for his money. We had tried everything to weather the storm. Some ideas were more successful than others.

Our very popular Corvette raffle had infused some much-needed capital into the dealership accounts. Still, we needed more avenues to boost our stability in a tough market. Our use of local girls to model in our car ads proved to be a positive–especially among the 18–35 age group. By attracting younger buyers, we opened up whole new markets.

It may have been coincidental early on, but we developed a reputation for stocking and selling flashy, sporty cars–especially the Camaro. During the calendar year of 1979, in spite of the recession and lack of consumer confidence, we sold over fifty Camaros. The previous year, we had only sold four. We had discovered our own niche, unique to our operation, and it brought us notoriety among buyers and, more importantly, with the zone office. One day my father received a phone call from the zone manager in Tarrytown, New York, congratulating us on being the "Camaro Kings" of northeastern, Connecticut. After all the mistakes Chevrolet had made throughout the 70's with such poorly manufactured and unpopular cars as the Vega, the Monza, the rear wheel drive Impalas and Caprices, and of course, the Luv pickup, the Camaro was a revelation. Most importantly to our market, it was reasonably priced. Younger buyers could afford it. The styling was gorgeous, and the reputation of the car for performance and resale was extraordinary. It was the right car at the right time. Along with our strong truck sales, the Camaro saved the day at Cassidy Motors. Now we needed some good news on the national front.

The 1980 election was just the remedy we were looking for. Ronald Reagan, a moderate conservative, who believed in business as the cornerstone of a democracy, won the election. Immediately, the pride of the American people was restored when Iran released the American hostages, and a new feeling of confidence in our government and its new president was born. Within months of Reagan's election, our business took off in a positive direction. The pent-up consumer demand, of which we had heard so much, became a reality and we embarked very quickly and very thankfully into the golden years of our dealership. The decade of the eighties had begun.

"Happy Days are here again.
The skies above are clear again.
Let us sing a song of cheer again.
Happy Days are here again."
- Ben Selvin

The strangulation of our country's domestic agenda created by astronomical gas prices, high interest rates and roaring inflation, and our sorry performance in international politics were soon just a long difficult memory. Indeed, happy days were here again. Our optimism for our future was sky high.

Three weeks after President Reagan was inaugurated, Pierre walked into my office, gave me a big hug and a letter. It was a letter of resignation.

Chapter Fifteen

Downtown

> "When you're alone and life is making you lonely
> You can always go, downtown."
>
> -Petula Clark

On November 24, 1979, Tucker Cassidy joined Jimmy in our family after a relatively easy birth compared to our first. To say that Tucker was a delight from the beginning would be to understate the moment. Katie wanted two children, and although once again the gender didn't matter, we were blessed with a boy. Unlike Jimmy who chose to stay in his mother's tummy for two extra weeks, Tucker wanted out. Perhaps I was a little too cavalier that night, but when Katie informed me it was time to go to the hospital, we were lying in bed watching reruns of "You Bet Your Life." I told her I was ready but I just wanted to see the end of the Groucho show. After a good punch to my bicep, I realized that maybe Groucho would have to wait.

For late November, it was a particularly nasty evening. An early season snowstorm snuck up the coast and was dropping some significant snow onto the roads just when we were about ready to drive to the hospital. The ten-mile trip was difficult as conditions were close to a whiteout. We arrived a little after midnight. The nurse on duty in the birthing unit knew Katie and made a big deal about her being there.

She was immediately taken into a room for an examination to ascertain how far along she was. Within a few moments, she reappeared in the waiting area. The examining nurse had determined that she was hours away from delivery and we were free to go back home if we wanted. Tucker had a different idea.

After a discussion of driving back home in the blizzard conditions or just sticking around the waiting area to see what happens, we decided to wait at the hospital at least until the storm subsided. The movie that was playing on the television in the waiting area was "Helter Skelter," the story of the infamous Manson family and the butchering of the very pregnant Sharon Tate. This was certainly not the kind of story that someone who is about to give birth would choose to see. Katie said she wanted to go for a walk. As soon as she stood up, she screamed and said she thought the baby was coming. The same nurse that was going to send us home came running and rushed her into the birthing area. Having religiously attended Lamaze classes with Katie, I went into the room with her to assist with her breathing. I noticed our doctor wasn't there yet and asked the nurse about that frightening detail. She said he had been called and was on his way. I hoped she was right because Katie's contractions were getting closer and closer. The nurse was becoming nervous as the time was getting near. She finally asked me if I had ever delivered a baby before. Of course the answer was a very definitive, "No!" She said maybe I ought to get ready to help her.

Just as I was preparing to faint at the thought of delivering my own baby, Dr. Behar appeared and literally within seconds, Tucker was born. He entered the world smiling, unaware of what he had just put his father through.

The next couple of months were a blur. Not only did we have a very active little boy learning his first steps and wandering all over the house, but we had a new baby boy to add to the mix. Life was crazy. Work had gotten busier and therefore required more of my time. Winter meant snow and snow in the car business is a nightmare. Some days I would work all day, come home for a few hours and then go back and plow all night. There were too many days with too little sleep, but somehow, someway, we got through it.

Winter was holding on with a death grip. Baxter thought it was time that we went back to the Racquet Club and played some tennis. It was early March, and because of the exhausting schedule that Katie and I had both undertaken since Tucker's birth, tennis had been put on the back burner of things to do.

"Katie, this is Baxter. Can Sean come out and play tonight."

"Baxter, where have you been? Sean wondered why you haven't been over."

"Babies scare me. They remind me that I shouldn't have done all those things I did in Boston. I wouldn't want to bring another me into this world. I'm surprised Sean did."

"Baxter, you will never change. I'm glad you called, though. I think Sean could use a night out playing tennis. Don't worry about staying out too late. Pam, the girl next door, is going to help me with the boys' baths and then I'm going to bed. Just behave, though, Baxter. I don't want to get up in the middle of the night to bail the two of you out of jail.

"Katie, its just tennis. What trouble could we possibly get into?"

I have to admit, as much as I loved those two kids, it was great to get out of the house and go hit some balls with Baxter. Katie was astute enough to realize that I was showing signs of wear and tear from the hectic pace I was keeping. I was also aware that before long, she too would need a break. I was hoping to surprise her with a spring trip–the result of a sales contest we were in at the dealership. We were currently leading in our group and if we won, we would be going to Palm Springs, California as a reward. I hadn't yet told her of the trip because I wasn't sure how she would react to leaving the kids for a few days. Anyway, tonight it was going to be tennis.

The people at the club were glad to see us. It had been weeks since we had made it there. Baxter and I played a singles match and then combined to play doubles against some friends of ours. I couldn't believe how much I enjoyed the physical activity. I had missed working out and doing something athletic. I guess these are the sacrifices fathers make all the time–at least until the kids are old enough to coach, or worse, to compete against you. Nevertheless, I thoroughly enjoyed my couple of hours playing tennis. It was still early when we finished so Baxter and I decided to have a few beers on our way home. We stopped at Hank's Restaurant in Brooklyn for a couple of brews. Hank and his family were customers of Cassidy Motors and I always liked to go there to reciprocate with my business. We stayed for an hour or so, long enough for a couple of rounds, when someone came in and said there was a big fire on Main Street in Danville. It was on our way home so we decided to see what was going on downtown. At the top of the hill near Day Street, we got a horrifying glimpse at what we thought was a small blaze. It looked like the whole town was on fire. As we approached the highway bridge that crossed the Quinebaug River into Danville, all we could see was a huge rose-colored cloud sitting on top of the buildings on Main Street. Police vehicles blocked the road heading into town so we went around the downtown area by way of Broad Street. We were blocked again as we got to Canyon Drive so we turned up to the highway bypass and came down Raymond Street on the far end of town. The view coming down the hill was frightening. There were flames and smoke covering the downtown area and fire engines and firemen were everywhere. As we got to the bottom of Raymond Street, I looked to our right and spotted a tenement house that was on fire. Flames were engulfing the upstairs area. We drove to the edge of the downtown fire and looked for firemen to tell them of the fire on Raymond. They were all busy.

Baxter and I were far from heroes, but we decided to go back and knock on the door to see if we could get any of the occupants out of the house. When we got to the front door, we knocked and yelled as loud as we could. Finally, after what seemed like an eternity, an elderly lady in a bathrobe appeared. She was visibly upset at our intrusion but we finally convinced her that she had to get out of the house. When she was safe outside, she told us that an elderly man lived in the upstairs apartment. We ran to the back door and yelled his name to no avail. I could see that the fire was coming from his apartment, so I kicked in the door to the hallway that led upstairs. Baxter and I went into the house and started to scream his name and try to get his attention. We got nothing. We decided to go upstairs and see if we could find the man's apartment. When we reached the second floor landing, a wall of smoke almost knocked us down the stairs. I got on my hands and knees to get under the smoke and began to crawl down the hallway as Baxter continued to scream out the man's name. The wall of smoke began to choke us and we had to retreat. We went back to Main Street and were able to alert a fireman of the possibility of an elderly man being trapped in his home on Raymond Street. Several rescue workers hurried to the scene and went into the smoldering building with gas masks on. They were able to find the man unconscious in his room and removed him by stretcher. Unfortunately, the old man died that evening of smoke inhalation.

Baxter and I had shared many adventures through the years, but the one of the old man who died in the fire because we couldn't reach him was one that we rarely ever spoke of again. The fact that we probably saved the life of the elderly woman on the first floor was small consolation. That night a corner of Main Street in Danville that included a hardware store and an office building had burned to the ground. Because of the quick work of the various volunteer fire departments in the area, the rest of Main Street was saved. There were no casualties reported in the downtown blaze, but an old man who lived a lonely life by himself in a second story of a tenement building on an adjacent street was pronounced dead at the scene of the house fire.

The next morning, Katie was reading the newspaper account of the Main Street inferno. She said a man died in the fire. Reading on, she asked if we saw any of it on our way home. I just shook my head and said, "We saw more than I care to talk about."

Chapter Sixteen

Time to Reload

"There is no substitute for hard work."
Thomas A. Edison

Pierre's resignation came at the worst possible time. Business was picking up rapidly and customers were once again finding their way to the showroom. These were the good times we had longed for through some very difficult months. The shame was that Pierre wouldn't be with us to benefit from the increase in traffic and the opportunities to make more money. His reason for leaving was understandable. His father had offered him a position working with him at his marina in Florida. After a long hard winter and sluggish sales, who could blame him for wanting to make a change? Everyone at the dealership would miss him. It would be very difficult to replace him, but we had to find someone quickly to gear up for what looked like a great spring selling season. In spite of the loss of Pierre, the dealership had to move forward.

The sales contest for the trip to Palm Springs had ended in March and we were declared the winners. It was somewhat unusual that a dealership our size would be in a position to win one of these contests, but Chevrolet had modified their rules, pitting dealers of similar size in groups. We were selling against a quota and the final percentage of sales against that quota would determine the winner in each group.

Because of our modest performance in past years at the old dealership, our assigned quota was relatively low. With the good effort my guys put forth in the last several months, we almost doubled our quota and won easily. The trip wouldn't be until the fall, but it would give Katie something to look forward to and prepare for.

For me, it would give me added incentive and time to replace Pierre. I knew that wouldn't be easy. Where do you find someone to replace the ace of your staff? Mediocre salesmen were a dime-a-dozen and we had gone through our share of the misdirected, the inept, and the moronic. I was looking for another Pierre and that would be very difficult. After a particularly exhausting day interviewing new candidates for the job, most of whom were woefully inadequate, Francois asked me if I would join him for a drink at Hank's. I cleared it with Katie and told him I was good only for one and that would be it. After several drinks, I spotted a big man sitting at the other end of the bar.

"Frenchman, is that the guy who works at the Ford dealership in town? Let's talk to him to see if he has any desire to come in for an interview. He can't be happy working for the lunatic who owns that dealership."

Francois said that he thought he was the manager. I made up my mind to find out what kind of guy he was. I went over to him and introduced myself. He looked at me like I was some sort of predator.

"I know who you are," he said. We use your picture on our dart board."

I wasn't sure how to take that remark. Then he laughed and formally introduced himself.

"I'm Bob Shanahan. I was only kidding about the dart board."

We chatted some more and I realized that although his sense of humor was very dry, he was, in fact, quite interesting. I told him of our job opportunity and invited him to come in and fill out an application. He said he would, but warned me that he had always been a Ford man. Selling Chevrolets might not be something he would want to do. We concluded our conversation and when he stood up to shake my hand, I was amazed how big he was. Bob stood six feet, five inches tall with broad shoulders like a lumberjack. He towered over me.

"Did you ever play basketball?" I asked.

"Yeah, I played for Sterling High. I actually played against you guys from Danville. We gave you a good game, but you beat us by a couple of baskets."

I vaguely remembered him playing against us. I recalled that he was a lot thinner in those days. Oh well! I always said athletes make the best salesmen. Their competitive instincts give them an edge over the non-athlete. I guess it could be said that I was inclined to use athletic profiling.

'Big' Bob, as he soon became known, was hired later that week and began a long career as a trusted employee. He was quickly elevated to the role of sales manager, a position he held for many years. Even though he was unfamiliar with Chevrolets, Bob took over the chore of ordering all the new cars and trucks, one of the many responsibilities I had inherited when I came into the business. Bob's specialty was trucks. He was very knowledgeable about the technical specifications of trucks and which options were the most popular among truckers. He quickly gained a reputation as the man to see when purchasing a new Chevy C10 or bigger. Consequently, our sales in this very important segment of the market rose dramatically. Things were looking up. It was time to find another ace to join the staff.

Like a stray dog that wanders into your yard in search of a home, Frankie Peloquin roared into the dealership the day after the help wanted ad hit the paper. Frankie was the son of the former dealer in Westchester, just a few miles north of Danville. He had been associated with the car business since he was a teenager and felt betrayed when his father sold his dealership a year before. The timing of our ad was perfect for it came at a time when Frankie wanted to prove to the world that he was the consummate car guy. There was little doubt that he came with a chip on his shoulder and a score to settle with the new dealer in Westchester. We would try not to make too big a deal about that for it was important to me to get along with the local dealers.

Frankie was the eternal "rebel without a cause." He drove a hot, 1965 Corvette with a muffler that gurgled like a vacuum cleaner with a screw loose. He must have been born with a toothpick in his mouth and his collar up because both were part of his everyday appearance. Frankie had an irreverent way of looking at things and a cocky manner that somehow fit the image of someone in the car business, a business he absolutely loved. He had maverick good looks that attracted some outstanding looking girls to share his unorthodox lifestyle. He never was without a joke that he would laugh and slurp through as he was telling it. Frankie was indeed a character, hopefully a perfect fit for our sales staff, but he came with some considerable baggage. I had known Frankie for many years and we had always gotten along.

"Sean, my good buddy. How the hell are you?"

This was Frankie's idea of a job interview. I introduced him to Bob, and it was apparent immediately that two people couldn't have been less compatible. Bob was a solid family man who cherished his life with his wife and two daughters. Frank would have dated Bob's daughters if they were old enough. Bob didn't like cocky and arrogant people. Frankie was cocky and arrogant. This arrangement at first seemed doomed by the painfully obvious differences in personalities and lifestyle. I made my pitch to Bob about the good things that Frankie could do for us, but I thought it was best if I left the decision to hire Frankie up to Bob.

"Bob, this is what I know about Frankie. He's a handful, but he can sell cars. He can deal with people that you and I probably wouldn't even talk to. We can't become one-dimensional in our approach to this sales team. We have to be able to adapt to the different kinds of customers that come in here. We'd have to watch him and try to control him the best we can, but I think Frankie could be a big asset to us."

"Sean, this is your dealership. It's your reputation that's on the line. I'm sure I could get along with Frankie if I had to, but if he crosses me the wrong way or jeopardizes what we're trying to accomplish here, I'll be the first to get rid of him. Just so you know, I'm willing to give it a try, but it will be a short leash."

"That's fair enough. I've got a feeling this could work out just fine. I know you told me you have a bad temper. I can only hope that Frankie doesn't get to see it."

With the hiring of 'Big' Bob Shanahan and Frankie Peloquin, the cornerstones of a potentially spectacular sales team were set. With a few more additions to compliment our staff, we would be ready to take advantage of the expected boom in the car business. We were ready for the eighties.

Chapter Seventeen

Go West, Young Man

"Mamas, don't let your babies grow up to be cowboys"
Willie Nelson

I was brimming with enthusiasm when I came home for dinner. I knew Katie would be busy feeding and doting on our two little boys, but I couldn't contain my excitement as I entered the door.

"Katie! Are you sitting down? I've got something to tell you."

"Sitting down? Hardly. With these two, there's not much time to sit down. What do you want to tell me?"

"Have you ever ridden a horse? What do you think about rubbing elbows with Bob Hope?"

"Sean, I have to feed the kids. They're not going to wait for me to figure out your riddle."

"Katie, we're going to Palm Springs, California. Five days and four nights in paradise."

"You won the contest! You're kidding. I thought you said only big dealers win these contests."

"I didn't want to get your hopes up. It's not until September, but we're heading west!"

Katie suddenly became introspective.

"How are we going to be able to go? We can't just leave the kids."

"Oh, they'll be all right. Jimmy's almost two. He could take care of his younger brother."

"Sean!!!"

"Look. I called your mother today and asked her if she would come down that week and take care of the kids. You know how much she loves these two little rug rats. She was thrilled. I don't think your father was quite as happy, but he said he would come along too. You see. They'll be in good hands while we're living the lifestyle of the rich and famous. What do you say? Five days in the desert and it's not costing us a penny."

"Well, it sounds great, but I don't know if I'll enjoy myself knowing that the kids are back here. What if the plane crashes?"

"Your parents can show them pictures of us. They'll be fine."

"Sean, you know you'll miss them as much as I will."

"Katie, of course I'll miss them, but we won't be the first parents to ever go on vacation without the kids. And, it's not as if we're leaving them with strangers. They'll be fine."

"You already said that. It's not them I'm worried about. I don't know if I can leave them for a whole week. I'll miss them terribly."

"Do you want me to give the trip to somebody else?"

Katie thought for a long moment and finally responded, "No, I'll go. But I'm not going to ride any horses."

I had no idea that Katie was going to be so difficult to convince to go on a vacation that was all paid for by Chevrolet. I was thankful that we had a few months before the trip so that she could get used to the news. Personally I had never been that far west, yet I grew up watching westerns on television and dreaming of being a cowboy. I could just imagine life on the range with folks from a wagon train, sitting around a campfire singing songs by the "Sons of the Pioneers." I was very much looking forward to this trip.

The sales continued to be strong through the spring and summer months. Bob and Frankie learned how to co-exist and became a very effective team. It's amazing to me how people from two completely different backgrounds, with two totally different views on life, can manage to coalesce. As different as they were as people, they shared a great sense of humor and a common goal of doing their respective jobs well. There were those times when one or the other would fall off the wall and react to adversity like a juvenile, but those times were few and far between. Frankie would avoid confrontations with Bob for fear of his physical wellbeing and Bob would occasionally go outside into the parking lot and let out a primeval scream that would have the effect of a teapot boiling over. He would return to the showroom minutes later, refreshed and ready to take on the next crisis. I had learned from working with Pierre that the good ones can be high strung and it was wise for me to just let these small diversions happen. Successful results were always the bottom line–no matter how you got there.

As sales continued to increase, we added to the sales staff. The first addition was my sister June's son, Jack. Jack had been working in the service area at the dealership since he left college to find himself. In spite of some insecurity, he possessed a charming personality and an ability to approach his job with a great deal of organization. In many ways he was the antithesis of Frankie who generally made his sales on the run with very little planning or method to his madness. Frankie relied solely on his magnetism and the loyal following of some misguided acquaintances from his many years in the car business. Jack and Frankie became good friends and worked well together. The team was growing in a positive way. With Bob as the sales manager that summer, the dealership was in good hands. It made the upcoming trip to Palm Springs much easier to undertake. I was confident that my being away for a week would not affect the business negatively. I hadn't always felt that way.

Katie's mother and father arrived on time to take care of our two cherished little boys while we were away. Leaving them was tougher than I had imagined. I thought Katie was going to have a nervous breakdown as the time neared for us to leave for the airport. After many kisses and hugs, we were off, determined to have a good time. Katie was more relaxed after we boarded the plane and prepared for takeoff. The flight was long, but once we arrived at the Palm Springs Airport and saw all the palm trees and beautiful flowers and vegetation, we couldn't wait to get to the resort. We checked into a beautiful room that bordered a golf course, A pond was right outside our first floor bungalow and our backside patio faced the outside restaurant that was no more than a hundred yards away. As we were to soon find out, Chevrolet rewarded their top performing dealers by sparing no expenses on these trips. Everything was first class and everything was paid for. Hesitant to take advantage of that at first, it didn't take me long to figure out that excess was not only expected, it was encouraged. Even Katie, who had grown up in a frugal family and was prone to live on a budget, couldn't avoid being caught up in this totally unfamiliar world. We were in paradise with an unlimited expense account.

That evening was the introductory social where we would meet all the other winning dealers and the Chevrolet executives whose jobs were to make sure their dealers had a good time. We walked into the social and were immediately greeted by Chevrolet people who couldn't have been more gracious. Katie was still a striking blonde and attracted a great deal of attention when she walked into the hall. I introduced myself as "Sean Cassidy. I'm with her."

It was really easy moving about the room meeting new people. There were dealers from all over the country. The older dealers tended to gravitate to each other and the younger ones, of which we certainly qualified, did the same. We were chatting away when all of a sudden this couple came over to us and introduced themselves. My God, I thought to myself, this couple belongs on a wedding cake. Benny Dick Hicks and his wife, Joy, from Dallas, Texas, sought us out because we gave the appearance of a couple that liked to have fun. Benny was a former football player at Kansas State who had movie star good looks and Joy was a former Miss Texas runner-up. Katie and Joy could have passed for sisters. They immediately hit it off and were quite adept at the art of non-stop conversation. Benny and I both drank Bourbon. We were great together. We spent the rest of the evening getting to know each other and planning some joint activities together. They were great people with big personalities and Joy had an accent that I could have listened to all day. Katie's not one to gush, but even she mentioned to me how good looking these two were. We struck up an instant friendship that lasted for the whole trip. The next morning at breakfast, the four of us were laughing and comparing notes on our families when another couple approached and asked if they could sit with us. They were a bit older than us but seemed like really nice people.

"Y'all mind if we join you. You look like y'all are having so much fun. We got stuck with some old fuddy-duddies last night and we can see that y'all are here to have a good time."

"Please. Have a seat." I said. "The more the merrier."

"We're Corwin and Bonnie Decker from just outside of Lawrence, Kansas. We are truly pleased to make your acquaintance."

We exchanged introductions and proceeded to have a lot of laughs at breakfast. Corwin was a small town dealer who was blessed with a fabulous sense of humor. Bonny possessed a great deal of mid-western charm. They were lovely people and fit right in with our new group.

The next few days went by like a blur. We had a fantastic time with our new friends and the six of us participated in all the activities together. These were people that we had just met, but because of their warmth and personalities, it seemed like we had known them forever. Benny was from a large dealership in Dallas, and much to my chagrin was a Dallas Cowboy fan. I grew up as a die-hard New York Giant fan. We had many discussions about which team was better, but it was all in fun.

The last day of our trip came too quickly. The activity we chose for that day was horseback riding. I recalled Katie's remark before the trip about not riding a horse, but Joy and Bonnie convinced her it would be fun. We soon found out that the stable of horses was on the Apache reservation. I had never been on a horse before so I was worried about affecting my ability to produce any more children. The trip coordinator assured me that I had a docile horse that was good with beginners. So off we went onto the reservation for our afternoon ride. As I looked around on my barely moving horse, I could easily imagine Geronimo leading a war party over the hills to attack our group and take our scalps. The landscape was gritty and stark. It was hard to believe I was on the same sacred ground where the great warriors of the old west had ridden. My boyhood fantasies were being fulfilled.

After about an hour, we came to the end of the trail. We turned around and headed back. My horse was the slowest, and because I was last in the pack, I swallowed a great deal of trail dust. With only a couple of hundred yards left before we returned to the stables, my horse suddenly came alive and bolted for home. I was holding on for dear life riding along at a gallop. When my horse bounced up, I bounced down. My privates were getting beaten up as I hung on. Finally, the horse darted into its stall as I ducked to miss the top of the stable door. The ride was mercifully over as was my horseback-riding career. Katie and

Bonnie were laughing so hard they could barely speak when they asked if I was OK. As painful as it was to talk, I answered as best I could.

"Don't worry about birth control tonight, Katie. I'm good."

The group was in hysterics at my expense, but I was plotting my next move, provided I would be able to move at all.

That night, we all met at the lounge to spend our last night in Palm Springs. A Country and Western band was playing and I went up and requested a song to be dedicated to our new friends, Benny Dick and Joy Hicks, and Corwin and Bonnie Decker. We raised our glasses as the band played a Willie Nelson classic.

Mamas, Don't Let Your Babies Grow up to be Cowboys.

Don't let 'em pick guitars and drive them old trucks
Make 'em be doctors and lawyers and such.
...They'll never stay home and they're always alone
Even with someone they love.

The next day we said our good byes to our new friends and vowed that we'd get together again someday. Of course, we never did. We exchanged Christmas cards for a number of years, but eventually that also stopped. For one week, however, in the fall of 1980, we shared a wonderful time with some great people whom we will never forget.

Chapter Eighteen

Promises Fulfilled...Promises Broken

> "My heart leaps up when I behold
> a rainbow in the sky."
> -William Wordsworth

When I returned from my first Chevrolet trip, I was rested and invigorated. The day-to-day wear and tear that goes with working ten hour days, six days a week, can sneak up on you and leave you in a robotic trance. Your mind becomes numb and your body begins to tire. Days begin to meld together forming a mystifying conundrum. You begin to question your place in the world and your significance in society. You're exhausted. A vacation can cure all these ills. You return with a renewed purpose and a desire to improve your lot in life. You are renewed. Your batteries have been recharged. Sometimes busy people forget they need a break. That never seems to turn out well. I had a great vacation and I was once again ready to tackle the world.

My father was surprisingly happy to see me. He had enjoyed his week in the showroom–I'm sure the same wasn't true for the sales team–but he was ready to go back to his gardening and morning muffins at Berris's Coffee Shop. He had earned the privilege of setting his own schedule and coming and going as he pleased. I could see contentment in him that had been missing during the turbulent times of the past few years.

He had hatched a dream of a busy and profitable modern dealership. Now that the business was living up to its potential, it was obvious that he had derived a great deal of satisfaction in the fulfillment of his dream. He never said it directly to me, but I knew he was also pleased with the job I was doing. It was nice to be appreciated–even though it was never expressed. My first day back on the job provided my father with the opportunity to just go home and tinker. I think there might have been a nap planned for some part of the afternoon. Naps are good when you are contented.

The following day, Dad showed up dressed in his best suit. I asked him what the occasion was. He said there was a dealer meeting in Hartford and it was time that I went with him.

"If you're ever going to take over this business, you're going to have to start going to these meetings. It's a great way for you to meet all the other dealers in the zone and also introduce yourself to the factory people. I'm not going to be around forever. Someday, you'll be going to these meetings alone. Why don't you go home and put on a suit–you know, make a good first impression."

I knew my father pretty well at this point. We had worked together for over five years and I knew it was a rare day when he would volunteer even a hint of stepping aside. Long ago, he had made his intentions known of turning the dealership over to me, but he had never totally fulfilled his promise. I wasn't comfortable pressing him on this point and was placated, at least temporarily, by the knowledge that I was fully in control of the operation. He was satisfied with my job performance but he was reticent to give up control of the ownership. I compared his intentions to those of an old sea captain who is reluctant to leave the bridge of his ship. For the past few years we had sailed through troubled waters, but now it looked like we were headed for calmer seas. I could feel that he might be getting ready to fulfill his aging promise.

"The person I want to introduce you is to is the zone manager, Ken Culver. He's been after me to initiate an ownership transfer of dealer stock. Because of tax ramifications, and quite frankly, my reluctance to give up total control, we're going to do this in twenty-five per cent increments. You will initially be in control of twenty-five per cent of the stock. I will own the remaining seventy-five per cent and will distribute to you the remainder in a timely fashion over the next couple of years.

Your stock will satisfy Chevrolet's minimum requirement for ownership transfer so we can begin the process of making you the Dealer-Operator. It's not as complicated as it sounds, but we still have to go through the necessary steps. Ken Culver's a very impressive man. He represents the image of the kind of individual you would want in the position of zone manager. He's brilliant, compassionate, and extremely capable. If it wasn't for his positive reinforcement throughout the whole relocation process, I doubt if I would have ever built a new facility. You'll do well to listen to any advice he has for you. He told me on the phone yesterday that he was anxious to meet you."

I called Katie to tell her what was going on and she was all excited. She told me to call her again the minute we got home from the meeting. My adrenalin was pumping, much the same way it had before an important athletic event. Six years ago, the promise was made to me that someday the dealership was going to be mine. At that time, I had no idea that I would have to serve a six-year apprenticeship before anything was done. Katie and I had even talked often about moving on to another career in another part of the country. My father's announcement had probably come at just the right time before we made a radical decision to leave the area.

It had been years since my father had gone to one of these dealer meetings. He told the factory representative who came regularly to the dealership that if the zone people wanted to talk to him, they knew where to find him. He was one of the last of an independent breed that ran their dealership with very little guidance from Chevrolet and very little interference. Chevrolet tolerated these old timers because their fierce independence was a sign of strength. When my father decided to build a new facility in a great location, it must have come as a tremendous shock to the power structure in the zone office. My father was now in his seventies. They were looking for a successor plan, and that plan included me. Our appearance at a dealer meeting was the first step in establishing that succession.

I wasn't nervous as we entered the Ramada Inn ballroom in Hartford, but I was uncomfortable. I had certainly been exposed before to many important people during my days at NASA in Boston. This was different. It was like I was going to a cattle auction to be prodded and evaluated and bid on. I was going to be judged by people I had never met before. I was confident I would make a good first impression–after all I didn't have any tattoos, or piercings, or long greasy hair. I spoke the King's English, had a college degree from a reputable college, and had a secret government clearance. I was married to a beautiful woman and had two terrific young boys. I didn't smoke, cursed only when I was with my friends, and could drink socially without getting drunk. I thought to myself: 'for God's sake, what else could they be looking for?'

My growing fears were immediately dispersed when my father introduced me to Ken Culver. He was the epitome of a gentleman. He made me feel welcomed in a warm and gracious manner. He told me that he had heard good things about me from his factory reps and was happy that he finally had the chance to meet me. After several minutes of small talk, we sat down at his table for a catered lunch. During our meal, Ken dispensed cursory advice solely for the purpose of making me feel comfortable. I respectfully listened intently to his every word. He outlined the procedure my father had to follow to add my name to the ownership papers. He expressed his approval of my father's decision and added that he looked forward to many years working with me. I wasn't sure how long all this would take, but I was encouraged by the direction we were headed. Finally, after six years of unfulfilled promises, I was becoming part of the ownership of Cassidy Motors. Katie would be pleased. I couldn't wait to get home to tell her.

Chapter Nineteen

Priorities

"...only if you've been in the deepest valley can you ever know how magnificent it is to be on the highest mountain."

–Richard M. Nixon

The bridge between decades is sometimes littered with the carcasses of ill-fated outcomes of well-conceived intentions. The Seventies were distinguished by the absurd, the mismanaged and the unimaginable. President Jimmy Carter's one-term presidency was a glowing example of the wrong man at the wrong time. Whether it was foreign or domestic policy, he seemed inept at making the right choices. Facing heavy criticism for his economic policies, he was suddenly faced with the Russian invasion of Afghanistan. Carter's response was a boycott of the 1980 Summer Olympics in Moscow, which did little to punish the Russians but deprived our Olympic athletes of the opportunity to compete on the international stage.

The economic news continued to be bad. Citing poor quality control, rising import competition, and a severe economic downturn, Chrysler Corporation and American Motors were near bankruptcy. Ford was also going through a bad stretch. Only General Motors seemed to be weathering the hard times. To top off the decade of turbulence, Mount

Saint Helen erupted killing 60 people and John Lennon was gunned down outside his Dakota Apartment in the Upper West Side of New York, effectively ending the era of the Beatles. With the conclusion of the decade came the hope of a new beginning. People were looking for new leadership.

As big a mess as Jimmy Carter had made of the last part of the Seventies, the election of a new president, Ronald Reagan, heralded fresh optimism. The fact that he was a Republican certainly sat well with one member of the Cassidy family. My mother could have been the standard bearer for the Republican Party. She was still convinced that Richard Nixon got a raw deal and that Watergate was the result of a Democratic plot to discredit his presidency. My mother was a stubborn woman. Once she made up her mind about something, you weren't going to change her thinking. She was thrilled that Ronald Reagan was our new president. Not the least of her reasons for being thrilled was the fact that she thought he was handsome. My mother's leaders had better be good looking or she didn't trust them. Obviously, she had no use for Lyndon Johnson.

As the eighties began, my mother became a more frequent visitor to the office. She loved Josette and often her visits were extended as she took the time to get to know the new girls that joined Josette's team as well as the new guys that were hired to work in sales. Frankie, in particular, went out of his way to be nice to my mother, always opening the door for her when she arrived and waiting on her hand and foot. He would often have a new joke to tell, or a story that would make her laugh. If you made my mother laugh, you were assured of her allegiance and support. I was sure that Frankie was sincere in his attention to my mother, but I also knew he was aware of how his bread was buttered. It became apparent to me that my mother was making an effort to be around the dealership more and I wondered why. One day I decided to ask her.

"Mom, are you worried that I'm not doing a good job?"

"Not at all, Sean. I can see your employees like you a great deal. Your father hasn't been feeling too well lately, so I thought that I would come down here in his place."

"To check on me?"

"Come on, Sean. Don't be so sensitive. I enjoy coming in and seeing everyone, and that includes you. You know, you and Katie don't come over to the house very much anymore, and this is the only time I get to see you."

"Message delivered. We've been busy with the kids and the dogs and getting our house squared away. The only day I have off is Sunday, so that doesn't leave much time for visiting. We'll make a point of coming over this weekend. I hope you're ready for two non-stop little boys who will probably get into everything."

"Sean, you know I don't mind. Clinton and Jaime are coming down this weekend, but I'm sure they'd love to see the kids too. June and Rick will probably also be there with their clan. It might just be the medicine your father needs to feel better. He's been very tired lately–sleeps all the time."

"Is Clinton still his charming self. He seemed pretty ticked off when I started at the dealership. He must have thought Dad was going to make him his successor."

"Don't be silly, Sean. That was never going to happen. Your father and Clinton just don't get along. They've learned to tolerate each other, but that's it. Boy, you're very paranoid today."

"Paranoid or justifiably suspicious. I've heard some of the disparaging remarks Clinton's made about me since I've been back. He doesn't think an English major is the right fit for the dealership. He thinks I'm over my head. I personally don't like him and I certainly don't trust him."

"Oh, Sean. Don't cause a big scene over some imaginary grudge. Let it lie."

"OK, Mom. We'll be there in the afternoon after church. After all, someone in this family has to go to church. I always tell the kids when they start whining about going to Mass: 'If you don't have time for God, He won't have time for you.' They're still young, but not too young to understand. It's propaganda from my good Catholic education that you guys so kindly paid for."

"Well, it will be good to see them. Your father really lights up when he sees those two. He knows they're the torchbearers of the family. It's up to them to carry on the name. I also think they both remind him of himself when he was a small boy. It's tough getting old. You're only left with memories."

"We'll be there, Mom. I'll even do you a favor and leave the dogs home."

Our two dogs were very much a part of the family. Goldie, our blonde Cocker Spaniel, was still with us from our days in Boston. She was a sweetheart and was very tolerant of the physical abuse she got from the boys. Our other dog, Sam, was a stray that we had gotten from the Boston pound. He was an all black, mostly Labrador retriever that was very feisty and very protective of Katie and the kids. The last time we took him over to my parent's house he put on quite a show. It was summer and the Cassidy clan had gathered outside the house by the pool. Sam and I were in the yard tossing a ball and Katie and the kids were poolside. Clinton ominously was hanging around Katie attempting to be charming. I noticed him staring at Katie uncomfortably. He suddenly lifted her up in his arms and attempted to throw her in the water. She screamed at the sudden move and was fighting to get free when Sam noticed her yell. He was off like a shot and in full stride, hurdled the fence that surrounded the pool. Clinton's' eyes became as big as saucers as Sam settled in front of his crotch, growling. He quickly let go of Katie, putting her down very gingerly so as to not upset Sam any further. I took my sweet time calling the dog off. I thought the whole scene was quite humorous but I guess Clinton didn't share my humor. We barely spoke the rest of the day, but I made sure that he heard me say to Sam, "Good boy."

Chapter Twenty

Planned Obsolescence

"Don't be so busy making a living that you forget what you are living for."

-Unknown

Promotions were a big part of the sales strategy that we unveiled in the early Eighties. People needed a reason to trade their car and purchase a new one. The car business had been built on the theory of "planned obsolescence." The theory was based on the fact that cars and trucks were not built to last forever. Sooner or later, parts would fail; tires would wear down; exteriors would rust. Any number of problems could develop as the vehicle aged, all traceable to the planned obsolescence of the car or truck. The manufacturers never admitted to this practice, but it only made sense that the future of their business rested on this theory. A dealer's success or failure could be dependent on the ability to appeal to the basic human desire to purchase something new. Promotions were designed to give that basic human desire a kick-start.

Spring was always a great time to run a promotion, especially in the northeast part of the country where people endure long, hard winters from which they eventually begin to suffer from a horrible human condition called "Cabin Fever." The symptoms of this condition include: a desire to be outside for more than the time it takes to shovel the driveway; an abhorrence for the color white; skin so dry you could peel it with a knife; a real need to barbecue some meat wearing your Bermuda shorts; and a strong eagerness to once again use bug spray while roaming some golf course with lush green fairways. Cabin fever can be serious, but it can also be the catalyst for a successful spring selling season. Once people are turned loose in the good weather, their buying patterns change immediately. It was paramount that we make our product as appealing and affordable as necessary to take advantage of the change in season.

The reputation that we had worked diligently to establish as the place to buy a new Camaro was the basis of our spring promotion in 1981. We had over twenty Camaros in stock, each equipped differently and each sporting one of the many color variations available that year. It was quite a sight driving by our dealership with the many different Camaros parked on the front line, all of which were being offered at greatly discounted prices. We were prepared to blow the competition away with our prices and our selection. To further spice up our promotion, I hired some young local girls to model for our cars in our ads. The ads proved to be quite popular and reached many neighboring communities drawing in customers from areas that we would normally not reach. Our salesmen were pumped. As the week progressed, our sales were good, but not great. We were looking forward to a big Saturday. Bob decided to bring some trucks up front near the road to attract a different clientele than we had earlier in the week. The mix of the trucker crowd and the sports car enthusiasts was just the blend we needed. All day Saturday, we were packed. Some people just came to get a free hot dog or hamburger that we were cooking outside on the grill. One elderly gentleman went so far as to bring an empty bag with him to the promotion and when he thought no one was looking, he scraped a dozen or so hotdogs off the grill into his bag. He would have gotten away with it if he hadn't gotten greedy and tried to take the mustard and ketchup bottles that were on the table near the grill. Francois noticed him and quickly confiscated his bag. We decided to just let him have the food if he was that desperate, but we did tell him never to come back to the dealership for any reason. This incident illustrated the nature of promotions. They drew real customers into your showroom, but they also attracted many people who were just looking for the free stuff. Unfortunately, these people would hang around most of the day, generally in the area of the grill, and take advantage of the dealership hospitality. Some were driven to desperate measures to makes ends meet. Most, however, were degenerates or delinquents. In either case, it was Francois' job to control the unruly portion of the crowd. He was eminently qualified for this duty because of his years as an army cook. Mess with Francois and he'd hit you with a spatula. The grilled food was just a part of the promotion. The real action was in the give and take of negotiating the price of an automobile. The rest of our sales staff was busy concentrating on the potential buyers that came to enjoy a day of fun with the ultimate goal of buying a car. The haves and the have-nots–such was society in 1981.

It looked early on in the day that we were going to set a record for a Saturday sale. Our previous record was eleven sales set several years ago during our first Corvette raffle. On this Saturday, we sold eleven before noon. We ended the day at five o'clock with thirty written deals. Not all the deals would make it through financing, but the majority was solid.

The only casualty of the day seemed to be to the ego of my nephew, Jack. Sometime during the busiest part of the afternoon, Jack greeted a young man who was interested in a new Z28 Camaro. Having had a big day already, Jack relished the fact that he could make a good commission on this sale. The young man said he was from Rhode Island and had been attracted to the dealership by our ads in the Rhode Island papers. Jack was anxious to make the last big deal so he forgot to go through the basics of selling by asking the young man for his license. Instead, he consented to take a test drive without verification of the man's identity. The young man asked Jack if he could drive into Rhode Island to see how the car handled on the back roads in Foster, the first town over the state line. Jack agreed and off they went. When they got fairly deep into the remote areas of Foster, the young man asked if Jack heard the noise coming out of the back end of the car. Trying to be accommodating, Jack told him to stop the car and he would get out and attempt to identify the noise. The young man started the car and moved slowly forward maintaining the charade until he was clear of Jack. He then waved good-bye, sticking his arm out of the window as he roared away with his freshly stolen Z28. He was quickly over the horizon and out of sight. Embarrassed and more than a little pissed off, Jack began the long walk down the deserted road. We wondered what had happened to Jack back at the dealership for it had been over an hour since he left on the test drive. Mortified but unhurt, Jack eventually reached a house and was able to call and tell us of his adventure. We sent a car to pick him up. He arrived back at the dealership about the same time the state police did. He sheepishly re-entered the showroom to a chorus of catcalls and laughter and then he had to explain what happened to the police. Several days passed before the police discovered the car–or rather what was left of it–in a chop shop in Providence. Insurance covered the loss of the car, but nothing would lighten Jack's mood. He was emotionally damaged, easily susceptible to the barbs and the sarcasm that Big Bob, Francois, and Frankie were laying on him. It would be some time before he regained his sense of humor and his self-respect. Promotion Saturday had been a big success–thirty sales and only one badly bruised ego. Not bad for an early spring day in March.

Chapter Twenty-One

Man's Best Friend

"Walk beside me, and just be my friend."
Albert Camus

When the boys were old enough to walk around, they became my constant companions when I was home. Their favorite thing to do was to help Daddy with the lawn. We bought each of them a plastic mini-mower with which they followed me around the yard as I mowed. We didn't have a big yard, but it was a huge deal for them to be outside helping me keep the lawn in good shape. The dogs would join in, frolicking about between the boys. The parade around the yard was something to see. It amazed me how well the dogs had taken to the boys. They had never been around small humans before but they somehow sensed the need to be patient and tolerant of the kids. Goldie was a very mellow dog so her behavior was not surprising. Sam, however, had a feisty demeanor that included fighting any dog that came close to our family or our yard. He wasn't very popular with the neighborhood kids, but our boys loved him. Sam would have been happiest on a farm with lots of acreage to explore. To confine such a free spirit on our little three quarters of an acre lot posed some problems whenever he was loose. Even though he was harmless, big black dogs scare people.

Our last year in Boston had been particularly exciting for Sam as he was constantly in dogfights with breeds ranging from poodles to Great Danes. He was a scrapper with a tremendous heart. The combination of guts and glory provided me with too many occasions when I would have to break up a dogfight before one of the dogs got hurt. Risking my own health never occurred to me because Sam was like my brother. His fights were my fights.

His last fight in Boston may have been his most memorable. A cocky young guy showed up one day in the field at Chandler Pond, where we lived. Even from a distance, I could tell by his demeanor that he and I were probably not going to be friends. He had with him the largest German shepherd I had ever seen. The dog stood waist high to his owner and had a huge head with visibly forbidding teeth. Noticing right away that this dog was possibly dangerous I looked for Sam to bring him inside before an altercation could develop. He had wandered down to the far side of the field about a hundred yards away. When he looked up to see where I was, he spotted this massive dog entering his territory. Without as much as a hesitation, Sam took off in the direction of the behemoth. The owner, whom I guessed was compensating for his insignificance by walking his huge dog haphazardly on private property, unleashed his hound. The monster took off in Sam's direction. The fact that this dog was at least twice as big didn't deter Sam for a second. The two came together like battling buffalos. I ran as fast as I could to the fight when I saw that there was no way Sam was going to win this one. The other dog, whose name was Cannabis, had his huge mouth around Sam's throat. Sam continued to fight, but you could tell he was losing his will. I yelled at the young guy, who had unleashed this monster, to call off his dog, but he just smirked as if he was enjoying the one-sided outcome. Without thinking of the consequences, I burrowed into the middle of the fray. I managed to grab the skin on Sam's back and pried him away from the vicious beast. I put him on my shoulder shielding him from the teeth of the monster, exposing myself to the crazed animal. Miraculously, the dog backed off. I looked at the owner who was still wearing a smirk on his face happy with the vicarious victory his dog had secured for him. Incensed, I shouted at this pompous jerk that had been brazen enough to bring his savage dog onto private property not caring if it would maim or kill another animal. I remember losing complete control at that point and yelling a string of vulgarities at him.

His response was short and way too bold for somebody hiding behind his dog.

"What's the matter, buddy," he replied. "Is your dog too small to fight mine."

I could barely contain my fury, but I knew I had to take Sam back to the apartment to tend to his injuries. Still, I was furious and wanted a piece of this little coward. I told him to meet me in an hour at the same place without the dogs.

He never showed. I found out later that he was visiting a girlfriend at the neighboring apartments. Some guys attempt to make up for their lack of testosterone by driving a sleek sports car or by owning a big dog. This guy had both. It was the classic case of this little twerp trying to compensate for his shortcomings. As angry as I was at the time, it's a good thing he didn't show up for I might have been arrested for aggravated assault.

Tending to Sam was something that led to the formation of a lasting bond between us. He looked at me with adoring eyes as I cleaned his wounds. I could only admire his courage because he had fought bravely in a fight that he had little chance of winning. His eyes told the story of a battle lost, but they also displayed the love of a dog for his master.

There were other less violent incidences–other territorial fights–that only cemented our relationship. A man couldn't have asked for a better pet. He was fearless, brave and loyal. Sam was a man's dog. After each confrontation, he would settle down next to me on the couch in our living room. His instincts were to be free and to roam the countryside unfettered, but his loyalty kept him from going too far. He enjoyed his quiet time with Baxter, Goldie and me. However incongruous the four of us appeared, we were a family. Later, he would allow Katie into his life, but he was very careful whom he let in.

When we moved to Beverly Avenue in Danville, his life was far less exciting because he had to be tied up when he was unsupervised outside. His world, which once included a great deal of the neighborhood in Boston, now was confined to a small area near the tree he was tied to in the back of the yard. Whenever he was allowed to run free, his old spirit would resurface and he would proudly prance about like the stud that he used to be. Sam's life had indeed changed, but he remained the loyal guardian of the family. As long as Sam was around, Katie, the kids, and, of course, Goldie, felt protected.

Chapter Twenty-Two

Clarence

"There is a great deal of human nature in people."
Mark Twain

The tedium of the long days in the showroom continued to be a problem for me. I was used to the fast paced work environment of an editorial group that included deadlines and panic and controlled bedlam. Achieving success was totally dependent on being able to think on your feet while those same feet barely touched the ground. After a while, it became addictive to be frenzied. The tighter the schedule was, the more exciting the atmosphere. There was tremendous gratification when the job was completed. Days in the showroom rarely approached the chaos I had been used to. To compensate, we would look for diversions to keep us busy until the next customer came in. Often these diversions came from the lineup of characters that would find their way into the showroom on a regular basis for their morning coffee and chat with whomever was free to listen to them. Most were harmless and therefore were welcomed. Some were more colorful than others.

One of our first regulars was Clarence. He was a retired painter who became our first driver. Every dealer needs someone to run errands, give customers courtesy rides, and generally just be available whenever we needed them. Clarence made himself available and with him he brought a great personality that included a daily sick joke that we all looked forward to. He was a big man with a checkered past. Some people in his neighborhood remembered him as a tough guy, but in his retirement, he had mellowed into a loveable teddy bear. Clarence and Francois were good friends and frequently claimed that they "plowed many of the same fields." For Clarence, his big moment at Cassidy Motors came during his participation in one of our seasonal promotions. He would volunteer for whatever we needed him to do, including helping Francois on the barbecue. On this particular day, he was busy flipping burgers when he noticed a demandingly difficult customer giving Frankie a tough time–so much so that it seemed he was intentionally trying to frustrate Frankie and make him look incompetent in front of the man's wife. Clarence watched the entire proceeding from within earshot. His reaction would provide a lasting image of Clarence and his loyalty to our dealership. He waited for the right moment when he could sense that the man's wife was definitely interested in the car that Frankie was showing her husband. Clarence went to work.

"Hey, Frankie," he started. "I don't mean to interrupt you, but I've got some good news. I'm glad you held that car for me. My wife gave me the OK to buy it. Do you mind if I take it home to show it to her?"

Frankie had been in the business a long time and caught on very quickly to Clarence's ruse. He looked first at the wife with a shrug and then turned to the disrespectful husband.

"I'm sorry, guys," he said. "This man was looking at the car yesterday and…"

The suddenly courteous husband interrupted him.

"But we're ready to make you an offer."

Frankie and Clarence huddled in mock discussion until Clarence feigned an angry reply. He spoke loud enough for the customers to hear: "If they don't buy it, you had better call me right away."

Frankie was always good at closing deals so it was easy finishing what would have been a marathon negotiation without Clarence's interference. The customers got the car they wanted; the wife was especially happy; and Frankie was able to make a nice commission on a deal he would have probably had to give up most of the profit to close. Such was the nature of the business. Sometimes the simplest of negotiations could turn ugly over a few dollars. In this case, with a little help from the Oscar performance delivered by one of our drivers, everyone was a winner. Frankie and Clarence would team up on other occasions, often successfully.

Clarence would always end his day at Cassidy Motors with a warm adieu. "Good day everyone. May all your dreams come true."

Unfortunately for all of us, Clarence's time with us was too short. Not long after his double team sale with Frankie, this big robust man who was full of life and who was well liked by the entire dealership personnel, died suddenly in his sleep of a heart attack.

Chapter Twenty-Three

Dad

"The doors of wisdom are never shut."
Benjamin Franklin

Much has been said about my father. He was an individual of great contradictions. He was a man of letters, with a high intelligence and with knowledge of many subjects. He majored in accounting in college, but knew as much about History and English and Philosophy. He could quote Irish poets and describe in detail the battle of Hastings in 1066. He had a strong love for his family, nevertheless had a difficult time expressing that love. He was not a big man, but seemed larger because of the commanding presence of his voice. He was extremely frugal yet was known for his generosity to local causes. He was principled and reserved–still he could drink a bottle of Irish whiskey with his friends while singing the Whiffenpoof song. Harmonies with my mom, his sister, Peg and her husband, Jim in our kitchen on Broad Street always included a rendition of this famous tune that is generally associated with Yale University. As kids, we called it the 'Baa, Baa, Baa' song. It was obviously his favorite.

From the tables down at Mory's
To the place where Louie dwells,

And the dear, old Temple Bar we love so well,
Sing the Whiffenpoofs assembled,
With their glasses raised on high,
And the magic of their singing, casts a spell.

We are poor little lambs
Who have lost our way,
Baa! Baa! Baa!
We are little, black sheep
Who have gone astray,
Baa! Baa! Baa!

Gentlemen, songsters, off on a spree,
Doomed from here to eternity.
Lord! Have mercy on such as we,
Baa! Baa! Baa!

Melody attributed to Tod Galloway

Edward Cassidy was Irish to the core. He openly admired his parents who had come over from Ireland at the beginning of the Twentieth Century. His father was the equivalent of a professional baseball player in an era when local teams were challenged by barnstorming major leaguers who in their offseason travelled around the country to earn a few extra bucks. Grandpa loved to tell stories of pitching against the likes of Babe Ruth and Ty Cobb. When he was in his seventies, he could still throw a mean sinker and a screwball that I couldn't even catch, let alone hit. He was a gregarious, wonderful man who unfortunately possessed the Cassidy addiction gene. In the last years of his life he succumbed to a dependency on alcohol and Copenhagen Snuff. He survived the alcohol addiction, somehow avoiding the family ban on supplying him with booze, by storing bottles of beer behind the garage. The snuff, however led to throat cancer and the removal of his voice box. For a man who loved to spin a good yarn and emboss a tasty tale, not being able to speak was too cruel a punishment for him to bear. He died a silent, sad man who nevertheless always was able to perk up when he saw his grandson coming. I shared my father's love for the man whom he affectionately called, 'The Old Gent.'

Dad followed his own athletic path. While a young boy in his hometown of Manchester, Connecticut, he learned the art of diving at the local YMCA. He became so proficient at the sport that he earned a scholarship to Boston University from which he graduated in 1933, at the height of the Great Depression. Our house was full of his many trophies that celebrated his diving prowess. He never spoke of his athletic achievements–he let Mom do the bragging for him–but it was obvious by the open display of his awards in the cabinets surrounding the fireplace that he was proud of what he had accomplished. To be a champion diver, you have to be without fear, and there was no doubt that Dad was a bit of a daredevil. He co-owned a plane and was often seen skimming the treetops for kicks. He stopped flying completely when his co-owner crashed while flying solo and was killed. Shaken by the tragedy, but not deterred, he continued to drive his car faster than the other parents we knew and would always be willing to take a dare. Sometimes my mother would be annoyed by his recklessness, but often she would look like a star struck young girl. He was daring, dashing and fun. He loved his home; he loved the car business; and he loved having a good time. He possessed a rapier wit and a zest for life bordering on obsessive. His obsession with drinking robbed him of his middle age, nonetheless it was clear that he had conquered his demons in his later years and was reveling in the success of his business that he had started in the early 1940's and restarted, with his new building in its new location, when he entered his golden years. His master plan was to leave the dealership to his youngest son to carry on his legacy. He was well aware of my initial reluctance to come into the business, but was obviously pleased with my final decision to leave the playground of Boston and return to my roots in Danville.

Despite my reservations about working with my father, we established a comfortable business model with my Dad as the corporation head and with me as the engineer that drove the corporate train. It truly amazed me how little we disagreed on important matters concerning the dealership. While I was growing up, our relationship was functionally non-existent, but somehow we were able to create an ownership of mutual respect. True to his image of contradiction, there were family members that he didn't treat as fairly. Chip, of course, was a constant malcontent and often a disgruntled distraction. Their relationship had included years of animosity that precluded its repair. He looked much more kindly on his three girls, although he had very little good to say about Jaime's husband, Clinton. His first born, June, maintained a special spot in his heart; and Pat, his rebellious daughter, was special to him because her personality was a reflection of his. My mother was his partner, yet like many Irishman, he sometimes forgot about the "for better or worse" part of his marital vows. She was the glue that kept the family together during his mid-life crisis years, and I'm sure he felt his kids had a stronger allegiance to her than to him. Whether that allegiance caused tension between the two would be easy to answer if my father were not such a complicated man. It was part of his personality–some say it was part of his charm–that such feelings were never exposed. It was a rare day when you could get a true barometer of what he was thinking. Because I often wore my emotions on my sleeve, I most admired his controlled demeanor. It was therefore with some degree of alacrity that I accepted his request to go over to his house with Katie to chat about the future of Cassidy Motors.

After a few awkward moments in which he attempted to be hospitable, Katie and I sat down in his living room. He started by saying that he didn't know how much longer he would be active in the dealership and he wanted to make sure that I was aware of his wishes.

"At my age, with my past history, who knows how long I'll be around?"

You could tell he was uncomfortable speaking so openly to us, but he nevertheless continued on.

"There are a few things I want to talk to you about before it's too late."

"Dad, I …"

"No, let me finish. Katie, I want you to know how happy I am that you're my daughter-in-law. Sean couldn't have picked a better girl. And Sean, I hope you realize how lucky you are to have her. That being said, I want you to take care of some loose ends while I still have my wits about me. First and foremost, I want you to always take care of your mother. Make sure that she feels like she still is a part of the dealership. She should still get a new car every year; still have her special parking space, etc. You know … all the things that she's used to. Josette and the girls will continue to make her feel important. Do whatever you can to make her happy. I know you love your mother and I'm certain you'll do a good job of keeping an eye on her.

Next, take care of Francois. He's not getting any younger. Make sure that he's provided for and not just turned loose when his best days are behind him. He's quite a guy and I would hate to see him treated poorly. I know I really don't have to ask you to look after him because I know how much you like him, but I didn't want to just take it for granted. The same goes for Chip. He needs you. He's never been on his own. Brothers need to look after their brothers and I'm sure you'll do the right thing where he's concerned."

"Dad, you didn't have to ask me to help anybody. Katie and I have already talked about the future. Our plans were much the same as you requested. We'll do our best."

"There's one other request. Your brother-in-law, Clinton, will try to stick his nose in your business under the guise of helping manage your mother's money. Don't let Clinton near the dealership. If you do, you'll regret it, because his motives will not be in your best interest. Just beware!"

"I hope you're wrong about him, Dad, but I'll be careful. Anyway, we hope you'll live forever. Then we won't have to face these issues."

The meeting ended as it began–awkwardly. Katie and I left with the same questions on our mind. Was my father OK? If anything did happen to him, what kind of a mess would we be in? Why didn't he mention the remaining shares in the corporation? Did he just forget? And what about Clinton? Was he someone who was so deceitful that he would try to use his influence with my mother against us? Unfortunately, the answers would come sooner than we anticipated.

Chapter Twenty-Four

Service with a Smile

"You're never fully dressed without a smile."
Martin Charnin

As much success as we had in the last few years building our sales department, the opposite was true of our service. We had become adequate, sufficient, acceptable, passable, satisfactory, decent–even pretty good; but we most certainly weren't great. We had gone through a line-up of competent and semi-competent service managers who all possessed the fatal flaw of not keeping our customers happy. Not since Maurice, our French-speaking manager who I inherited from my father's old dealership, had we had a manager in our service department that engendered all the traits of a great service coordinator. Unfortunately, Maurice was literally driven from the business by the enormously unpopular Vega, Chevrolets' attempt at building a small, gas efficient car that could compete with the new wave of foreign competitors. The Vega had a stylish design, but also had an aluminum engine, the brainchild of some moron in Detroit that didn't foresee the problems of overheating an aluminum engine block and literally burning up the cylinders. Because the Vegas were constantly in for service and because Maurice was frustrated with having to make excuse after excuse to his loyal customers, he became so discouraged with the ineffective cylinder repair outlined by the Chevrolet technical support team, that he finally threw up his hands and quit. The Vega was a Chevrolet nightmare, and in this case, cost us a valuable member of our team. It also cost us many of our loyal customers who swore they would never buy another Chevy.

Chevrolet eventually replaced the Vega with the Monza, a glorified clone that used much of the same technology that had doomed the Vega. It, too, went the way of the Vega, disappearing from our line-up of economy cars and dragging many of our repeat customers with it. Not until the Chevette, the most simply designed small car Chevrolet ever made, did the fate of our small car business change for the better. Unfortunately, the years between the Vega and the Chevette were punctuated with one failed service manager after another. The few that were good at the mechanical side of the business were lousy with the customers, and the ones that were good with the customers couldn't tell a wrench from a screwdriver. We were looking for the perfect blend of knowledge and personality, but we were beginning to think that person didn't exist. Then one day, almost miraculously, Josette came into my office and said Leonard Laperriere was on the phone. I had known Leo since high school and he had done a great job of building a solid reputation as the quintessential service guy in our area. He had been with the same Ford dealership as long as I could remember, so I didn't think he was available for our position. I took the phone call with more than a little interest.

"Sean, this is Leo Laperriere. I've been noticing your ads in the newspaper for a service manager. I think we should talk. I might be able to help you."

"Leo," I replied, trying not to show my excitement, "let's get together. I'll be looking forward to seeing you." I couldn't disguise my exuberance after I hung up and let out a loud, "Yes!" Bob came running to see what was going on. Bob had been openly critical of our past service managers, often describing them as buffoons. He knew Leo from his days working for a rival Ford dealership and said I should do whatever it took to hire him. He was quick to add: "Your service problems would be over."

If there was such a thing as a legend in the car business, it was Leo Laperriere. I had heard time after time from our legion of showroom visitors how competent a job he was doing. In addition, he was a solid family man who seemed to have the respect of everyone he dealt with. He was an officer with the Danville Volunteer Fire Department and was active with our local Catholic church as a Eucharistic minister. Was he too good to be true or would this meeting uncover ghosts in his closet? Whatever the outcome, I viewed the opportunity to meet with Leo as some sort of Divine intervention. Anxious to find out the answers to my questions, I scheduled the meeting for the following evening.

"Leo! How the hell are you?" I realized after I greeted him that I should have avoided the reference to hell. "Have a seat. What's it been–twenty years since we've seen each other?"

"Close. I was a couple of years behind you in school. I used to enjoy watching you play football. You played hard."

Two things were evident from the beginning: Leo knew how to schmooze with the appropriate compliment, and he instantly created a favorable impression with a solid handshake and a big smile. He was blessed with the kind of smile that elicited trust. It was big and genuine. When you first met him, you knew you could trust him. In a lot of ways he reminded me of Pierre–not a bad comparison in my book.

"Sean, as you probably know, I've been working with a Ford dealership out of town for twenty years. I don't have any real knowledge of Chevrolets, except I love some of their new cars. To be quite honest, I'm considering moving to a dealership closer to home. My kids are involved with sports at the high school and I want to be close enough to go to their games. I've been noticing there are a lot of Cassidy Motors stickers around town. I think you guys are doing a hell of a job, and if the situation were right, I think I could add a lot to your business." (I guess the reference to hell was OK.)

I was as noncommittal as my excitement allowed me to be because I knew I had to run it by my father first. I told Leo we were interested and would get back to him in a couple of days. I knew in my mind what my answer was going to be but Dad was still the final say on a big hiring like a service manager. His answer was resoundingly affirmative. He had long admired Leo's reputation. He told me if we could afford him, he was in favor. Once again, true to his image, my father was thinking with his wallet. Nonetheless, I made Leo an offer that was fair for both parties. My father's response was, "I hope he's worth it."

I got back to Leo the next day and we came together on the terms of his contract. I closed the hiring with a paraphrase from my favorite movie, Casablanca. "Leo, this could be the beginning of a beautiful relationship."

Chapter Twenty-Five

Leaving on a Jet Plane

"All my bags are packed; I'm ready to go.
I'm standing here outside your door.
I hate to wake you up to say goodbye."
John Denver–lyrics

With Leo inspiring a great surge in our service business and with the sales team working like a well-oiled machine, our record in sales contests continued. Still sporting a relatively low quota of sales based on a five-year history, our record in these contests was almost automatic. It was getting to the point that I was beginning to feel sorry for the dealers we were in competition with because it seemed they had little chance. We were setting new records every month, and we learned to anticipate these contests–usually held in March–by holding some delivery reporting until the contest began. It was a little trick I learned from a neighboring dealer who always competed in a different group. I questioned the ethics of such a practice until he convinced me that all the dealers did it and the only chance you had of winning was to go along with everyone else. It wasn't unusual for us to begin a contest with ten to twenty new vehicle sales right from the start that would put us in a commanding position and usually made us the dealership to beat. As my French compatriot, Francois would say: "C'est la Vie."

This spring's contest was an unusual one because it awarded double points for the sale of the hot new addition to our lineup, the Cavalier. Up to this point in time, Chevrolet had a history of screwing up its new car introductions. The most recent debacle was the launch of its first front wheel drive compact, the Citation. The Citation hit showrooms in the fall of 1979 as a 1980 model. Underestimating the impact of this vehicle, Chevrolet under produced the car resulting in long waiting periods of up to nine months for ordered units. From the initial car that was sent to us for display on its introduction date, we sold over thirty more that we had to order. Most customers were tolerant of a two-month waiting period when ordering a new vehicle from the factory, but when that waiting period ballooned to eight and nine months, their enthusiasm waned considerably. The salesmen spent a great deal of time putting out customer fires that year resulting in many disgruntled and lost buyers. It didn't help matters at all when Motor Trend magazine selected the Citation as its 'Car of the Year.' For us, it was the nightmare of the year and left us bruised by consumer anger and leery of the next new car introduction in the fall of 1981, the debut of the all-new 1982 Chevrolet Cavalier.

This launch would be different. There was ready availability and with its superb handling and attractive style, the car was a winner from the beginning. In a rural area like northeastern Connecticut, driving is more of a lifestyle than in metropolitan areas. The Cavalier was fun to drive; it was priced right for the market; and there were plenty to sell. For us, getting two points in the spring sales contest for selling Cavaliers was a slam- dunk. We won the contest going away. The Cavalier, not only helped us win the contest, it became our best seller for years. Finally, Chevrolet had done something right.

Katie knew when we were in another spring sales contest, but she had no idea of the winner's prize. She would get excited during the final weeks of a contest, but I made it a practice that I wouldn't tell her where the victorious dealers were going until after the winner was declared. When we got the official notification that we had won, I rushed home to tell her that we were going to Maui. After I explained to her that Maui was one of the Hawaiian Islands, I thought she was going to pass out.

"Hawaii! Are you kidding me? There's no way. Hawaii! You're kidding, aren't you?"

Her initial exuberance was almost instantly and understandably tempered by the thought of leaving the kids for an extended period of time. The distance to Hawaii was six thousand miles. She had never been in a plane for a prolonged period before and this trip required that we would be in a plane for more than nine hours. Once again I had to convince her that the kids would be fine with her parents and that once we got to Hawaii the length of the flight wouldn't matter.

"It's paradise, Katie. There's probably no place on earth that can compare with the Hawaiian Islands. We may never get another chance to go there in our lives and it's all for free. We'd be crazy not to go."

"Oh, I don't know. The other trips have been fun and we met some great people, but you know I always miss the boys terribly. They're right at that cute stage and I hate to miss any of it."

"Katie! That cute stage won't go away in eight days. The kids will be fine. When we get back, they'll be cuter than ever."

"Oh, all right. I wish you had told me we would be winning all these trips. I was half-heartedly hoping that you would lose this one, but the Hawaiian Islands do sound exciting. Can I call home every night to see how the boys are doing?"

"Sure!! They have electricity there and everything!"

"Sean! Don't make fun of me. I'll go, and I'll even try to enjoy myself"

With the expected separation drama out of the way, we made the necessary arrangements for Katie's parents to come down from Beverly, Mass. to take care of the boys. Katie was right about the boys being at a cute stage, but they were also at ages–four and three–that they were easy to take care of. I had no doubt that my in-laws would have a ball with our two little rascals, but I also knew that Katie wouldn't be the only one who would miss our sons. The trip to Maui was set for the end of May. We boarded the plane in Hartford along with all the other Connecticut winners, most of whom we knew quite well from various dealer functions. There were some very funny and entertaining people that boarded the plane with us. Katie was much more relaxed when she recognized some of our favorite dealers. This was going to be a great trip.

The flight was long; however, it was anything but boring. Sitting across the aisle from us on the plane were the Sassoons, Rachel and her daughter, Dina. I had met Rachel at a recent dealer meeting and was struck by her sophisticated style and extraordinary figure. She reminded me of Zsa Zsa Gabor, only with a lot more class. The Sassoons were one of the most prominent Chevrolet families in Connecticut. Their dealership in Hartford, the capitol city, was a paragon of a successful urban dealer. Unfortunately, Rachel's husband, Neil had recently passed away of a heart attack while working at his desk, only a few days after he had taken over the family corporation from the estate of his father, the founder of the business. From what I had read of the incident, there was a great deal of family discord when the dealership was awarded to Neil. His sister, Jules, and her husband, Stanley, felt that despite the wishes of the father that were clearly delineated in the will, they had as much right to the business as her brother. Jules filed a lawsuit contesting the will, lost their contest in the court, and immediately purchased a rival dealership in a neighboring town vowing revenge to her brother and his Austrian model wife, Rachel. Jules and Stanley had also won their sales contest and both parties had boarded the plane knowing their rivals would be on the same flight. The drama that unfolded during the flight to Maui had a great deal to do with the raw nerves that were still evident from the dispersal of the estate and the fact that the two warring parties were only two rows apart on the nine hour journey. It was our fortune, however good or bad, that we occupied the cabin space that separated the two.

Caustic remarks could be heard emanating from the back row where Jules sat and the subsequent weeklong confrontations that continued once we were settled in our five-star hotel in Kanapali were our introduction to family strife at its snippiest. Katie and I got caught in the middle of the feud because we had befriended the Sassoons and I had helped the two women carry their many bags at the airport. In spite of our inadvertent involvement in their family battle, we were determined to enjoy Maui, the beautiful gem of the Hawaiian Islands. We feasted on opulence and excess to a degree that only Chevrolet could provide its winning dealers. It was simply the most magnificent trip to the most beautiful place on earth.

There was a great deal of interaction among the dealers, which made the trip even more pleasant. Separately we got to know Rachel and Dina and Jules and her husband. For the most part they managed to avoid one another. Rachel was a gorgeous, middle-aged Jewish woman whom Neil had gone to Austria to find. He had lavished her with diamonds and pearls and spoiled her with a privileged lifestyle. Dina was a Jewish princess who could stop you in your tracks with her beauty. Both Rachel and Dina relied on Katie and me to assist them with their travel itinerary and their social schedule. Both were well meaning and at times very vulnerable. I became a surrogate to them and they depended on me to provide a male presence on their trip. Katie didn't seem to mind sharing me with these beautiful, rich women for she knew that I was only trying to be helpful. The two joined us for dinner every night and we all became great friends. Before the week ended, Rachel confided in us that the death of her husband and the subsequent battle in probate court with Jules and Stanley for control of her husband's estate had taken an enormous toll on her. She thought the trip was just what they needed to bring some joy back in their life. She was determined to make the best of it on the trip despite the presence of her main adversaries. She found Katie to be a wonderful girl and a great match for me. When she learned that I worked with my father and that he was still the majority stockholder, she warned me of the possibility of family interference in the business in the event of his death. She strongly advised me to protect my interests legally and to not assume that all my relatives would be cooperative. The long flight back home gave me plenty of time to think about her warning. It was difficult to imagine that my family would ever get to the point that the Sassoons had. Nevertheless, I decided to consult with my lawyer when I got home to discuss any possibilities of a family conflict with the future settlement of my father's estate–just in case.

Chapter Twenty-Six

While the Cat Was Away

"Where large sums of money are concerned, it is advisable to trust nobody."

Agatha Christie

My arrival back at work after my extended vacation to Hawaii was greeted by a strange quiet from my two young secretaries that sat closest to the office door. A curt hello was followed by an ominous silence. Josette was not yet in her office and her impending arrival had somehow signaled the girls, who were normally very chatty in the morning, to be reticent about engaging in light conversation. Their countenances alerted me to a crisis that I guessed only Josette could address. I awkwardly made some inane conversation in anticipation of Josette's arrival. What could this problem be?

Thankfully, Josette arrived and was her usual pleasant self. The other girls seemed to loosen up considerably when she arrived and were full of questions about the trip. The atmosphere had definitely changed for the better–until Josette asked if she could talk to me in private. I entered Josette's office as I could hear the other girls whispering in the background.

"Sean, thank goodness that you're back. Something happened when you were gone that made me very angry." Her French accent became more pronounced as she began to detail what had occurred. "Your brother-in-law came into the office and started demanding financial statements and bank balances. He said Mrs. Cassidy had told him that I would cooperate with anything that he asked."

"And what did you do?"

"I told him that I worked for you and Mr. Cassidy and that unless one of you told me to help him, I wouldn't. He seemed a little upset, but I don't care what he thinks. Did I do the right thing?"

"You definitely did the right thing. What did my father say?"

"Your father has been home all week. He didn't feel well enough to come down here and I didn't want to bother him with this problem."

"Again, you did the right thing. Did you ask my mother what this was all about?"

"Your mother apologized for Clinton's behavior. She said she told him that if anything happened to her husband, she had no idea of the status of the dealership or his own personal finances. Clinton took it on his own to attempt to research your father's financial status. Sean, I believe that he did it this week because he knew you were away. I wouldn't trust that man, Sean. He's evil and he's up to no good!"

"Well, Josette, there is no doubt where your allegiance is and, believe me, I appreciate that. I'm not surprised that my father has kept his personal finances to himself. People that survived the Depression are very protective of their money. I never mentioned this to you, but my father told me to keep Clinton away from the dealership. He suspects that he's up to something and he fears that my mother will be susceptible to his offers of help. Thanks for your astute handling of the problem and let's be vigilant in the future to any more of his schemes."

"Thanks, Sean, and, by the way, welcome back."

"It's great to be back. Tell the girls they don't have to whisper anymore. The cat is out of the bag."

The crisis was temporarily averted, but I wondered if my father was sicker than I had originally thought. All of a sudden, Rachel Sassoons' warning about the stability of the dealership in the event anything happened to my father took on a whole new life. The health of my father was paramount at the moment, but I knew I would have to be cognizant of a potential problem if anything happened to him. I was beginning to think that I was living in some sort of movie of the week plot with an outcome that was going to be too obvious. Forewarned and armed with a great staff of workers, I embarked on another successful selling season. The problem faded into memory, but there was always doubt that it would ever disappear.

Chapter Twenty-Seven

5:35

"The hour of departure has arrived and we go our ways; I to die, and you to live. Which is better? Only God knows."

Socrates

Summer- 1983

Dad was dying. His once indefatigable spirit was wafting away. The Irish wit, the charm, the indomitable personality–were all but gone. There was a deep resignation, a sense that he had accepted his fate.

For a while it appeared that he had rallied and would be around for a good deal longer. But cancer is a horrible guest whose delight is in sapping its host of the will to live. His decline was rapid and painful to watch. All that remained was for him to tie up the loose ends of his estate and say the appropriate good-byes to his family and friends. He left by ambulance for the hospital in August presumably to receive treatment for his cancer in a feeble attempt to prolong the inevitable. He never came back home.

Each of my siblings made it up to the hospital for a last visit. I was to be the last one. I waited for late afternoon on Saturday because I wanted to see the end of a meaningless Red Sox game. I left for the hospital a bit after 5:00 p.m. I was filled with anxiety, knowing that this might be the last time I saw my father alive. I began to think about some of the good moments we shared over the last eight years. Working together to build a respectable business was rewarding and afforded me the opportunity to truly get to know my father. In many ways, I felt inferior to him. He was a robust, daring man that had accomplished a great deal in his life. He had taken gambles where I would never have had the nerve. He was intellectually classified as a Mensa, a mathematical genius with a very high IQ, who could take long columns of numbers and add them in his head without the use of a calculator. Dad's genius, however, was not limited to math. He had a great historical perspective and was a gifted raconteur, who could tell a host of wonderful stories with colorful anecdotes and outcomes. He was a witty and musical Irishman, who could quote Irish poets or sing the songs of his youth. His grammar was always impeccable and while he was at Boston University, he felt the need to master the Spanish language. His thirst for learning never stopped. In his late 60's, he took a correspondence course to learn how to speak German. The search for knowledge was interminable.

As I approached the hospital, I hoped that he would be awake so that I could tell him how much I respected him and his accomplishments and, possibly for the first time in my life, tell him how much I loved him. I was too late. My father, the man whom I had admired as a youngster, feared as a teenager, pitied as a young man, and appreciated and loved as an adult, had passed on at 5:35 p.m. on the 17th of August, 1983. His death came only a few minutes before I arrived. No one else was with him at the time. He had died alone.

The funeral was three days later. The large numbers of people who came to pay their respects were an indication of the position my father held in society. He was a true representative of northeastern Connecticut who dedicated his whole life to his family, his business and his community.

As my sisters and my brother joined me in the back seat of the limousine that was taking us to the church, the driver asked if he could play the radio as we drove. The song that came on the radio had special significance for me. It was a song by the group, The Police, and it sounded as if the lead singer, an Englishman by the name of Sting, was singing directly to me. It's a song that has haunted me since the funeral.

Every Breath You Take
The Police

Every bond you break, every step you take,
Every move you make and every vow you break
Every smile you fake, every claim you stake,
I'll be watching you.

The words attacked my consciousness and filled my soul with a hope that I would do the right things to make my father proud. When it was mentioned by June in the car that it seemed that Dad was trying to communicate with us, we all looked at her in disbelief, but none of us could respond. The great mysteries of life certainly weren't going to be explained by a popular song that we were sure my father never heard of. Yet, it did leave us separately wondering how coincidental this song was. We may have all gotten our answer several hours later when we gathered with our spouses and kids in the living room of my parent's home. Stories of my father were circulating as we each took our turn recalling the good times we had as kids. Only Chip's story was less than complimentary, but that was to be expected. As always, my turn came last because I was the youngest. Just before I began, I noticed that no one had sat in my father's reclining chair in the corner of the room. I placed no great emphasis on that fact other than it was a tribute to him out of respect. As I began to regale my family with the story of my father diving for coins at the lake with a cigarette in his mouth and resurfacing several minutes later with the cigarette still lit and the coin in his hand, I was interrupted by a loud noise. The footrest on my father's chair suddenly sprang to the reclining position. We were all startled. Was this some kind of message from the other side? I'm not sure we believed the answer to that question until we looked at the clock hanging irrepressibly on the wall and it boldly read, 5:35.

Chapter Twenty-Eight

The Void

"If you judge people, you have no time to love them."
Mother Theresa

For days after my father's death my boys would ask, "Where's Grandpa?" Jimmy had just turned five and Tucker was only three. It was difficult finding the right words to describe to a child what happens when someone dies. At their ages, there is only light and hope and dreams. Death is something they are simply not prepared to deal with. Initially, it was hardest on Jimmy for he was reaching the age of understanding. Jimmy's world was his family. His grandfather had always been the funny old guy who made him laugh with silly songs or funny expressions. Any of my father's parenting skills that were doubted by my siblings and me growing up in the dictatorship we knew as home, were never again doubted when we saw him entertain his namesakes. It was obvious that he loved those boys by the way he would visibly light up when he saw them. I'm sure he envisioned a great deal of himself in their freckled faces and Irish bright eyes. He would get the biggest kick out of the things Jimmy would say and Tucker's unending laugh made him smile, realizing that his legacy was going to be carried on by two pretty special kids. Grandpa's passing was, to them, an unexplained mystery.

Katie was so concerned with Jimmy that she asked me if I would try to clarify everything for him. When he was told that his grandfather had died, he grabbed his favorite blanket that he had named "Quilty" and disappeared into the living room. We found him there minutes later sitting in a corner behind the rocking chair hugging his quilt and sobbing. It not only broke my heart to see him this way–it shattered it. I knew that my own composure, which was shaky at best, would be an issue if I lost control of my emotions, so I literally bit my tongue and went over to him and sat down next to the fetal shell he had escaped into in the corner. For a minute, I just leaned back and said nothing. Jimmy was rocking back and forth enveloped in his quilt. Something he couldn't fathom had just happened to one of his favorite people and he didn't know how to handle it.

"Jimmy," I finally said as softly as I could. "I want to talk about Grandpa."

"No," he interrupted. "Mommy said something bad has happened to Grandpa. Why, Daddy?"

Sometimes the one-word questions are the hardest to answer.

"Jimmy, do you remember when Grandpa would tickle you with his cane. You know Grandpa didn't always have a cane. He needed it to walk because he was sick. And you know how you love to run and play sports. Grandpa used to love to do those things too. Unfortunately, when people get old they sometimes lose their ability to do the things they've always been able to do. Life becomes more difficult to enjoy, but do you know what Grandpa enjoyed more than anything?"

"What, Daddy?"

"He enjoyed seeing you and your brother. You guys made his days a little brighter. All he talked about was the two of you. He loved you very much. You know, Jimmy, I believe that Grandpa is still with us, watching over us and laughing at the funny things you and Tucker do."

"Really, Daddy. Will I be able to see him again?"

"No, Kiddo, I'm afraid not, but you can believe that he's in heaven. That's where people go and wait for their families to join them again someday. When you get a little older, maybe I'll be better at explaining all this to you."

"Will you be able to explain it to me tomorrow?"

"Maybe not tomorrow, but someday soon–when you're a little older. Today, it's OK to miss your Grandpa, but just remember him with a happy face watching you play."

"Daddy, isn't today yesterday's tomorrow?"

I looked at him quizzically for what felt like a long time. All I could say in response to his question was, "Yes, it is, Jimmy. Yes, it is!"

The depth of the philosophical question I just got from my five-year old son was enough proof to me that my father's spirit was, indeed, still alive. It was no wonder that my father was always so excited to see him for he must have sensed an intelligence that was befitting his legacy. When I told Katie about Jimmy's question, she just shook her head and said: "he says some unbelievable things to me all the time." We both gave Jimmy a huge hug when he came out of the corner and he and his quilt retreated to his bedroom. Still amazed by what I had just heard, I kissed Katie good-bye and went out to my car to go back to work. I turned on the radio as I was backing out of the driveway and was greeted by the sounds of Sting singing, "Every breath you take, every move you make, I'll be watching you."

Chapter Twenty-Nine

The Full Moon

"The moon is a friend for the lonesome to talk to."
Carl Sandburg

Francois had once warned me that strange things happen in the car business when the moon is full. Before that, Katie had described to me the weird people that used to visit her emergency room at St. Elizabeth's Hospital in Boston whenever there was a full moon. I originally dismissed these stories as fantasy, as tales that grew from fertile imaginations. It was, however, scientifically proven that the moon affects the tides of the ocean and even has an effect on the menstrual cycles of women, but to translate that effect to the actions of seemingly ordinary people was simply, in my mind, empirically implausible. To me, the moon was nice to look at–nothing more, nothing less.

My first few years in the business, Francois, and then Josette, would refer to certain people who came into the showroom on a regular basis as "full mooners." Later, when Big Bob came to work for me, he too ascribed to the theory of the moon affecting people's behavior. They would point out incidents of individuals who acted peculiarly in conjunction cyclically with the moon. Ever the skeptic, I dismissed their theories as figments of their overactive minds. I gave the idea as much credence as the stories of werewolves appearing when the sky was lit by the full moon, or the notion that the full moon creates madness in humans. I did, however, acknowledge that there was a group of repeat customers who seemed to show up on a regular basis, not to buy a vehicle, but just to hang around. Some of them would occupy a salesman in inane conversation for as long as that salesman would tolerate it, and others would actually go to a different salesman every month to price out their dream car and even go as far as taking a test drive and filling out a preliminary purchase order. For some of these people we had a number of the same purchase orders in their files each dated curiously about thirty days apart. When Big Bob and Francois pointed this out to me, I decided to investigate this bizarre information further. Sure enough, there seemed to be a pattern to these visitors coming into the showroom and that pattern did seem to coincide with the cycle of the full moon. I decided to make a list of these people to monitor their appearances in the dealership. This list quickly became known as the "Full Moon List" and from that day on, we referred to it often. I was becoming less skeptical, but I still didn't believe in werewolves.

As the myth outgrew its importance, I did notice that when I saw certain customers drive into our yard, I could predict without looking at the calendar that the full moon was near. One such regular was Campy. Campy was a longtime customer who had done business with my father for years. He was retired now and spent his days driving around in his immaculately maintained five-year old S10 pickup looking for old friends to visit who had the time to listen to his same stories of the "good old days" when Danville was a booming commercial town. The town had steadily declined since the mid-1970s when the state thought Danville was a good place to recycle the degenerate populations of Bridgeport and New Haven and dump these people in what the residents of northeastern Connecticut called the Quiet Corner of the state. Crime, drugs, and undesirables were now the tenants of the downtown area and Campy's store on Main Street was just one of the many stores that were forced to close because of the new blight injected into our town by the powers that existed in Hartford. He was a good old soul but his visits were a harbinger of the advance of the full moon people. Campy's two brothers were also on the list, one an inveterate complainer who manufactured a crisis to complain about once a month on the full moon and spent hours milling about the showroom looking for someone to listen to his perceived grievances. He wasn't necessarily a werewolf, but he certainly was a pain in the neck. The other brother was the exaggerated version of Campy. Where Campy was harmless and, at times, entertaining, this brother was exhausting in his repetitive stories about how my father sold him his first car in 1948, how life was so much better in the old days, and how Francois and he used to chase "the ladies" back in the day. He found it necessary to seek me out during his monthly visit and wasn't shy about walking in on one of my meetings without knocking and just sitting down as if he were asked to stay. All three were brazen and self-absorbed, each thinking that we couldn't operate without their collective input. Thankfully, all three would disappear when the moon would begin to wane.

Other people on the list were less frequent visitors, but nonetheless obviously affected by the glow of the lunar light. Stasha, a gigantic young woman who lived on a farm and, quite frankly, smelled like the livestock, would come in with her compact car that somehow she was able to squeeze into. She would immediately go to the service area to flirt with any mechanic who was fool-hearty enough to ask her if he could help her. Her car was filthy and infested with fleas making service test-drives a horrible event. She would strut and stroll about like she was performing on the burlesque stage. One wash boy would hide whenever she came in for fear that someone would be nasty enough in the service office to offer her a free car wash. The mechanics would literally cheer when she left the yard. We found out later that we were the lucky ones for Stasha also visited the emergency room and was oftentimes belligerent and physically abusive to the emergency room personnel. She was deemed to have psychotic tendencies, but we were all convinced it was the moon.

As the three-day cycle of the moon would progress, we would literally check off the names on our list and quite often we would have a hundred percent visitation experience. As the list would continue to grow, one name always stood out as the most obvious full-mooner– Ted Marvin. Ted lived the farthest away, down in the Mystic area, and therefore had to travel the greatest distance to fulfill his monthly obligation. Ted resembled the 1960's television comedian, Professor Irwin Corey. He had the same disheveled hair and unkempt attire and his eyes would curiously focus in one direction by pointing two separate ways. He always greeted everyone in the showroom with a warm hello and then would seek out the one person he had never talked to before. We considered it a form of initiation for a new salesman to sit through a sales session with Ted Marvin. Somehow he knew his stuff, testing the rookies with questions about towing capacities, horsepower, gear ratios and the like. We had all been through it with him dozens of times over many years, yet he would come back to price out his dream truck once a month on the full moon. One month, he showed up with a brand new truck that he had just purchased at another dealership. We were all astonished. He said he had always wanted to buy from us but he got such a good deal he couldn't refuse it. Without reminding him that he never got a price from us, just information, we were nevertheless relieved that he would be doing business somewhere else. When he left that night, we wished him the best and hoped that his purchase meant the end to his monthly visits.

Six years passed and Big Bob and I were kidding each other about the full moon list of years past and telling stories of some of the more colorful characters to a couple of new salesman. When it was time to close the doors on another day, I got up to lock the showroom door. There on the other side of the glass, standing in the light of a huge full moon was Ted Marvin. He was back. Never again would I doubt the psychological influence of the moon on the slightly disturbed. As I let Ted in to price out a new truck that I knew he wouldn't buy, in the distance I thought I heard the howling of a wolf.

Chapter Thirty

Pent-Up Demand Unleashed

"The road to Easy Street goes through the sewer."
John Madden

The early 1980's were like a whirlwind. President Reagan's controversial economic plan, dubbed by the Democrats as "Supply Side Economics," was an attempt at unfettering businesses from governmental constraints thus creating an atmosphere more conducive to an economic recovery. The first year of his presidency was saddled with choking interest rates left over from the Carter years. Reagan's plan was based on the theory that government had become too big and taxes had become insanely high and would need to be cut to stimulate growth and investment. An emphasis on military spending would promote jobs and provide much needed security during the Cold War.

On March 30th, 1981, a disturbed youth by the name of John Hinkley, Jr. nearly ended the dream before it began. His attempted assassination of President Reagan was unsuccessful but did manage to critically wound the President. It was as if the country had to go through one more crisis to escape the clutches of recession and galvanize the people to spur the economic turnaround. After he recovered from his wounds, the President and the country were ready to act. The economy started to slowly show signs of new life. Interest rates were falling which had the effect of more people spending money rather than stashing their savings in Certificates of Deposit. The business atmosphere was clearly changing for the better and it was General Motors that came up with a plan to further jumpstart their slowly improving sales. After many months of double-digit interest rates, General Motors announced a 2.9 per cent financing sale that surprised even the dealers and set us up for a possible big weekend.

The sale started on Thursday with the support of a large national advertising campaign. Big Bob and I spent most of Thursday morning deciphering the details of the program to determine its veracity. We were pleasantly surprised with the simplicity and integrity of the program. There were no misleading promotional curve balls and no mumble jumble rules to be enforced. Even General Motors Acceptance Corporation (GMAC), the financing arm of General Motors, promised to be lenient with their qualifications of potential customers. Basically, if you had a pulse, you had a chance of being financed during this promotion. Bob and I were excited.

"Sean, this is the moment in time that we will remember for the rest of our lives. Let's get the salesmen pumped up for what should be an outstanding weekend. I suggest we put a moratorium on days off for Friday and Saturday. Let's get everybody on board and make some money."

I had never seen Bob so animated. His normal demeanor was very laid back. There were days when I would ask him a question and by the time he answered, I had forgotten the reason I had asked the question in the first place. Our relationship was an interesting dynamic, certainly not your typical car dealer/sales manager connection. We got along very well, but it was extremely evident that my wiring was hooked up to a faster pace.

"Let's get everybody, including the girls in the office and the key people in the service, to come to a meeting in my office to announce this program and establish a cohesive strategy for this weekend. Even the girls are going to have to work on Saturday because I think we are going to be deluged with customers. Bob, if you can think of anything else to add to our plans don't hesitate to mention it at the meeting. We're going to have to emphasize a sense of urgency and a plan to handle a sudden increase in business. Everybody has to be on the same page–'one for all and all for one.' We'll worry about commissions and sorting out incentives after the sale. Right now, it's all hands on deck."

Bob loved my nautical references. He gathered everybody in my office where we outlined our strategy for the weekend and alerted the personnel to the enormity of this sale. Maybe we were being too optimistic. Time would tell.

On Thursday afternoon we began to see the reason for our optimism. Early birds, the customers who had seen the advertisements first, were streaming in the doors. Our sales staff, Francois, Jack, Frankie and a newcomer, Philippe, were frantically scurrying about the showroom trying to get to every customer. People were staking themselves out next to the car they wanted with money in their hand for a deposit, waiting for a salesman to wait on them. Within hours, Bob and I realized that we were understaffed. We both took on the role of salesmen, which helped with the crowd of people in the yard. The girls were stationed in the showroom with receipts to accommodate the rush of buyers. Frankie caught on quickly to the frenetic pace and walked from customer-to-customer collecting deposits and taking names. He told each person he talked to that he would fill out paper work later but for the time being he would put a sold sign on the car with his or her name on it. Jack was quick to copy Frankie's lead and Francois was bringing his customers to Bob or me. Only Philippe, a veteran of several smaller dealers, never seemed to get into the right groove. He latched onto one couple early in the day and spent the whole afternoon with them without getting a sale. To waste this opportunity on some rote memorization of salesmanship he had learned somewhere was frustrating for all of us. A talking dummy in the middle of the showroom could have made sales this day, but Philippe came up empty. We stayed open late that night, knowing that Friday and Saturday could be even busier. The majority of our staff worked long and hard and the final results were breathtaking. We sold 85 cars and trucks in three days. Frankie, by himself, sold thirty and Jack sold twenty-five. The remaining sales were spread among Francois, Bob and me. Philippe never showed up for Saturday after going blank the first two days. He told Frankie that the pace was too hectic for him and he was going to look for a less stressful job. Some people rise to an occasion, others shy away from the moment. We hoped Philippe would find an unchallenging, less hectic position.

The success of the 2.9% promotion was phenomenal. I was so thrilled with our results that I called a few of my dealer pals on Monday to brag a little. My first call was to Carter Chevrolet, a similar sized dealer in Manchester where my father had begun his career in the car business many years ago. Steve Carter was also ecstatic with his weekend. When we compared totals, he congratulated me on our 85 sales. He then stole my thunder when he told me that they sold 160 vehicles. In the car business, it's tough to be number one for very long.

Chapter Thirty-One

Good-bye Old Friends

> "You think dogs will not be in heaven? I tell you, they will be there long before any of us.
>
> Robert Stevenson

Baxter and I had seen less and less of each other in recent years. He was busy with his new family and his new career at the aerospace factory. We had both stopped playing tennis when the tennis boom that had enveloped the late seventies was dying out with the retirement of Jimmy Connors, John McEnroe, and Bjorn Borg. It was no longer cool to be a tennis player. Occasionally he would call to talk about the Red Sox or the Celtics or stop by to play with the dogs. Our lives were headed in two different directions. I was occupied most of the time with the activities of the dealership or with whatever time I could muster with my family. In effect, the boys had replaced Baxter in the pecking order. He, of course, had his own family to enjoy. In addition, he had started running with a group of long distance runners. His new passion precluded my participation because I simply didn't have any desire to train to be a distance runner. Baxter was always a good athlete and in no time at all, he became quite accomplished in area running circles. I headed in a different direction. Whenever I could, I worked out with weights and machines at the local Nautilus facility. Exercise can become addictive. I found myself skipping lunch on a regular basis to work out. Going to Nautilus provided me with the benefit of losing the middle-age paunch that had appeared disturbingly around my mid-section. Within a few short months, both Baxter and I were in superb shape. It was unusual that we would find different venues for our pursuit of more athletic bodies, but it was not unusual that there would be some banter between us on the merits of those two pursuits.

"Sean, my Nautilus junkie, you don't know what you're missing. There are so many good-looking girls running these days and most are wearing the shortest of shorts. I just settle in behind a good-looking chick with a nice ass and I could run for miles. It's like being hypnotized by a perfectly formed apple. I tell you, it's better than going to a strip show."

"I'm sure the girls you are stalking from behind would be thrilled with that description. And by the way, there's nothing too shabby about a girl with zero percent body fat, dressed in tight spandex shorts, working out in the gym. The only difference is they're not running away from you, and they are all very friendly. Anyway, is that the only reason you started running . . . to check out the chicks?"

"No, my goal is to run in the Boston Marathon someday. Just think about it-hundreds of girls to run behind. Paradise!"

"Yeah, but there is a reason they call that mountain you have to run up, Heartbreak Hill. It's way too tough a climb to enjoy the scenery."

"Sean, you know I'll find a way. Say, how are my dogs doing? They didn't look too great the other day when I stopped by."

"Bax, to be honest, I'm worried about both of them. Sam's fourteen years old now and is stumbling and falling. Goldie is thirteen and we think she's almost totally blind. The kids have become very attached to both of them and it would be a shame if something has to be done."

"You're not thinking what I think your thinking, are you?"

"Katie and I have talked about it. It's painful to see them suffer and not be able to do the things they used to do. I guess we'll have to make a decision soon."

"I'm with you, Pal. Whatever you decide, don't forget to include me. Those dogs were part of my life, too."

"Thanks, Bax. I may need your help. I'll let you know when we decide."

That night at feeding time, Sam barely touched his food and Goldie just sat there with a glaze over her eyes. It was tough to watch. I began to reminisce about our days in Boston when Sam would gallop free in the field next to our apartment, proud and majestic as he lorded over his kingdom. And I remembered Baxter using a very cuddly and cute six-week old Goldie to attract girls. She never failed him. These were more than just dogs to us–they were roommates and buddies. They played with us and slept with us and partied with us. Their lives had been filled with happiness and love, but the time had come to put them to rest. The call to Baxter was difficult to make.

"Bax, I made an appointment for the dogs. The Vet said to come in around three o'clock tomorrow. I told Katie to take the kids to her mother's house for a couple of days. They'll say their good-byes before they leave this afternoon. The boys are still too young to understand what's going on. We'll try to explain everything to them when they get back home."

"I'll be there around two o'clock to give you a hand. I hope you bring a lot of Kleenex."

The dogs perked up when the kids came to say good-bye. Somehow they sensed their destiny. Katie left me with a kiss and a hug for she knew my emotions were going to be challenged when I was alone with my two longtime friends.

That evening I tried to make the dogs as comfortable as possible. Because of their advanced ages, their incontinence made letting them in the house impossible. I brought blankets and straw out to the garage where I planned to feed them their last meal. Neither dog had eaten very well lately so I prepared a special meal of boiled hamburger and rice. When I brought their meals to them, they both ate heartily and for the briefest of times perked up to play like in the old days. I sat down on the blanket and both dogs came to me and lied down on either side of me. As I stroked Sam behind the ears, he looked up at me lovingly with his big brown eyes assuring me that his affection for me was undying. Goldie wiggled as close to my leg as she could and snuggled. I looked down at both of them as I petted their aging fur and I began to cry. Uncontrollably the tears flowed as I hugged my two dogs. I sat there for hours–in the garage, on a blanket, just me and Goldie, my beautiful Cocker Spaniel, and Sam, my loyal Black Lab. When I finally put them to bed for their last night it was nearly dawn. A new day was beginning, and yet I knew that on this day a chapter in my life was ending.

Baxter came at two and it was obvious he had already been crying. We gingerly put the two dogs in the car and drove silently to the Vet. Baxter took Goldie in and I took Sam. For two dogs with different breeding and from different sides of the track, they had always gotten along very well. As we sat in the waiting room, the dogs nuzzled each other as if they knew their fate. Finally, the Vet's assistant came out and asked which dog did we want to go first. We both hesitated and then decided Sam should be first. I took Sam inside and stayed with him to the end. When finally it was Goldie's turn, there wasn't enough Kleenex to go around. I took the bodies of my two dogs home to bury them in my backyard. For all the joy and love that they had provided us through all the years, first in Boston and then back home in Danville, Sam and Goldie deserved a proper burial.

Chapter Thirty-Two

Parameters of Potential

> "Patience and perseverance have a magical affect before which difficulties disappear and obstacles vanish."
> John Quincy Adams

The 2.9 per cent sale had the effect of indicating to us the potential of the dealership. The haunting question had always been how big could we get? With that thought there was also the considerations of just how many cars and trucks should we stock at what time of the year and with the increase in inventory, how many new salesman would we need to handle the additional sales? Each consideration brought with it added overhead costs including a huge increase in floor plan expense. Any added personnel would mean additional and costly payroll expenses and a tremendous increase in employee benefits. We were also getting some pressure from the factory to stock more vehicles–an indication that Chevrolet expected big things from us in the future.

Bob and I discussed the situation at length. Bob wanted to expand the inventory-especially the trucks. He said he believed we could double our truck sales with a bigger and more varied array of stock. I trusted his opinion immensely, but I had to let him in on my biggest secret. I had been operating the dealership on a string since my father died. Two weeks before his death, he had come into the dealership and emptied all his reserve accounts with the sole exception of twenty thousand dollars that he instructed Josette to put in the checking account. When Josette asked my father why he was removing most of his money from the dealership, his terse reply was, "that's all the money I had when I took over. Sean will have to learn, as I did, to make his own money."

Only Josette knew of the financial hardship we had been left with and together we had been able, with a great deal of planning and saving, to weather the storm. The first week was particularly harrowing for us as that week's payroll included commissions from the previous month and totaled just over thirteen thousand dollars. There wasn't much left.

By adding more inventory and more personnel, we were jeopardizing the future of Cassidy Motors. Bob understood my dilemma, but he still thought a gradual increase over time was the best plan moving forward. I told him I agreed with him but, at the same time, I wasn't growing money on any trees. I assured him that I would keep him abreast of our financial situation so he could better prepare his future new vehicle orders. I told him not to panic and go looking for another job or anything. My father's concern with his money was more a reaction to his loss of immortality. He literally was trying to "take it with him." Knowing that his son-in-law Clinton was going to have a profound influence on my mother when he was gone probably triggered his reaction. It seemed that I was already paying for Clinton's role in the family–however dubious.

"Bob," I said. "What I told you today has to stay in confidence. If our competitors knew of our financial shortcomings, they would come after us with all their resources. It wouldn't be pretty. The situation is improving financially. The 2.9% sale helped a great deal, but it didn't cure the long-range picture. I was talking to Pete Ward today and he believes all the 2.9% did was rob sales from our next two months. By creating a firestorm of activity, it drew a lot of people out of the woodwork that were on the fence about buying a car. He fears a huge drop off coming. I hope he's not right."

"Sean! My feeling is that it awakened a sleeping economy. Let's see what happens in the next couple of months, but it's my belief that we've got some big months coming."

As it turned out, they were both right. The next month was very slow, as we had squeezed out every sale we could during the promotion.

The following month, however, was encouraging, spurred by another low interest rate from General Motors. Our bank accounts were beginning to look healthier and the climate of enthusiasm was contagious at the dealership. Bob and I had another meeting and we decided to add more sales personnel. Our inventory was well stocked, but not irresponsibly large. We had some great product; the economy was beginning to percolate; and even the weather was improving as we were coming out of winter. Things at Cassidy Motors were looking up.

Chapter Thirty-Three

If the Spirit is Willing...

"It's hard to beat a person who never gives up."
Babe Ruth

Confronted with the financial crunch at work and the inevitable emotional crisis at home facing me when the boys returned from Katie's parents' house, I firmly resolved that I would tackle both problems with all the energy and imagination I could muster. The problems at work were monumental in scope and terrifying to conceptualize. As daunting as the task was of recovery without the necessary capital, the task at home of explaining the deaths of our two beloved pets to a six year old and a five year old was going to be far more difficult. The sound of Katie's car in the driveway signaled the necessity to rise to the occasion and be as sympathetic and as understanding as I could be. The door opened and the two boys spilled into the house as only two small boys can. They were happy to see me and greeted me with a big double hug. I picked both of them up and spun them around. It was great to have laughter in the house again. Katie quickly followed. Although it had only been a couple of days, it was wonderful to have everyone back together. Surprisingly, the subject of the dogs didn't come up until the boys went outside and saw the empty doghouse in the backyard.

Jimmy's bottom lip began to quiver as he suddenly realized that the dogs were no longer there. Tucker 's response was more verbal.

"Where are they, Daddy?"

The emotional ups and downs of parenting were suddenly confronting me. I tried to explain to the boys that the two had gone to doggy heaven together. I started by saying that both dogs were very sick and were far better off now. I told them to always remember that the dogs loved both of them, and that they were the lucky ones to have such nice boys as their friends.

"Never forget Goldie and Sam because they were great dogs. We'll let some time go by before we do anything, but some day soon we'll get another puppy for you two to play with. Your mother and I have already talked about this and we decided that we would even let you guys pick the dog you want. "

The innocence of youth can be masked with resiliency. Suddenly the boys were dancing about trying to think of new names for the puppy. After moments of frolicking around uncontrollably, Tucker went in the house with Katie for a snack. Jimmy stayed behind and slowly came up to me and said, "Don't be sad, Daddy. We'll all miss Goldie and Sam." He then hugged me and I realized how quickly role reversal happens in a family. Jimmy was comforting me. The worries I had of how to handle the emotions of two little guys were assuaged by the compassionate gesture of my six-year old son. I guess Katie and I were doing pretty well at this parenting game.

The crisis at work was the next cross to bear. I went to work the next day determined to find a way to maintain our sales momentum and still have enough money in reserve to operate effectively. It was the end of the month and Josette greeted me with the preliminary financial statements for the different departments. She had a very pleasant look on her face, like someone who was harboring a positive secret. I began to go over the statements and was quick to point out the significant improvement in profits we had made in sales.

"Josette! The sales did very well. Is this the reason you have such a pretty glow on your face?"

"Thank you, Sean, but I want you to read on."

My curiosity was overflowing as I turned to the back end report, the once boring story of the service, parts and body shop that had for many years been a drain on the dealership's overall profits. I was astonished at what I saw.

"Josette! We made money in the parts? How did that happen?"

"Leo has performed miracles. Read on, Sean."

"The service department made that much! Wow! Are you sure all the expenses have been deducted?"

"Sean, everything is complete. Look at what the body shop made. And the 'piece de resistance'–check out the finance office. I think your father would have been very proud of you if he had seen this report."

"This is great, Josette, but is it all paper profit?"

"Sean, that's the most wonderful part. Your bank accounts are filling up fast. It may be just one step forward, but I think we're on the right track."

"Josette, I love to listen to your wonderful accent when you have all these good things to say. Let's have a meeting with Bob, Leo and Denny in parts. Everybody deserves a good pat on the back. And that also includes you, Josette."

"Thank you, Sean. I'll call the meeting right away."

The meeting quickly became a mutual admiration society. The performance these people accomplished was extraordinary. The beauty of it for me was the way that everyone worked together to achieve our goals. We weren't completely out of the woods yet financially, but with this great staff I was fortunate enough to put together, I was confident that soon our troubles would be a thing of the past.

Chapter Thirty-Four

The Metamorphosis

"...those who look only to the past or present are certain to miss the future."

John F. Kennedy

1984 was flying by. Month after month, the sales were steady and profitable. Leo's influence on the entire service operation was responsible for record months and increasing business. In Leo's case, I learned a valuable lesson about reputation being important in the car business. People trusted him. He was a solid family man and an active member of his church and various other service organizations. A large percentage of our new service business was coming to Cassidy Motors, not because we were a convenient Chevrolet dealer, but because Leo Laperriere was running the service department. Service with a smile-what a unique concept!

Cassidy Motors had long built its business on new vehicle sales. We weren't alone. Discussions with fellow dealers disclosed an unhealthy trend in new vehicle operations that centered on the growing competition from franchised repair facilities. A flood of advertising was hitting the various media markets extolling the merits of discount auto centers for automobile repairs. Coupled with the low-ball pricing of franchised auto parts chains, the threat of losing a significant market to these independents was becoming the reality rather than the exception. New car dealers were also saddled with the burden of having to hire certified mechanics that were required to undergo expensive dealer financed training and were asking for competitive wages equal to or better than the wages offered by other new car dealers in the market. Good mechanics cost money to hire and train. The small repair facilities could care less if their mechanics were certified or not. They would hire anybody who had a wrench and some oil stains on their pants. These facilities would advertise cheap repairs that new dealers couldn't compete with. Customers would understandably take advantage of these cheap prices but often would eventually end up at the new car dealer to get their car fixed properly. With someone like Leo Laperriere on our payroll, many customers that would have normally gone to these discount havens thought twice about getting the job done correctly the first time. There was little doubt about the effect Leo had on our bottom line. Although there was no way to empirically calculate his impact on the entire dealership, it was my opinion that he had a significant influence on sales as well. His considerable presence was becoming the face of Cassidy Motors.

Big Bob more than once used the words, "I told you so," whenever we discussed the good things that were going on in service. Bob had long been a proponent of Leo's ability and although he was happy with Leo's success, I could sense some concern that his own role was being diminished. Bob's easygoing countenance betrayed him whenever he had something to get off his chest. It was time for a one-on-one meeting.

"Bob, it's apparent to me that something is on your mind. Do you want to talk about it?"

"Well… I've been here now for a couple of years. I know that it hasn't always been easy to make ends meet, but I think maybe it's time to look beyond the past and gear up for the future."

"By gearing up, do you mean more inventory?"

"That would be a start. Quite frankly, I think we need more salesmen. Sean, I know you are basically very conservative and I certainly don't have a problem with that, but if you ever want the business to get bigger, we're going to have to have a bigger sales staff. If it all works out, and I think it will, you're also going to need a general manager, not a sales manager, to help you run things. I just want to go on the record that I would be interested in such a position if it ever opens. That's all. Whatever was on my chest is now on the table."

It was obvious that Bob was concerned about Leo's burgeoning status in the dealership and he just wanted to make sure that I didn't forget about him if and when I ever promoted or hired a general manager. It was great to have two solid guys in my organization to rely on. Whether or not I would need a general manager in the future would be determined by the growth of our business in the coming months. In terms of seniority, Bob was the guy.

The following morning I placed help wanted ads in the various local newspapers for new salesmen. I included emphatically that there was no experience necessary, a beacon for new applicants to apply that in no way were remotely qualified to sell cars. The response was overwhelming. Initially I left it up to Bob to filter through the applications, but eventually the task became too time consuming, conflicting with his responsibilities as the sales manager, so I chipped in as I was always prone to do. The number of applicants was astonishing. It was a good sign that our reputation as a fair and honest dealership was spreading. I made a vain attempt to interview in person each applicant, but quite frankly, I was forced to make many quick value judgments on some of the people to save time and weed out the ones I didn't think would fit in with our group. After several hectic days, I had narrowed the big field down to a precious few. Predictably, I hired three ex-athletes who were well known in their respective communities-one from Jewett City, one from Cargill Falls and one from Danville. By spreading out the demographic profile of the dealership with the hiring of well-known athletes from outlying communities, as well as one local legend, I believed we would be able to further expand our business. Bob was thrilled with my choices and couldn't wait to meet with the three new salesmen. The golden age of Cassidy Motors was about to begin.

Chapter Thirty-Five

Spoiling the Broth

"A business that makes nothing but money is a poor kind of business."

Henry Ford

"What's happening?"

I looked up unnecessarily when I heard the knock on the door. Baxter had already entered my office and sat down on my red faux leather couch. It wasn't unusual for him to just stop by unexpectedly, and of course, it was always a welcomed break from the tedium of the day.

"Hey, when you get ready to get rid of this couch, I'll take it off your hands. This would have been great in Boston. Girls love red leather. Of course, I'll have to clean off all the stains you've left."

"The only stains on that couch are probably from Francois. I think he uses it on Saturdays after we close. Anyway, what possible purpose would you have for a red leather couch now that you're happily married?"

"I'm married, but I'm not dead. Sometimes you just need a little kink in your life. If you weren't so preoccupied with work, you might realize there is a whole world of crazy women out there."

"I'll be sure to tell Katie about your suggestion. I'm sure she'll be thrilled and anxious to thank you in person. So, what's happening with you, Bax? I haven't seen you lately."

"I've been busier than a one armed paper hanger. When I'm not cutting wood for my wood stove or playing basketball with my boys, I'm running. Carol and I have gotten friendly with a bunch of runners and we all run together on Sundays. Some of us have entered a number of the big races in the area. My specialty is 10K, but I'm still planning on someday running the Boston Marathon. Who would have believed years ago that I would be the picture of health at this stage in my life?"

"Certainly not me, but then again I hear running can become addictive and you've had a history of being addicted to something. What else is going on?"

"Well, my car dealer buddy, I'm looking for a small truck to carry wood in. I told Carol that I was coming down to see you because I know you won't screw me too badly. By the way, what the heck's going on in your showroom? There's a whole bunch of new faces out there and they all asked if they could help me. It was like running a gauntlet to get to your office."

"We just hired three new salesmen. You remember Jake Richmond. He was the point guard on Danville's team a couple of years ago. The other two are from out of town. Bo Archer was a big time athlete from Cargill Falls, and Mike Hayes was a football player from Jewett City. We're trying to improve our company softball team."

"It's getting crowded out there. You must be making all sorts of money. I hope that means my deal will be a little sweeter."

"Your deal will be like three teaspoons of sugar in your coffee."

Although he had no idea, Baxter's deal was almost too good. I barely made a hundred dollars on the deal. It was so good that even Bob had a comment.

"Where were you weak? Did you have a hard time closing the sale? What's that deal going to do to my average gross per vehicle?"

The first two questions I knew were good-natured ribbing because of the low profit. The third question I expected. All sales managers are concerned with their gross profit per vehicle. It reflected on their performance and in cases like Bob's, reflected on his standing in the sales manager's contest he was in. I assured him that I would list it as a wholesale purchase and it wouldn't be included in his totals. He was satisfied with that as he realized that Baxter was my best friend.

Unexpectedly, I also got some flack from Frankie when I went out in the showroom.

"Sean, when are you going to throw me a bone? If you're handling customers, what do you need me for? I've known Baxter since I started here. I'm sure I could've handled him for you. It's bad enough out here now that we have a showroom full of salesmen."

I realized Frankie's comments were fraught with frustration. He had long been the top performer on the staff, the one person I could count on for fifteen to twenty cars every month. His concern was that there was only so many deals in the dealership pie, and with all the new guys, his cut of the action would probably be significantly less. In addition, Frankie had never been into athletics. He could have cared less who was playing whom or what team was doing what. The conversation in the showroom among the new guys and Jack was almost exclusively sports oriented. He was left out. I could tell his nose was out of joint. He had gone from the top dog to the lone wolf. Bob was going to need my help in keeping this group happy.

Chapter Thirty-Six

The Lake

> "Do not bite at the bait of pleasure, till you know there is no hook beneath it."
>
> Thomas Jefferson

I couldn't wait until the end of the workday to hurry home with my news. I was almost giddy as I pulled into the driveway. The kids were in the yard with Katie making a snowman. The boys both stopped what they were doing and ran over to greet me with hugs. Katie followed and asked why I was home so early. I told her that there was something I wanted to tell her, but maybe it would be better if we went inside. It was January in 1985 and the kids were home for school vacation. We all went into the house and the kids went to their rooms to change out of their wet winter clothes. Katie and I went into the living room where we were out of earshot of the boys.

"What's going on, Sean? You're so mysterious."

"Katie, brace yourself. I just met with our accountant. Last year's figures were fantastic."

"That's great, Sean. But why all the secrecy."

"Katie, the accountant says the dealership made too much money. Because of what the business would pay in taxes at the corporate rate, he suggested I take a rather large bonus. Our personal rate is considerably less and would result in saving a great deal of money. He said in his opinion, I've been underpaid for years compared to my fellow dealers. He suggested an end of the year bonus and added that he felt I deserved it. God, I love that man!"

"Should I get really excited about this, Sean? How much is he talking about?"

"It's almost as much as I made for the whole year."

"Sean, that's unbelievable. I'm not sure what to do with all that money. What are we going to do? Does your mother know about all this? Is she going to be upset?"

"Katie, I don't know. She probably would be upset if she knew how much, but I did tell her the accountant recommended a bonus and the reasons for it. It's probably best if she not know the amount. Clinton would fill her head with all sorts of false accusations to make me look bad. No, I think it's better off not mentioned. After all, it is dealership profit, payable to the dealer principal only–nothing to do with her."

"I hope you're right. This could get messy."

Katie's concerns were well founded. The specter of a family blowup had been ominously lurking in the background ever since Clinton was asking for the dealership records when I was on vacation. He was, in my opinion, a slippery individual who would go to any extremes to undermine my place in the hierarchy of the family business. His tentacles had attached themselves to my mother after my father died. He assumed the role of her financial advisor, her investor, and her guru. He had also begun to work on other members of the family who he had identified as potential heirs. His approach was simple; if he could get the majority of heirs to believe that their inheritance would increase if the dealership were included in my mother's estate, their influence on my mother would guarantee that I would have to go along with the rest of the family. His presence was a constant threat to the sovereignty of the dealership. It was like a movie-of-the week with Clinton cast as the antagonist. My hands were tied and my reaction to his constant interference was tempered by his influence on my mother. I had a difficult time believing that my sister was his accomplice, but as the years were unfolding, it became apparent that my sister's role in his master plan was significant. It became difficult to trust anyone in the family.

When the bonus was paid, I looked for something to invest in. As I was searching through the real estate ads, I came across a house on Lake Alexander in the neighboring town. This was the same lake where my father had a cottage when I was a kid and where I spent all my summers when I was a young boy. I had nothing but fond memories of the lake and the good times the whole family had there. I recognized the house that was for sale as one that had belonged to a prominent family in town. The figures jumped off the page. The price was nearly the same as the bonus. I called the realtor to inquire about what I thought must have been a misprint, and he said that was the price. I hurried over with a deposit, forgetting entirely about telling Katie. When I arrived home and told her, she was less than enthusiastic.

"Sean, what are you doing? We should be saving money right now for the boys' college education. Where is this house and what kind of condition is it in? Honestly, Sean, some times you act way too impulsively."

"Katie…Katie…Katie! It's been a good ride so far. Has it not? Trust me. This is going to be a great move for the kids and us. Just think, summers on the lake, swimming and boating. It gets pretty hot here on Beverly Avenue in the summer."

"Before I agree to your latest adventure, I want to see the property."

Katie's conservative upbringing was something that I battled against our whole marriage. It was also the one element of her personality that I admired and admittedly relied on to make sound decisions. If it weren't for her reluctance to gamble with our hard earned money, I probably would have put us in financial trouble years ago. The fact that we suddenly were dealing with a large sum of money didn't change the dynamic that seemed to work so well for us in the past. I promised to listen to her opinion–after we saw the property.

The next day, I arranged for us to meet the realtor. My memory of the house in the real estate ad was of a regal colonial that was one of the bigger homes, nicely situated on a hill overlooking the water. I knew that the real estate market had been slow to rebound, but I still couldn't believe how low the price was. It didn't take long after we were led into the front door by the realtor to realize why the price was so cheap. The house, quite simply, was a disaster. The property had changed hands several times since it was one of the elite addresses on the lake. As we entered the home, a toilet surrounded by three walls and a shower curtain for privacy greeted us. I could hear Katie gasp. The kitchen was adjacent to the toilet and it was tough to ignore the hideous orange and brown cabinets and rusted sink. As we walked further into the structure, it got worse. What once was a spectacular home with a cathedral ceiling and a balcony that surrounded the living area that included an original stone fireplace, was now a two story house with an enclosed stairway that led upstairs. The open expanse of the cathedral ceiling had been replaced with a cheaply installed plywood floor creating space for four additional bedrooms. The walls of the bedrooms were crooked and the floor creaked when you walked on it like it was about to give way. The electrical wiring for the rooms was stapled to the outside walls. The rooms were small and dark.

"This looks like a whorehouse," Katie said, as she tried to control her emotions. "Sean, I'm never going to live here."

I could understand Katie's disappointment for I was also disillusioned by what we were seeing. I pulled the realtor aside and told him we were probably going to ask for our deposit back. "This place is a mess," I told him. "How could people live like this?"

His explanation struck a chord with me. He said the previous family had a lot of kids and they needed extra bedrooms. He said the structure of the house was sound. If I invested in repairing the house to a livable condition, he was sure I could recoup my investment and make a healthy profit on resale. It sounded like a great deal of work just to get it in resale condition, ultimately putting a huge dent in my dream of owning my own home on the lake. I told him to give us a day or two and we would let him know our decision.

After consulting with a handy-man carpenter on what reconstruction would cost, I was better prepared to make a decision. He told me I could save a great deal of money if I decided to gut the interior myself. I ran the idea by Frankie and Jack the next day at work and they both agreed they would help if that were the way I wanted to go. That following weekend, Frankie, Jack and I–each armed with a crowbar, a sledgehammer and an axe–began the demolition of the hideous interior of the house on 1500 Peninsula Rd. We opened the upstairs window and literally threw the interior, piece-by-piece, of the old house into the huge dumpster below. Though it seemed like my dream was still a fantasy, and I still had to convince Katie to share the dream, I knew that with a whole lot of effort, a couple cases of beer, and the help of two of my salesmen, the fantasy could some day be a reality.

Chapter Thirty-Seven

Start Spreading the News

> "Winning isn't everything, but it beats anything that comes in second."
>
> Paul "Bear" Bryant

The constant banter in the showroom had become a common everyday distraction. Jake, Bo, and Mike talked sports from the minute they entered the building until they went home, some ten hours later. Jack often chimed in although his athletic achievements paled in comparison to these three. To their collective credit, whenever there was a customer to take care of, the banter would stop, and a modicum of professionalism would take over. Bob could have put a lid on all the yapping, but he decided that in some weird way that the chatter was keeping them all sharp for when they needed to be on their game.

Jake was the most talkative and the most entertaining. He had a fast paced manner of speaking that somehow made his devilishly good looks palatable to the other guys. He was cocky and arrogant, yet in spite of his endless bragging and editorializing, he was extremely likeable. Bo was a former three-sport athlete going through a divorce that became way too public during his daily phone calls to his wife. Saturday, the busiest day at the dealership, never was officially launched until Bo had screamed into the phone at his wife and thrown his blotter and all his pens and pads of paper on the floor. He would then storm out of the building, screech off in his demo, only to return moments later with a dozen donuts and say, "OK, let's go!" Saturday was a day you didn't want to be late for work because you would miss all the drama.

In spite of Jake's success with women, which Bo unsuccessfully tried to emulate, Jake and Bo became good friends. Bo jokingly called Jake "quick draw," a cloaked reference to his premature performances with woman. Jake didn't seem to care and neither did the scores of girls who wandered in to look at cars and asked if Jake was free to help them. Most of Jake's sales were to the fairer sex. On one memorable occasion, a middle-aged married woman who wanted a Camaro propositioned him on the test drive while her husband was filling out a financial statement for credit in the F&I (Finance and Insurance) office. The couple bought the car and the woman became a frequent visitor–Jake would describe her as a stalker–who found all sorts of reasons to come to the dealership without her husband. Jake became quite adept at disappearing whenever her blue Camaro came into the yard.

Mike, the third member of the intrepid threesome, was far more reserved than the other two. He was quickly indoctrinated into the Cassidy way of doing things and became an effective member of the team. He was part of a huge athletic family in Jewett City and attracted a great deal of new customers from that area. To his credit, he managed to stay out of some of the more heated sports debates, although his allegiance to the hated Yankees was stressing everybody out. Frankie stayed out of sports talk, instead becoming reticent and moody. He was obviously bothered by the introduction of new personalities into what was once his domain. Unwittingly, we had created an atmosphere of conflict that initially had sparked competition that resulted in an increase in sales. It would still be a matter of time before we would get a true picture of the dynamics of this group. As for the present, it was obvious that: Bo didn't like Frankie; Jack didn't like Jake; Big Bob didn't like Bo; Mike didn't care for Jack; and Frankie didn't like any of them. Only Francois seemed to be immune to all the drama. He quietly went about his business taking care of his large following of past customers. He did warn the new guys not to mess with any of his people, a warning that came with a roguish smile, for he had a habit of claiming customers that he didn't even know. The spring selling season was beginning and it was evident that in our showroom, at least, there wasn't going to be a dull moment.

In February, Bob and I talked about the likelihood of another Chevrolet sales contest beginning soon. We prepared ourselves by again delaying delivery information of new car sales in case a contest was forthcoming. Our gamble paid off. The new contest was announced and we began with a bang, reporting all our delayed deliveries. The contest was set up for us to compete in group competition for a trip to New York City. Both Katie and I loved to go to Broadway plays so the trip to the Big Apple was appealing. It also was only hours away so her anxiety of being separated from the boys wouldn't be so great. She liked the glamour of the city, the restaurants and the double-decker tourist buses. I liked the danger of the city. It was a much larger version of Boston where the excitement and the danger were magnified.

One of our personal trips to New York took place the year after Jimmy was born. We caught the train from New London to eliminate the hassle of having a car in Manhattan. It was just a three-day trip because that was all we could afford in those days. I was able to get tickets for the play, 'Forty-Second Street', which we both thoroughly enjoyed. Prior to the play, we had dinner at the world famous Sardi's Restaurant on West 44th Street where we took great pleasure in rubbing elbows with all the celebrities and upper crust citizens. We were in the heart of the Theater District, experiencing all the flavor of Broadway. After the play, Katie had mentioned she was getting tired. It was still relatively early so I told her that in New York the beautiful people don't come out until after ten o'clock at night. We were only a few blocks from 54th Street so I convinced her that we should go to Studio 54, the infamous nightclub where all the "A" list celebrities partied until the wee hours of the morning. After a longer walk than we anticipated (ten blocks is approximately equal to a mile), we arrived at the famous nightclub where a long line of people was waiting outside the entrance. It didn't take long to discover that this wasn't 'a first in line gets in' kind of nightclub. Three rather large doormen would walk down the rows of wannabes and pick whomever they thought would fit in the best with all the beautiful people inside. That night, Katie had outdone herself. She was dressed to kill–a knockout by any standards. She was wearing a short mini-skirt and very trendy short black boots with a high heel.

Her blonde hair was crowned with a beautiful, black bandeau that was the style of the day. She was striking. It wasn't long before one of the doormen noticed her and asked if she wanted to come in. She said sure. He then condescendingly asked if I was with her. When I said yes, he reluctantly allowed me to enter as her escort although I'm sure he would have preferred if she were alone. I was proud of my beautiful wife that night. She stood out among the glamour queens of New York. Without her, I would still be stubbornly standing in that line looking at perpetual rejection.

When we entered the building where the notorious and famous people of New York were spotted on a nightly basis, we were presented with a cover charge of fifty-four dollars each. I only had two hundred dollars with me so just the entry fee to get in put a huge dent in our funds. Drinks were ten dollars so it was quickly apparent that we wouldn't be there very long. Once we walked into the club, it made our investment more palatable. The clientele were eclectic to say the least. Actors and actresses, stockbrokers, hookers, bankers, transvestites, and Wall Street investors mingled on the crowded dance floor grooving in harmony to the decadent music that resounded throughout the club. The waitresses were all knockouts and the male bartenders were all shirtless. As the clock struck midnight, an hour my wife rarely saw, the crowd got even rowdier and more bizarre. Katie nursed her drink for quite a while knowing we didn't have a great deal of money left. Soon she had to use the ladies' room. The rest rooms were up the stairs of the former television studio in an area that included couches and secluded tables for privacy. I accompanied her to the loft where the rest rooms were located and as she disappeared into the ladies' room, I got an eyeful of the real Studio 54. It had been some time since I had been around drugs, but it was apparent that just about anything went on in the rest area lounge. Many of the loungers were sniffing cocaine off mirrors that were supplied for that reason at every table. Other couples were openly engaged in sexual acts in the back area booths. No one seemed to care if they were with the opposite sex or with the same sex. There was an orgy of activity. I thought about the safety of my wife and I was about to enter the ladies' room to check on her when she appeared and said quickly, "Let's get out of here. If this place ever gets raided, we'd be arrested for just being here." I agreed and we went downstairs to leave.

As we neared the exit, I looked back and saw some famous people acting as crazy as everyone else in the place. Had I been alone, I might have stayed just to witness what the night would bring, but I readily escorted Katie out of Studio 54 for her safety. All the stories we had heard about the place and all the future problems that resulted in the closing of the nightclub were true. There was a sense of relief when we left, and yet I was happy that we had gone, because we had experienced a lifestyle and an atmosphere that we would probably never see again. We both agreed that the experience brought us as close to hell as we would ever want to be. Katie was glad she survived the experience; I was glad that we had it. I guessed that our different way of looking at things was the ingredient in our marriage that kept it interesting. In spite of our Studio 54 moment, we always enjoyed visiting New York. If we won the spring contest, we would once again be headed for the "Big Apple."

Chapter Thirty-Eight

Castle to Castle

> "My Mama always said, 'Life was like a box of chocolates; you never know what you're gonna get."
>
> Forrest Gump

The realization that we had won the Top Performer trip instead of the trip to New York didn't really hit me until the package came from Chevrolet Travel. Because of our outstanding sales achievement in the spring sales contest, we had qualified for the Top Performer trip. I knew Katie would be disappointed that we weren't going to New York, but I was sure she would be thrilled when I told her of our new destination. I couldn't wait until I got home, so I called her with the good news.

"First of all," I started, "Our new trip is for ten days, half the time in Ireland and half the time in France. We'll fly out of New York on an early morning flight from JFK Airport to Shannon Airport in Galway on the western coast of Ireland."

"Oh, I can't believe it. I can't believe we're going to Ireland."

"Shhh," I said. "Let me finish before you get all excited. While in Ireland, we'll be staying at the fabulous Ashford Castle, in Cong County Mayo, once the estate of the Guinness family. After our stay in Ireland, we'll fly to Paris and be chauffeured to another castle in the French countryside, the Chateau d'Esclimont, situated between

Versailles and Chartres. We'll visit Paris by day and night and fly home on the Concorde.

"Sean, I can't believe it. This sounds like a fairytale."

"It is, and you're the princess. Just don't kiss any frogs before the trip because you're stuck with me." Maybe this trip would make up for buying the lake house.[3]

Chapter Thirty-Nine

Le Grande Voyage

"We'll always have Paris"
Humphrey Bogart-Casablanca

It was a clear autumn morning when we arrived in New York for our flight to Ireland. No one on the plane could have been more excited than I was to be flying to the land of my ancestors. It had only been two short years since my father died. In my mind I truly believed he had something to do with our winning this trip. I had mentioned that fact to Katie, and she admitted to thinking the same thing. The flight was shorter than I imagined it would be and the approach to Shannon Airport provided spectacular views of the Irish coastline and the Kelly green Irish fields. My mind rushed to thoughts of my father and his father, "the old Gent." They both spoke so lovingly of their homeland. My grandfather's accounts of his boyhood in County Cork were always spiced with fascinating tales and left me with a curiosity to see the Emerald Isle for myself. In many ways, I was flying home, although I had never before stepped foot onto Irish soil. Both Katie and I were brimming with expectations. What a trip this was going to be!

Chevrolet never failed to deliver when it came to providing first class treatment for its winning dealers. I could only imagine the extent to which they would go to make sure their Top Performers were going to get the best of everything. At home, we still lived on a budget and were careful not to spend money foolishly. On this trip we were going to experience an unlimited ticket to excess, surpassing anything that we had seen before. Katie was going to have to change her whole philosophy on spending because, not only were we expected to charge our expenses to an open Chevrolet account, we were encouraged to do so. For the duration of this trip we were going to have to get used to living the lavish lifestyle of the wealthy.

From Shannon we were chauffeured to Ashford Castle. The ride took less than an hour but included some hair-raising intersections and roundabouts that left us longing for our super highways. In Ireland the main roads are narrow, so narrow in fact that it appeared to me that a sheet of paper would barely fit between vehicles going in opposite directions. As we were leaving the airport, we spotted an interesting road sign alerting drivers to just how many fatalities had occurred on that particular road during the calendar year. Despite these harbingers of the bad things that could happen, the beauty of the Irish hills quickly hypnotized you. Once we arrived at Ashford, situated on the shores of Loch Carib, we totally forgot about the harrowing drive to get there. The castle personnel trumpeted our arrival. We were pampered and fawned over like royalty. As for Ashford Castle itself, it was stupendous in its appearance. It was the same castle where President Reagan had stayed on his recent trip to Ireland, a revelation that certainly impressed me. However, this grand edifice and the immaculate grounds that surrounded it was an Ireland with which I was unfamiliar. I was anxious to see the Ireland of my grandfather's stories, the Ireland of the working people. Tomorrow, I would be afforded the opportunity I was looking for. We would visit the pubs of Galway.

On the bus into town the next day, we met a lovely young couple from a small dealership in a remote town in the Midwest. They seemed overwhelmed by the opulence of the trip and the ornate trappings of the castle. Kevin and Myra were also surprise winners of the Top Performer award and were thrilled to meet us because they felt they were being snubbed by some of the stuffy older dealers on the trip. We struck up an instant friendship that provided Katie with a shopping partner, while availing me with a more than enthusiastic participant in my exploration of the pubs of Galway. Kevin and I lucked out on our first choice, Riley's

Pub, down by Galway Bay. It was filled with colorful local characters that were more than willing to share their pub with two curious young visitors from America. I looked around several times to see if there were any Leprechauns milling about carrying shillelaghs, but none seemed to be present. Due to the thick Gaelic dialect of the regulars at the bar, it was difficult to understand what they were saying. Even the few that claimed to speak perfect English were a challenge because of their heavy Irish brogue, but after a few mugs of Guinness, communication seemed to improve. These patrons loved to sing and oddly, when they did, they sang in perfectly understandable English.

Kevin was a good old boy from the plains of Kansas who obviously enjoyed an occasional brew. He was quick to join me in singing along to the songs of the locals. Of course, "*Danny Boy*" was our first request eliciting a response from the entire pub to join in. As the afternoon progressed, the singing became more raucous and Kevin and I, by this time arm-in-arm with our new friends, became a part of the chorus. It was the kind of spontaneous afternoon that you couldn't plan, but it was certainly one that we would always remember. This was the Ireland that I was seeking, the Ireland of my grandfather's stories, the one that made his eyes fill with tears when he recounted his memories.

After several hours and too many beers, it was time to meet the girls, who were probably wondering what kind of trouble we had gotten into. We announced to our new friends that we had to leave. They all stood and patted us on our backs and wished us luck on the rest of our trip. Then, in a farewell tribute that neither of us would ever forget, they sang one last song that they dedicated to us. Its words were sung from deep within their hearts, with their eyes closed and their glasses raised high.

Galway Bay

'Tis far away I am today from scenes I roamed a boy,
And long ago the how I know I first saw Illinois;
But time nor tide nor waters wide can wean my heart away,
For ever true it flies to you, my dear old Galway Bay.

Oh, grey and bleak, by shore and creek, the rugged rocks abound,
But sweet and green, the grass between, as grows on Irish ground.
So friendly fond, all wealth beyond, and love that lives alway,
Bless each poor home beside your foam, my dear old Galway Bay.

The blessing of a poor man be with you night and day,
The blessing of a lonely man whose heart will soon be clay;
'Tis all the Heaven I'll ask of God upon my dying day,
My soul to soar for ever more above you, Galway Bay.
Frank A. Fahy

The next morning, we met Kevin and Myra for breakfast. Fried fat in many forms seemed to be the staple of the menu, so we ate only the recognizable foods. After breakfast, we boarded the waiting helicopters for a trip to the Cliffs of Moher, the number one tourist attraction in Ireland. The helicopter ride was the perfect way to gain an overhead perspective of this beautiful country. The Cliffs lived up to their reputation as a required tourist stop rising more than 200 meters above the Atlantic Ocean on the western seaboard of County Clare. Much like driving on the Irish roads, there was very little regard for the safety of the tourists who wandered off the paths to get a closer look at the ocean pounding against the rocks below. I'm sure there were incidents of people falling, but it was the Irish way not to worry about things like that. From the top of the cliffs, you could see for miles in every direction, from Galway Bay in the north to the tiniest glimpse of the Ring of Kerry to the south. We all agreed that the daylong excursion had been worth it although we were anxious to get back to the castle to rest before dinner.

While my wife and travel companions went to their rooms to nap when we returned to Ashford, I decided to take a stroll down to the lake that surrounded the land on which the castle was built. I wandered along a moss-covered lane that led to a secluded sitting area where there was a plaque that described this as the very spot where Saint Patrick had driven the last snake out of Ireland. I sat there for the longest while, quite content in my thoughts, when I impulsively reached down in front of me and scraped some dirt from the spot and put it in my jeans pocket. I knew this kind of activity was discouraged, but without remorse, I decided that this sacred soil would have an appropriate place when we arrived back home.

The rest of our stay flew by and finally it was time to say good-bye to this glorious place. A fantastic feast ushered in our final night in Ireland. Toast upon toast filled our banquet hall, with Irish whiskey and Guinness and expensive wines being readily dispensed to the Chevrolet party. There was no limit to how much you ordered and no limit to the amount of money being spent. Chevrolet was going all out to reward their top dealers. They capped the evening by bringing in some Irish dancers and a lovely young harpist just to perform "*The Rose of Tralee*." Tomorrow we would leave for France, but for one memorable night, everyone in the room was Irish.

The Rose of Tralee

The pale moon was rising above the green mountain
The sun was declining beneath the blue sea
When I strayed with my love to the pure crystal fountain
That stands in the beautiful vale of Tralee.
She was lovely and fair as the rose of the summer
Yet, 'twas not her beauty alone that won me
Oh no! "Twas the truth in her eye ever beaming
That made me love Mary, the Rose of Tralee.

The cool shades of evening their mantle were spreading
And Mary all smiling was listening to me
The moon through the valley her pale rays was shedding
When I won the heart of the Rose of Tralee.
Though lovely and fair as the rose of the summer
Yet 'twas not her beauty alone that won me
Oh no! 'Twas the truth in her eye ever beaming
That made me love Mary, the Rose of Tralee.

Lyrics by C. Mordaunt Spencer (1845)

Daylight brought us an early wake-up call and before long we were being bused to Shannon for our departure to France. We were all commenting that it would be difficult for Chevrolet to top the experience of Ireland, but as we were to find out, their masterful planning and total disregard for fiscal accountability was about to result in an even more memorable stay in the French countryside, just outside of Paris. Upon arrival, we were told to pair up (Kevin and Myra quickly joined us) because we were being assigned our own limousine with our own driver for the remainder of the trip, who would be available to us, day and night. Our driver's name was Ephraim and he was a delight. He was seemingly as interested in us as we were in the French experience. He quickly became more than a driver; he became a tour guide. The drive from Paris to the Chateau d'Esclimont took about an hour and the entire ride was filled with Ephraim's rich description of various French landmarks. I have always been a history buff, so I was totally enthralled with his knowledge of his own country. I could see that this was going to be a special experience. Our train of limousines filled with excited Chevrolet dealers and their wives entered the access road to the Chateau. Suddenly as if out of a dream appeared this magnificent structure, a former fortress constructed during the mid-fifteenth century. The limousines circled in formation to allow an ornate bus to unload its passengers at the entrance to the Chateau. To our great delight, the passengers on the bus were actually a twenty-piece orchestra from Switzerland dressed in authentic Swiss garb. They set up their instruments outside on the steps of the main entrance and began to play as we disembarked from our vehicles. The concert lasted just a few songs but was a wonderful way to be greeted into this fairy tale castle. Befitting the incredible flamboyance of this trip, the Swiss band finished their brief concert and was herded back onto the bus for a return trip to Switzerland. Chevrolet once again displayed its willingness to spare no expense.

The rooms at the Chateau were huge. By the luck of the draw, each couple was checked in to a room with a different theme. If you were in a room in the middle, you were treated to a square space punctuated with the finest French linens and bedding surrounded by ornate walls and furniture. Those that drew a room on the end of the building were in the turret section of what was once the fortress towers designed to defend the Chateau against its enemies. Our room was on the end and to our great amazement the room and the king-sized bed within were round. Katie and I just looked at each other and laughed. We were truly living in a dream. We made several jokes about sleeping around and waking up not knowing whether we were at the foot of the bed or at the top. It made sleeping unusual and fooling around more possible. We both loved the room and the bed and wished we could stay in this fantasy world for a bit longer, but Katie's maternal instincts surfaced and she said she would much rather be in our own normal bedroom back home with our two boys sleeping next door. She did add however, "In the meantime, let's enjoy ourselves in our Cinderella setting in this fantastic room."

After a lovely, authentic French breakfast the next morning, Ephraim appeared and announced that today we would be visiting the Palace of Versailles. The short trip gave us just enough time to become better acquainted with our tour guide. His wealth of information was a tribute to his upbringing and his sense of humor was a welcomed addition to the daylong visit to the grandest Palace in Europe. The Palace was so huge that without Ephraim we would have wandered about aimlessly, but his succinct directions and colorful descriptions of life in the Palace built by Louis XIV in the seventeenth century kept our focus on a true learning experience. Louis was the "Sun King," so named because of the grand, gilded opulence of the Palace. Inside, there were separate wings for the King and the Queen and over seven hundred rooms throughout the structure. The most interesting bit of information that was supplied by Ephraim was that there were no bathrooms in the Palace. He must have known that Americans relish that kind of historical irreverence when it concerns the French. After a whole day of saying "Wow," we welcomed the suggestion that we head back to the Chateau. We were overwhelmed by the grandeur that we had just witnessed, but exhausted from walking literally miles around the grounds at Versailles. We had just spent the day in the home of Louis XIV, Marie Antoinette, and Louis XVI, and had walked the same hallways and paths that they had walked. The historical significance of that knowledge made the day a special memory to relish for the rest of our lives.

The next day, Ephraim arrived early for our trip to Paris. My whole life I had heard about Paris and was anxious to see it for myself. Ephraim was ebullient on this day, for it was with great pride that he presented "the City of Lights" to his eager passengers. Firstly, he took us to the

Arc de Triumph, then to the Champs-Elysees, and finally to the Eiffel Tower where we did the necessary tourist thing and went to the top. The view of Paris from the tower was predictably spectacular. Paris by day was wonderful, but it was Paris by night that I wanted to see, and tomorrow we would be returning for our dine-around. Ephraim promised us many surprises.

On the third day, we made the short drive to Chartres and toured the beautiful Cathedral. The village itself was quaint and served as a welcomed respite in our otherwise hectic schedule. We wandered around town, eventually relaxing at an outdoor café. It was a charming afternoon that allowed us to catch our breath and ready ourselves for our evening in Paris. Kevin left the choice of a restaurant in Paris to me. He said he wouldn't know one from the other. I had done some research before the trip and the one restaurant I wanted to go to was called Maxim's. I asked Ephraim his opinion. His reply was classic.

"Oh Monsieur, you could not have made a better choice. It is a fabulous restaurant. It is so beautiful there…and the women that go there are tres̀ magnifique. Pierre Cardin is the new owner and it has become the place to be seen. Bridgette Bardot goes there. You might dine next to Aristotle Onassis, or the Duke and Duchess of Windsor. Even Barbara Streisand has become a regular. You will not regret your decision!"

He could have stopped at Bridgette Bardot to get my attention, but obviously Maxim's was a good choice. The girls got all dolled up in their best outfits and looked stunning. Kevin and I dragged out our suits from the unused section of our closets and we were all ready for our big evening in Paris. Ephraim seemed more excited for us than we were. He was truly proud of his country and especially, Paris. He couldn't wait for us to experience the city, to feel the love in the air and the glamour of a Paris night. I suddenly felt like Humphrey Bogart and leaned over to Katie and whispered, "Here's looking at you, kid."

Maxim's didn't disappoint. The décor was fabulous, glamorous, even enchanting. Red velvet walls and ornate mirrors greeted us as we were escorted to our table. A strolling violinist added to the ambiance. A charming waiter introduced himself and I immediately asked him if Bridgette Bardot was there. He laughed and said he would let me know if she arrived. He took our drink order and to my surprise, Kevin ordered a magnum of Dom Perignon Champagne. I laughed out loud and said to Kevin, "Chevrolet is going to take your franchise away when they get this bill." He laughed and replied, "It can't cost as much as the Swiss Band that performed for a couple of minutes and was then flown back to Switzerland." We shared a laugh at Kevin's impertinent remark because the whole idea of impetuous spending was foreign to all of us, although it seemed that we were getting used to the concept.

Our table in the dining area was very close to the tables on either side of us. Before long, a young Parisian couple came in and was seated at the table to our right. They were a handsome couple that appeared to be very much in love. We finished our meals and our magnum of Champagne. I then proceeded to order a bottle of Courvoisier, an exclusive French Cognac dating back to the days of Napoleon. We had been chatting with the young couple at the next table and it became obvious they had struggled to afford their meals. Kevin and I had just a taste of the Courvoisier and were ready to leave. As we received our bill and signed "Chevrolet" across the top, I took the nearly full bottle of Cognac and offered it to the beautiful French lovers. "With our compliments," I said. The young man was very pleased with our gift. He excitedly shook my hand and said, "Merci beaucoup. Vive America!" I looked back and once again referenced *Casablanca* by saying to the charming couple in my best Bogie impersonation, "At least you'll always have Paris."

Before we left through the gilded doors of Maxims, Katie said she had to go to the ladies' room. She was feeling dizzy from too much champagne. While she was gone, Ephraim came in and asked if we were interested in going to an after-hours club that he knew would be full of the beautiful people of Paris. Kevin and Myra were game and I was always willing to walk on the wild side. As we excitedly discussed Ephraim's suggestion, Katie returned and I could tell by her pale look that she wasn't going anywhere but back to the room. I thought to myself that it was exciting taking Katie to places like Studio 54 in New York and Maxim's in Paris. My problem was letting her go to the ladies' rooms in these places. The Paris nightlife would have to wait. The mother of my children was ill. When we arrived back at the Chateau, Ephraim said that he regretted that he would have to say good-bye. He said tomorrow's activities would be at the Chateau and the following day buses would provide our transportation to Charles De Gaulle Airport for the trip back to New York. He gave each of us a big hug and said it was his extreme pleasure to be our guide during our stay in France. He wished us all a safe trip home and we, in turn, wished him the best in his future. Ephraim had made quite an impression on all of us. I would forever regret not going out to experience the late nightlife of Paris with him as our escort, but I relished the time we had with him and would certainly always maintain a warm spot in my heart for his guidance whenever I thought about our "Grande Voyage." We made our way into the Chateau and said good night to our partners in this wonderful adventure. It was certainly an evening we would always remember with great fondness. Katie celebrated her night in Paris by throwing up.

The buses were already running when we stumbled down the hall the last morning. We grabbed a couple croissants and two coffees to go and barely made the bus on time. Katie was feeling better, but her stomach was still unsettled. She seemed back to normal when we got to the airport but was now in a panic state about flying on the Concorde. Supersonic speed didn't impress her much; she just wanted to get home safely.

We boarded the plane from our own private waiting area. My first impression was that this was a very small plane compared to a commercial airliner. The seats, however, were much more comfortable and afforded each passenger with a great deal more space. Once we were in the air, we were served caviar and champagne, neither of which appealed to either one of us. After about a half hour in the air, a loud cheer from the rest of the passengers startled us. The digital gage on the front wall of the passenger compartment had just gone past the speed of sound. We were going Mach 1 and to someone who always liked driving fast, that was pretty cool. Katie was less impressed but she was delighted to arrive in New York in half the time it would have taken on a commercial flight. Our great adventure ended as we landed at JFK Airport in New York. We said goodbye to our friends from the Midwest, Kevin and Myra, and just like with other friends we met on our past trips, we promised to get together some time in the future. Once again, that never happened. The fairy tale was over. We couldn't wait to get back to Connecticut to see the boys.

Hugs and kisses greeted us when we arrived back home. We had many stories to tell of our fantastic journey, and we had a great deal to catch up on with Katie's parents who looked relieved that we had made it back. Once we were settled in our home and the kids were tucked safely in their beds, I excused myself and said I had to make a special visit. I took a small bag out of our unpacked luggage and drove to the cemetery. In a moment of reflection, I sprinkled the sacred soil of Ireland on my father's grave.

Chapter Forty

Roots of Conspiracy

> "He who has not a good memory, should never take upon him the trade of lying."
>
> Michel de Montaigne

Two weeks was the longest time I had ever spent away from the dealership. Of course, I had heard the stories from other dealers about their lengthy vacations and the time they spent away. One local dealer spent all summer on his forty-foot yacht anchored in Mystic harbor. He said he would occasionally call in to make sure everything was all right, but no one was allowed to call him. He often told me I was going to die a young man if I didn't get away from the rat race periodically to rekindle the competitive fires. To each his own, I thought. My way was old school, taught to me by my father who very rarely ever took a vacation. I was at the dealership every day. I opened the doors in the morning and closed them at night, some twelve hours later. I worked every Saturday and in the winters, I plowed the yard at all hours of the night until the pavement was clear to open the next day. Most weeks, I would work sixty-five to seventy-five hours, and I had been doing this for over ten years. For the first five of those years, I was suffering financially under the weight of my father's frugal pay plan that was based on forty hours and never included overtime. I never received a commission for selling a car and never got a bonus for reaching objectives that had never been reached before. I was motivated solely by my father's promise to turn the dealership over to me one day. My competitive instincts from my days playing sports pushed me to sell more than the other dealers and attempt to be the best that we could be.

In the last few years, my situation changed dramatically. My father's untimely death had thrust me into the role of the dealer-operator of one of Chevrolet's up and coming dealerships. We were highly thought of by the powers that be in the zone office in Tarrytown, New York, and had forged a solid presence in the socio-business climate of northeastern Connecticut. We were innovative, aggressive, and passionate in our approach to representing our dealership and our community. I was very proud of what we had accomplished and was looking forward to a long, fruitful future as a successful businessman. The look and feel of the dealership had changed as dramatically as I had. Our one floor building had a fresh application of the Chevrolet preferred color scheme of white and blue; we had upgraded our diagnostic capabilities with state-of-the-art machines; we had purchased a whole new computer system at a ridiculous price; we had repaved the yard for a more attractive curb appeal; and we had erected a huge pole which proudly displayed a giant American flag in front of the building. The investment in the changes was significant but was done to insure our place in Chevrolet's future. With more employees and a much larger inventory, Cassidy Motors was making its mark.

When I returned from Europe, I was confident Bob, Leo, and Josette had run the dealership efficiently. I felt blessed that I could count on such high quality people to take over the controls in my stead. I intended to step right back into the controls without missing a beat. The confidence I had in my management team made returning to work a pleasure rather than a concern. I was ready to go. Entering the showroom, I was greeted first by Frankie who had a huge smile on his face and his usual colorful joke. The other salesmen soon joined in. They basically wanted to know what the women were like in Paris. Next, the girls from the office came out, all smiley and excited, and then Leo came from the service area with two of his mechanics that wanted to know all about the Concorde. For a few minutes I felt like a celebrity.

Everybody seemed genuinely happy I was back, although Big Bob was noticeably reticent as he took in the whole scene.

"Thanks for the wonderful homecoming," I said. "It's nice to be missed. All I've got to say is we had a great time; it was a fantastic vacation; I missed all of you–now get back to work!"

I went into the office to see how the money situation was and Josette said everything was good. "Sean, you would have been proud of the salesmen. They did so well while you were gone. Everybody was trying really hard to impress you when you got back. Bob did a great job."

"Josette, this is the first time I've felt comfortable being away. I really did feel that the dealership was in good hands. Were there any problems?"

"Just a couple of things. I'm sure Bob will tell you all about them."

Josette was not one to cause trouble or speak badly about anyone, so I knew if there was anything wrong, Bob was the one to see. I went immediately to his office where he said he was expecting me.

"Bob, Josette said things went well and that you did a great job. I appreciate that. But, she also mentioned a couple of problems. I hope it wasn't anything too catastrophic."

Bob got up and closed his door. Whatever the problems, he wanted to deal with them in a quiet one-on-one conversation.

"Sean, Clinton was in last week, supposedly looking for a new car for your sister. Jack showed him some cars, but he made it well known that he would only deal with you. To be honest, I thought he was just snooping around looking for trouble. He was his usual arrogant, condescending self. Sean, I know he's your brother-in-law, but I don't trust that guy."

"Did he try to go into the main office again?"

"No, Josette barely spoke to him. She doesn't want anything to do with him. I hung around the office while he was here so he wouldn't try to bully anyone again."

"Bob, that's exactly what I would have wanted you to do. I appreciate your looking after Josette and I'm sure she appreciated it, too. It's apparent Clinton wasn't too happy about our European trip. The man is incredibly jealous of everything we do. I believe he truly hates me."

"Sean, there's something else. I don't think you are going to like this very much. When Clinton was here, he and Jack seemed very cozy... too cozy. There was a lot of whispering and ..."

"And?"

"Jack was bragging to one of the salesman that he broke into your office the other night using a credit card to jimmy the lock."

"Did you check my office to see if anything was missing?"

"Well, I don't know where everything is supposed to be in there, but Josette said she thought the center draw of your desk was opened."

"Last month's financial statement was in there. I suppose he could have made copies of it. Do you think he gave one to Clinton? Anyway, even if he did, the statement looked good. All he'd find out is that we're doing well. Wait a minute! He'd be able to see how much of a bonus I received last year. That's probably what he was after–ammunition to use against me in the future."

"Sean, as I said before, I don't trust that guy. And I guess we're going to have to keep our eyes on Jack also."

"Bob, to paraphrase an old bromide–you can pick your friends, but you can't pick your relatives."

'"Welcome back, Sean. Welcome back."

Chapter Forty-One

Triumph Amid Tragedy

> "It was the best of times, it was the worst of times; . . .
> it was the season of light, it was the winter of despair."
> Charles Dickens, A Tale of Two Cities

I faced the beginning of 1986 with a great deal of optimism and, unfortunately, with a good amount of trepidation. Never before had I experienced the roller coaster of emotions that awaited the New Year. The expectation of prosperity in a great economic climate was tempered by the reality that my oldest sister, June, was fighting a courageous battle against an unrelenting enemy–cancer. As fractured as my family had become with the internal bickering that went on with the posturing to influence my mother's structure of her estate, June had been the glue that kept the family together. She quite simply wouldn't allow bad behavior between family members. She attempted to foster an air of cooperation between factions that disagreed. Her task was a monumental one, yet was one that she championed with a great deal of alacrity. Katie and I relied on June and her husband, Rick for advice and council on a myriad of topics. They were the pros, the ones who had married at a young age and were quite successful at raising four active boys. June was involved in the community and at the local school, and Rick was a successful businessman and a coach in the local baseball programs. They were well respected by their peers and loved by their friends and family. Katie and I thought the world of June and Rick. We went to dinner together; we vacationed together; we celebrated holidays and birthdays together.

Katie's admiration for June grew over the years and she became her best friend. As for me, it was simple. No one knew me as well as June, and she used that knowledge to advise Katie how to handle my mercurial personality, especially when I acted "too big for my britches." She always seemed to know what buttons to push to get a favorable response and in my case, to diffuse my irrational temper. We loved her; our kids loved her; and the rest of our dysfunctional family loved her as well. It was incomprehensible to think of our lives without June. Her prognosis for recovery was not good, but we were all supportive and prayed nightly for a miracle.

....

Most Januarys in the car business brought plenty of bad weather, a few major snowstorms, and very few customers. January 1986 was an exception. An unusual warm trend created by a favorable jet stream kept the snow away. As a result, the customers that normally would have put off their purchase until the spring came pouring in. The salesmen, who were used to living on their base salary in January, were ecstatic to be making commissions in the middle of a Connecticut winter. Though not balmy, the temperature provided a nice crisp atmosphere to sell cars and trucks. For years, Chevrolet would stuff their dealers with new product in January to be prepared for the spring selling season. It was an aggravating practice that meant each new vehicle that arrived would have to be moved and cleaned off every time it snowed–the more vehicles, the more aggravation. This year Chevrolet was stuffing a hungry lion. New product was flying in and out of the inventory. The final tabulation for the month showed that this was the best January in our history. With the traditionally strong month of February approaching, we hoped that the ground hog would not see his shadow on Ground Hog Day, signifying the end of winter. It didn't. Business continued at a record pace.

One lesson that I learned back in the seventies when I was still new to the business was that nothing ever stays the same. If sales were going badly, you had to believe that things would eventually turn for the better. The opposite was also true. When you had the hot hand going, you had to ride the wave as far as it would take you. This current wave was being ridden hard, but I worried that sooner or later, the ride would be over.

It started with rumors created by gossip. So and so was unhappy. One of the girls in the office didn't like the assistant in the parts department. An unidentified salesman was having an affair with a customer. A mechanic had propositioned a buxom sales rep from a parts distribution warehouse. And the most damaging–the dealer principal was having affairs with any of a number of people that visited the dealership more than once: the girl who wore revealing dresses into the showroom; the young lady who flirted with whomever came into contact with her; the woman from the dress shop who was seen with me at lunch while we planned our next big promotion together; the nubile young instructor at Nautilus; or any of a myriad of other young women who my sales staff and I would speak to at any of the local bistros. I never realized how recognizable I was until I was linked to all these women. I wasn't necessarily innocent.

I had turned forty years old–the age of transition between youth and the advancing years. I was driving my pick of the nicest car in the inventory–a brand new Corvette convertible. I was regularly going out on Wednesday nights with my sales staff to a bar that was situated conveniently between Danville and the neighboring town of Cargill Falls. We would arrive with our full entourage and totally dominate the action. I would throw money around like it was water and the salesmen would invite all sorts of comely young women to join our group at the bar. Those were wild times, the kind of atmosphere that a young guy with his antennae up would relish for the opportunities of scoring with some lovely young thing. I wasn't one of those young guys nor should I have been. I was the very fortunate husband of my wife, Katie, and the father of Jimmy and Tucker Cassidy. I was neither a player nor someone that was addicted to the nightlife. I had already had my time in the spotlight, my fifteen minutes of fame. I was ready to return to the life I knew I was meant to live, but first I had to make some amends. After much personal soul searching, I prayed to God that Katie would be understanding and accept my apology for whatever transgressions she had assumed I had done. Before I could do so, reality slapped us hard. My apology would have to wait. It was March of 1986. After a prolonged, agonizing battle against cancer, my beloved sister, June passed away surrounded by her family and her many friends. My little personal confrontation with my demons suddenly seemed insignificant. Absolution for my perceived indiscretions would have to be put on hold. It was time to reflect on the life of the woman who meant so much to so many, a woman who had left a legacy of goodness that I needed to aspire to.

Chapter Forty-Two

Regrets

> "And the wild regrets, and the bloody sweats,
> none knew so well as I: for he who lives more
> lives than one more deaths than one must die."
>
> Oscar Wilde

It is the true bane of human nature that we get so intoxicated in our own existence that we fail to acknowledge the relevance of those around us. We polish our own ego with self-importance, eschewing the accomplishments of others and discarding their significance in our microcosmic world. Looking in the mirror we see a wonder, a true gift to mankind. We get caught up in a wave of narcissism. We function solely for the rewards of fame. We seek the accolades of our peers and snub the under-accomplished. The journey is lonely for it doesn't allow for others to participate. We are filled with ourselves. Where once there was doubt and uncertainty, now there was arrogance and conceit. As difficult as the quest for success had been, the notoriety of its attainment became far worse. Call it mid-life crisis where the fear of our own mortality triggers abhorrent behavior–decisions made without the thought of whom it might hurt.

Instead of bathing in the glory of achievement, I was awash in inglorious ego. Even I didn't like the person I had become. The dealership was doing very well. It was my less than humble opinion that I was the reason for that. I had never been conceited before so its attachment to my personality came unnoticed. I was measuring success on a material scale, devoid of concern for the struggles of others. I had become isolated in my own little world of self-worth. When ambition overrides what is really important–the relationship with your family and friends and your contribution to society, then that ambition becomes a blind dead end. I had become an awful caricature of success.

Katie was the first to notice the change in my personality. She saw first hand an obvious pattern of disturbing behavior. I wasn't the man she married. I was some mutant egomaniac who was too busy partying with new friends who were bringing out the worst in me. I was forsaking my responsibilities as a husband and father for a few moments of drunken revelry with people I barely knew. I was too caught up in my own world to relate to even my own wife–my life's partner. While I was waiting for the right moment to take responsibility for my actions, Katie was being pushed to the brink. She remembered a poem I had hung over my desk when we first moved into the house. She knew my passion for literature was a crutch that I often used to navigate through one of my ominous moods. She made a copy of the poem and sent it to me at work.

Dear Sean,

I'm sending you this copy of one of your favorite poems by John Donne in an attempt to get my loving husband back. We've somehow lost our ability to communicate. Quite often you seem so far away in your thoughts that I feel I'm intruding. Please read the poem and remember that I love you very much.

Your loving wife,
Katie

I opened the letter and was relieved by Katie's comments. My intended attempt at an apology was too late. I was working a lot of hours and partying too much, yet I honestly thought that I was doing a good job with the family. Obviously, I was wrong. I sat down and read the familiar words to the poem. This time I paid more attention to the message and not just the words.

No Man Is An Island

No man is an island entire of itself, every man
is a piece of the continent, a part of the main;
if a clod be washed away by the sea, Europe
is the less, as well as if a promontory were, as
well as any manor of thy friends or of thine
own were; any man's death diminishes me,
because I am involved in mankind.
And therefore never send to know for whom
the bell tolls; it tolls for thee.
John Donne (1572-1631)

Katie's message was clear. In order for me to restore the life we cherished, to become the husband and father that we both wanted and expected, I would have to abandon my island of conceit and come back to the mainland. Realizing what I was about to lose–what I had put in jeopardy, I planned on rowing a boat across that regret-filled sea that surrounded my isolation, back to the world of humility, as soon as possible.

Chapter Forty-Three

Independence Day

"Old wood best to burn, old wine to drink, old friends to trust, and old authors to read."

Francis Bacon

Despite the constant reminders from my wife that I was throwing our money away, the renovations on the lake cottage were complete in late spring of 1986. Katie, who had been the captain of the negativity team, had changed her tune a great deal when she saw the final product. We had restored the old lady on the hill to her previous status as a paragon of the old grandeur that once existed on the lake. Katie couldn't believe the transformation, and although I reminded her often of her protestations about the reality of ever living there, she was anxious to move into our cottage for the summer. It finally turned out that she admitted that it was money well spent. Despite her conservative genes, she was on board for this new adventure. The boys were excited to be able to go swimming and fishing whenever they wanted. Suddenly, I was no longer the fool who bought the old dilapidated house without consulting my wife. I reveled in my newfound status in the family. While I gloated, Baxter stopped by to get an update on the lake and see when he could come out with his boys to fish.

"What's happening?" he started. "Did you make your first million yet?"

"Baxter, isn't it enough that I'm rich in the knowledge that I have friends like you? That alone should be enough for anybody."

"Well, I'll tell you. There are a lot of girls that wish that was the case, but life is just too short to satisfy everyone."

"Yes, it is, but I know you'll give it your best. After all, that has always been your prime motivation. Without girls, what would you do?"

"I'd probably sell cars. You seemed to do all right, and I know if you could do it, so could I."

"Well, you've got the gift of gab, and you can lie with a straight face. Your values are questionable, and so are your morals. You'd be perfect–but not for a car salesman. You'd make a perfect politician. Maybe, you should run for office. I also think you'd do well as a pimp. You'd look good in a long velvet coat and a big wide brimmed hat. Either one. There's not a great deal of difference between a politician and a pimp."

"Pimps are mean to women. I only treat women with the greatest respect and admiration. That's why they all love me. By the way, my filthy rich friend, how's the cottage coming along and when is the first party?"

Conversations with Baxter were always filled with bluster and hyperbole. Somehow, after many years playing ball together, rooming together in Boston, and supporting each other through all our various mini-crises and tragedies, we remained the closest of friends. He knew that I was still hurting from my sister's death and his way of support was providing a healthy diversion. Talking about the Celtics, the Red Sox, or the New York Football Giants was like a dose of painkillers to numb the pain. All three teams were successful in 1986, making any discussion about them all the more therapeutic. He also knew of the criticism I had taken from my wife for buying the cottage. His reference to the first party was a way of letting me know that Katie would be thrilled with the cottage now that it was finished and that a party would be another diversion. Sometimes I had to step back and reflect on the true motives for Baxter's conversant bantering. It was obvious this time that his motives were exemplary. I made up my mind on the spot that the first party would be on the Fourth of July, the one day of the year when the entire lake joined in to celebrate our nation's independence. Baxter said he and his family would be there with bells on.

By the time the Fourth of July came along, the kids and Katie had settled into our new summer digs. The kids quickly became water rats spending most of their days swimming in the lake. Katie was even quicker in her acclimation, instantly making friends with our surrounding neighbors. Because I was so busy at work in June, I seemed to be the only one who got shortchanged in this deal. I hadn't spent enough time at the cottage to truly reap the benefits of our new summer home. I promised myself that would change in July. I decided to include my salesmen in the festivities on the Fourth. Katie had already invited all our friends and relatives, so a few more people certainly wouldn't matter. I told the guys that this was going to be the salesman's party that I promised. I also invited Pierre and his wife. We had kept in touch since he left the dealership and he was delighted to be included. Reuniting Pierre with Francois would be like providing an entertaining sideshow for the rest of us.

Our guests arrived shortly after noon. Many of the wives felt compelled to bring a platter of food or dessert. We supplied the hamburgers and hotdogs, the beer, the wine, and the bourbon. The crowd swelled early in the afternoon on a beautiful summer day that could have been the subject of a picture post card. Jake and Bo came together, but said they would have to leave early to meet their girl friends on the other side of the lake. Several hours later, they had forgotten that promise. Frankie roared into the parking lot in his vintage corvette convertible, ready to party with his ever- present tooth pick in his mouth. Francois came with his wife and was thrilled to see that Pierre was already there. It was a beautiful mixture of personalities, from car people to lawyers, to engineers and teachers, which made for some interesting conversations. The kids invited a bunch of their friends giving the party a youthful exuberance. The stereo blared patriotic music from John Phillips Souza to Kate Smith. Early in the afternoon, the men left the women out on the deck and went inside for some bourbon tasting. It was the consensus that Kentucky produced better tasting bourbon than Tennessee, although Jack Daniels was still the brand most often requested. After the bourbon tasting, a pickup basketball game in the driveway developed with several young high school players challenging some of us old bucks to a game. I must say we stayed competitive for quite awhile until the effects of the bourbon drained our stamina. We promised we would do better in a rematch next year.

As the afternoon progressed the lake was pretty much enveloped in merrymaking. The residents of the lake go all out on the Fourth of July. There are parties on every shore and a boat parade where people decorate their boats with patriotic themes and sing songs like "God Bless America," and "America the Beautiful" as they float by the cheering crowds that spill out of the cottages and homes surrounding the lake. The aroma of countless barbecues pervades the air and the raucous hooting and hollering of drunken revelers can be heard emanating from any of the myriad of parties. As the day progresses the singing becomes more pronounced and the noise levels continue to rise. The festivities culminate at dusk when the first of many residents begin the fireworks display. Soon other cottages join in and before long the lake is engulfed in a spectacular holiday light show. Smoke from the rockets and mortars that have gone off settles just above the water to create an atmosphere not unlike the aftermath of a battle. For those of us experiencing the festivities for the first time, it was an impressive display of patriotism. There was no doubt that from that moment on the Cassidy clan and all our friends would be celebrating subsequent Fourth of July parties at our newly renovated home on the lake–the resurrected grand old house on the hill.

Chapter Forty-Four

The Seeds of Deceit

"When I consider life, it is all a cheat.
Yet fooled with hope, people favor this deceit."
John Dryden

The beginning of 1987 was filled with promise. The economic climate was building momentum and business continued to escalate. I never quite prescribed to the theory that everything must come to an end, but I knew from some less than pleasant experiences in the past that change was inevitable. My mother's first visit of the New Year illuminated the possibilities of change.

"Sean, your mother is in your office. She said she'd like to talk to you." Josette seemed disturbed. My mother always visited with her before she saw me so I ascertained that there might have been something in their conversation that bothered Josette. Guardedly, I entered my office where I found mom seated at my desk, my father's old desk that I had refinished when I opened the new office. The walls of my office were covered with photos and memorabilia of the boys, pictures of the various teams the boys had played on, and many remembrances of my father, including his diploma from Boston University. I could tell she felt very comfortable in these surroundings. She was busy taking care of some of her personal bills. I never objected to her sitting at my desk for

I considered it to be a symbol of the continuity of the family. It was a large solid oak desk with heavy drawers that were difficult to open and close. In addition to its solid appearance, it provided me with a strong symbolic base from which to run the operation and to garner the respect of the employees who depended on me to make the right decisions, the ones that affected their futures. I believed my mother enjoyed sitting at the desk not only to be reminded of the essence of her husband, but also to remind me that despite my position as the dealer-operator of Cassidy Motors, she was still the president of the corporation and the majority stockholder–the titular head.

My mother was a wonderful woman with many close friends and a reputation as a generous philanthropist that contributed to many charitable causes. She was also extremely well received by the employees, who viewed her as the matriarch of the Cassidy family. Because she was always smiling and pleasant, everyone enjoyed her visits to the dealership. That's what made Josette's demeanor all the more alarming. Something was up and I was about to find out exactly what.

"Sean, sit down for a minute." I obliged just like when I was a little kid.

"Clinton was here this weekend and he believes the will I prepared two years ago before June passed away is now invalid. He suggests I write a new one because my beneficiaries have changed. He suggests I talk to an estate attorney he knows in Windham to more evenly distribute the estate among the remaining four children. What do you think?"

What I really thought was that Clinton was a snake, but I knew because of his influence on my mother, I would be looking for trouble if I expressed those feelings.

"Mom, I think you should still have five beneficiaries. June's kids should be included as a separate entity. Leaving them out only enhances what the rest of us get and that includes you know who. I don't think that's fair, do you?"

"I don't know. Sometimes I wish I didn't have any money. Then I wouldn't have to worry about things like this."

"Mom, as I told you before you made the last will, I don't want anything from your personal holdings–your bank accounts, your stocks, or your property. All I want is the dealership. That's what was promised to me by Dad, and, quite frankly, I believe after all these years building this business into what it is today, there should be no question about the ownership of the dealership. Besides, Chevrolet would never go along with multiple owners of the franchise. We'd be looking for trouble."

"I don't know, Sean. Clinton says your share of the estate would be disproportionate to the others because the dealership business would be worth more than the rest of my holdings."

"And… what did Clinton have to do with that?" I could feel my face getting red, a true indicator that I was about to blow my stack.

"Oh, I don't know what to do! What should I do, Sean?"

"Maybe you should go see this estate attorney, but don't agree to anything until we have a chance as a family to agree on what's fair. Don't get all upset over this. We'll all talk and hopefully come to a solution that keeps peace in the family."

"I wish you and your brother-in-law would get along better. He says one thing, and then you say another. My head is spinning."

"If it makes it easier on everybody, buy me out. Katie, the boys and I will go merrily on our way."

"Sean, don't be silly. I'll go see the lawyer."

"Oh, Mom," I said stopping on my way out of the office. "Say hi to Clinton for me."

Chapter Forty-Five

Back to Reality

"A Time to Build, a Time to Breakdown"
The Byrds

Winter into spring, spring into summer–the endless march of time forgets not the progression of the seasons. The car business dulls your appreciation of the beautiful changes that New England has to offer. Equinoxes and Solstices come and go without a semblance of regard. Commissions, quotas, prospecting, follow-ups are all that is important, leaving little time to marvel at the vivid colors of autumn or the glistening freshness of a new fallen snow. Seasons flash by without a single thought of the majesty that they present. The car business is not for dreamers. This harsh reality is at the core of the unexplainably high rate of turnover that exists in our line of work. The status quo changes quickly and the feeling of complacency is never allowed to develop.

Today, Frankie gave his notice. His reasons were unclear, but I surmised that the endless sports chatter in the showroom had finally gotten to him. His spot at the end of the showroom, right by the door that beckoned buyers into his self-described "web of doom," would be difficult to replace. People that worked for me as long as Frankie were not just employees; they were friends. He had come to the dealership with a great deal of baggage, but he had done a wonderful job for us.

Even Big Bob was rattled when he first heard the news. He and Frankie were on the opposite ends of the integrity scale, but they had managed to co-exist for the last few years and had produced a great many sales for Cassidy Motors. There was little doubt that he would be missed, not only for his salesmanship, but also for his inimitable personality and quick wit. Our sales and our chemistry were taking a big hit. Bob and I were determined to move on without our number one producer, but we knew it would be difficult to replace him. Two weeks later, Leo gave his notice. Suddenly, a lone defection had become a crisis of identity. Arguably, our two most recognizable employees, the two that most defined our image, were leaving. I told Bob I had to go for a drive to sort out the impact of these resignations and think about a new direction in which we would have to go. Bob, who musically still lived in the 1960's, gave me a cassette to listen to as I drove into the countryside. I listened intently to every word.

TURN, TURN, TURN
The Byrds

A time to buildup, a time to breakdown
A time to dance, a time to mourn
A time to cast away stones,
A time to gather stones together.

Even without Frankie and Leo, our business continued to be steady, if not spectacular. Our young sales staff was gaining experience, and in spite of the constant distractions with young girls and the incessant sports banter, was showing signs of great promise. I moved Jack to service as a stopgap until we could find another service manager, a feat not unlike finding the Holy Grail. Bob said we could use another professional to replace, not only Frankie's production, but also Jack's. A search began to find the missing link in our sales organization. It began in late summer of 1987 and continued into the early part of fall. Several viable candidates were being considered when on Monday, October 17th, the stock markets around the world suddenly crashed. The U.S. markets dropped 508 points or approximately 22 percent. It was the largest one-day decline in stock market history to that point. Suddenly our search for a new salesman was set aside for another day. The next few weeks would be about survival.

"A time to cast away stones, a time to gather stones together."

Chapter Forty-Six

Preppies, Elitists and Snobs

> "We must ask where we are and whither we are tending."
>
> Abraham Lincoln

During the Reagan administration, there were myriad opportunities to improve our status in life. Although Katie and I were happy with what we had accomplished to that point, our latest concerns centered around the boys' education and their selection of college after high school. Both boys were good students so we often discussed the options that were available close to home. Danville High School, where I attended, was not without its problems, most of which were brought about by the dramatic increase in enrollment over the last few years and the declining space to accommodate this increase. If you put too many students with roaring hormones in a space too little for them to grow peacefully, generally trouble ensues. We had heard too many horror stories about what was going on at Danville to be comfortable with that as our only choice. We disagreed, however, on the merits of raising the kids in the only house that they ever knew.

"I know you love this house, Sean, but let's look around and see if there is anything interesting in Essex or Westchester. Think how cool it would be to live in Westchester."

This wasn't the first time we had this discussion. Our house was a symbol to me; it was our first house and the home in which our kids had grown up. I was a strong believer in establishing roots and providing the kids with a feeling of security–a place to call home. I remembered how much my family's house on Broad Street had meant to me and how devastated I was when my parents sold the house while I was living in Boston. They never even bothered to tell me until after it was gone. Painful–that's all I remembered about that time.

"I'll look around but don't get too excited. I'm sort of attached to this house. Besides, since we bought the summer cottage on the lake four years ago, moving there for three or four months a year is enough to satisfy my wanderlust. We've got some nice neighbors here on Beverly Avenue. They're not all idiots."

"Oh, Sean! You and your roots! You're not a plant, you know."

"I know, but sometimes I feel like a geranium."

It was easy to make a joke of Katie's desire to move to one of the more affluent areas of northeastern Connecticut. It wasn't because she was becoming infatuated with the opulence of the wealthy. It was more a fear of sending the boys to Danville High.

Her interest in Essex and Westchester came from a desire to see our boys enrolled in one of the exclusive schools in those towns, either Essex Prep, a highly rated private secondary school on a par with Phillips Andover and the like, or Westchester Academy, which provided students with a college atmosphere on its rustic campus. Both schools had excellent reputations and spectacular college placement histories. Essex was located on a nationally designated historic road that meandered through the beautiful countryside of northeastern Connecticut. Magnificent brownstone buildings complete with ivy covered walls and spectacular views of the surrounding hills and valleys represented the school's mission as a feeder school for the Ivy League. Its biggest drawback was the tuition that rivaled that of many colleges.

Westchester Academy was a public school, but it had the look and feel of a prep school. It offered many advantages unavailable in most public schools. Its college preparatory courses were second to none. Both schools defined the opportunities of class distinction. Katie and I were in agreement that a little class in our boys' lives wouldn't be a bad thing.

Both choices were very interesting, even if it meant having to move from Danville. Jimmy and Tucker were well rounded academically and gifted as athletes, a combination that would appeal to either of the two schools. The choice of colleges would have to be dealt with in the very near future. Any advantages in that process, including the reputation of the secondary school they were attending, would be helpful. The choice of high school to prepare for college was an intelligent long-range plan. We wanted to give the boys every possible advantage. What we didn't take into consideration was the preferences of the boys.

When approached on the subject of attending one of these schools, Jimmy spoke for both of our sons.

"No way!" he said quickly and emphatically. "I can't stand preppies. Both schools have one gigantic thing in common–they're full of obnoxious, elitist snobs. I wouldn't last a minute in either place. I'm going to Danville with my friends."

One look at Tommy and I realized from his distorted countenance, that it was unanimous. Jimmy's outburst in defiance was not something that Katie was going to ignore without a fight, but I knew from dealing with Jimmy's stubbornness and Tucker's deference to his brother's sentiments, that she was going to lose this battle. The kids had made up their minds. We acquiesced eventually and hoped that Danville High was ready for regular parental visits because the Cassidy brothers were coming.

Chapter Forty-Seven

Benny and the Bear

"Friendship is a sheltering tree."
Samuel Taylor Coleridge

My mother's appearance in the afternoon was a surprise. Normally, her visits were in the early morning. For a woman in her late seventies, she had an active daily schedule that usually started with dropping by the office to chat with the girls. She loved her time with Josette and the girls and they reciprocated that love. My mother was charming, gracious and a concerned listener. The girls would tell her all sorts of things that they were up to including some intimate details of their personal lives. She usually giggled at their funny stories and offered advice when she thought they could use it. She was, indeed, a special lady. Still, to see her coming into the showroom in the late afternoon was unusual. I imagined that it had to be bad news of some kind. This time she walked right by the business office, waving to the girls as she came directly to my office.

"Are you too busy to talk to your mother?" she stated with a smirk on her face.

"Well, that depends, Mom, on what tidings you are bringing me today." She liked it when I went along with her moods.

"You're probably wondering why I'm here at this time of the day?"

"Not at all. You know you're always welcomed regardless of how busy I am."

"All right, knock it off, Sean. You don't have to impress me with all your schmoozing. I just want you to know that I just came from the lawyer and he suggests that we put any discussions about my estate on hold until he can meet with you. He liked your suggestion about the five entities instead of four and he says he can understand why you wouldn't want multiple interests in the dealership. He told me to tell you that unless you approve any change in the ownership, nothing would change."

"And, what did Clinton have to say about these new developments?"

"He said he would take the lawyer's suggestions under advisement and get back to him. I thought you might be happy with everything so far."

"Well, Mom, as I told you before, I only have interest in the dealership. That's what Dad wanted, and that's what was promised to me. If that doesn't sit well with the other members of the family, let them come down and work sixty-five hours a week for twenty years, and then maybe they would have the right to complain."

"I just wish this whole mess was settled. I can't believe what's happening between you and Clinton. You used to get along."

"That was a long time ago when I wasn't a threat to his master plan."

"Oh, Sean. You're so dramatic."

"And so right in my assumptions."

"OK, I'm leaving. Try to look at things a little differently. It would be better for everyone, especially me."

"I'll try, Mom." With that empty promise, I kissed her goodbye and went back to work.

Bob was next to come to my door. He said he had some interesting applicants to fill our two vacant salesmen positions. One was Benny Chapman, the slick dressing young man who handled our newspaper advertising. Benny always wore a fitted suit and a bright tie for our appointments and was extremely creative when it came to our ads. I thought he was very competent and quite amusing, but because of the way he acted and the way he walked, I wondered if he wasn't a little light in the loafers. Bob laughed when I brought up that observation adding that he thought the same thing. I told Bob to bring him in later in the week for an appointment and we could make a better value judgment.

It turned out the other applicant was waiting in the showroom to see me. John "the Bear" Upton was an old friend and classmate who disappeared down south after high school. He was a big old country boy who was prone to sing at the drop of a hat. I remembered him to be occasionally, unnervingly boisterous and always at the ready to defend his principles regardless of how much they were watered down with liquor. The most memorable thing about John was how big and intimidating he was. He was well over six feet five inches tall and was too heavy to be weighed on a normal scale. After exchanging warm hellos, I shook his massive hand and was immediately drawn into a rib crunching bear hug. When I got my breath back, we sat and talked for more than an hour, reminiscing about many of the dumb things we did in high school. We were teammates on the football team, a fact he used as a suggestion that we team up again to "put asses and tail lights down the road." I guessed correctly that that was a southern expression for selling cars.

When I asked John what he had been up to in the years since our misspent youth, he sat down on my couch and sighed, "Let's see. Where do I start?" I too got comfortable because I knew this was going to be a colorful and interesting story.

"After school, I enlisted in the army and served in an artillery unit in Vietnam. That's why I'm hard of hearing now. I also lost my teeth in a barroom fight somewhere in Saigon. That accounts for my beautiful smile. See–all false. After Nam, I settled in Texas, sold cars and conversion vans, and married my ex. We had two beautiful daughters together and too many Pina Coladas." Somehow I knew it was coming, but it still humored me to hear him sing. "All my exes live in Texas, and Texas is the place I'd dearly love to be."

I thought to myself that having John around would be good for me–to keep me entertained and in touch with my inner self, the happy-go-lucky side of my personality that I had placed somewhere deep in seclusion while I fought life's seemingly endless battles of survival. Without thinking about Bob's opinion, I hired John on the spot. I knew working with old friends was a dangerous scenario because it often led to the ruin of a good friendship, but I was willing to take a chance on that not happening. Losing Frankie and then Leo had left me sullen and moody. Hiring John was the elixir I needed to pick up my spirits.

At the end of the week, Bob and I interviewed Benny and offered him the other vacant position. In one memorable week, my mother had given me some good news about the ownership of the dealership and we had hired two talented and personable people to fill our sales vacancies. Hopefully, the crisis of recent days was a thing of the past. Once again, time would tell.

Chapter Forty-Eight

Decade of Thunder

"Thunder is caused by the collision of clouds."

Aristotle

The smooth ride of success came to a crashing halt at the end of the Eighties. George H. Bush became the 41st President of the United States on January 20th, 1989. His term was christened by a world in turmoil. Communism was losing its grip on many Eastern European countries. After twenty-eight years of a divided Germany separated by a large concrete wall patrolled by armed East German troops, the Berlin Wall, one of the last symbols of Communist rule in Europe, came down to the cheers of a suddenly reunited Germany. It was an historical turning point for the waves of revolutions that swept the Eastern Bloc, starting in Poland. Dubbed the Revolutions of 1989, they heralded the death of the Soviet Union two years later. In effect, it was the beginning of the post-Cold War era of United States' dominance in world affairs. (Source: Wikipedia)

Elsewhere in the world, signs of change were just as evident as they were in Europe.

The last Soviet troops left Afghanistan in February, signaling the end of their nine-year war. In China, a student protest in Tiananmen Square in Beijing, led to a bloody conflict with Chinese troops. In Iran, the warring cleric, the Ayatollah Khomeini died, closing the book on the Iran Hostage crisis that had haunted the Carter presidency a decade before. Of interest to a great deal of Americans was the news that during his funeral, his corpse fell into the mob of mourners. At home, new President Bush declared a war on drugs. With all the ramifications of what was happening in the world, the glory years of the Eighties appeared to be over.

I was truly sorry to see the end of the decade in which we had made great strides in becoming a successful and influential business. I felt deep down in my gut that these were probably our best years and regrettably, they were most likely behind us. It was a pessimistic way of looking back at how well we had done in the past ten years instead of looking positively ahead to a new challenge. I felt we had reached the apex of our potential. The hiring of John and Benny gave me some optimism that maybe we might be able to duplicate the golden years that we had just experienced. John and Benny instilled new life to the showroom. Both were enthusiastic about their new positions and both brought with them a sense of fun. Unfortunately, it was like letting two strange roosters loose in the hen house. John was loud and boisterous and, at times, threatening. He was full of stories of his life in Texas and his many brushes with the law. His size and aggressiveness made the remaining staff uneasy. Benny was much more flamboyant. He came from a musical background and played many instruments including the piano and the accordion. He was great fun at parties, often taking over on the piano and playing anything that was requested. Unfortunately for the harmony in the showroom, both newcomers loved to party. Drinking at lunch and after work became the norm rather than the exception. Too often, I would join them.

Jake and Bo were the first to show signs of discontent with the new hired hands.

Whether they were turned off by the bluster of "the Bear" or the eccentricities of Benny, we could never be sure, but before long, both left to take sales positions at a foreign car dealer in Windham, about thirty miles away. Their friendship, forged while they were members of the Cassidy sales team and the various Cassidy sponsored athletic teams, led to their joint resignation to try their luck at another dealership. It's funny how they must have viewed the situation they were in, expecting somehow, despite the downturn in the economy, that it would be better somewhere else. They both had achieved different levels of success and both had done a good job of representing our dealership. I wished them well. It was not surprising, however, to hear that they moved on to another dealer several months later, and eventually left the business altogether. Jake settled into a position of hosting at a restaurant where Katie and I often dined. From his very animated tales that he was quick to share, it was evident that Jake had more success with the waitressing staff than with his new career, but when Katie and I went to dinner at that restaurant, we always got the best of service. Bo bounced around working several different jobs before he settled into the role of a part-time wholesaler. Bo and Jake were part of some very good years at Cassidy. I would always view their contributions to our dealership with a great deal of fondness.

With two more defections from our sales staff, Bob and I once again went to work finding capable replacements. The difficulty in replacing such dynamic personalities was duplicating the camaraderie that existed with the old group. While sifting through the new applications, I reminded Bob of the time that Jake, Bo, Frankie and I took off one Sunday afternoon in my new twelve-foot sailboat, *The Blue Nun*, to visit one of Jake's girlfriends on the other side of the lake. We left with a brash confidence in our sailing ability, a large dose of trash talking, a pinch of doubt in our ability to get to other side of the lake, and a case of beer. Jake's girlfriend's cottage was only about a half mile away, but the route meant navigating around an island and a couple of hidden sand bars. It also meant tacking through several wind direction changes because we were going from the protected side of the lake to the open end.

This was not exactly an America's Cup crew. What we lacked in sailing experience, we made up for it with bravado. Jake never stopped talking from the minute we left. Frankie kept insisting that he was a champion sailor during his youth, although he never offered his help to sail this boat. I was new at sailing and was just getting used to the main sail, the jib and the rudder and trying to work them in unison while holding a beer in one hand. Bo was petrified of the water and kept saying, "Get this boat to the other side. I can't swim." Two hours into our ten-minute trip, we started to wonder if we would ever get there. Bo was in a panic because he had to pee. Frankie was laughing hysterically and Jake was talking even faster than ever making fun of Bo. He told him to "jump in and pee. We'll come back and get you."

Bo's voice was full of fear. "I'm not jumping in, and don't you dare throw me in. You guys wouldn't come back and get me. You don't know how to go in reverse. I would never get home. I'm serious! I can't swim."

We somehow managed to navigate past the sand bars to the other side of the island where Jake's girlfriend and her buddies were waving at us from their dock. We had no problem seeing them. We just couldn't get there. Another hour passed before a wind change seemed to send us in the right direction. By this time, we all had to pee. Our landing was less than textbook as we crashed into the dock, knocking it over and eventually capsizing *The Blue Nun* in several feet of water. As soon as we all went into the water, four yellow clouds rose from below. We had made it!

Just recounting this story of our sailing journey was a microcosm of the way it was in the Eighties. We struggled through adversity, but we had fun doing it. The loss of my three erstwhile salesmen left me a bit sad. Thinking about them reminded me of how good those days were and how much I would miss those guys. But one thing the car business doesn't let you do is live in the past for too long, because tomorrow was going to bring a whole new set of challenges. I enjoyed reminiscing, but it was time to gear up for the Nineties.

Chapter Forty-Nine

A Respite from the Insanity

"Put me in, Coach–I'm ready to play today."
John Fogarty

The old saying goes, "Hope springs eternal." For me and every other baseball nut in the world, the true saying should be, "In spring, hope is eternal." Of course, I'm not referencing the economy or the car business, but rather the real passion in my life other than my family and my God–Baseball. When I was a young boy, I couldn't wait for winter to end. Spring trumpeted in baseball season and that meant spending ninety per cent of my waking hours somewhere on a ball field. I loved everything about baseball. I loved the smell of the grass and the feel of the infield dirt. I loved the sound of hitting a ball with a wooden bat and the thrill of making a good play in the field. I loved running the bases, throwing to cut off men, stealing, turning two at second base, playing pepper on the sidelines before a game, wearing metal spikes for the first time, pitching in a close game, or hitting one out of the park. I loved it all. Before I was old enough to play Little League, I spent hours in my back yard with my brother, Chip, just playing catch or an old game called "hit the bat." We would play every day after school until my mother would call us for dinner. She never had to look too far for us. We were always playing ball nearby.

Little League became a part of my life at nine years old when my baseball career was launched. I played until my twelfth birthday and then moved on to senior league, school ball and eventually American Legion and semi-pro ball as an adult. I enjoyed every minute I was on the field, whether it was a game or just practice. I was that rare bird that loved practice. I could do infield drills all day, and batting practice was never long enough. As long as I was active on a baseball field somewhere, I was truly happy.

Our boys didn't have a chance.

Centerfield
John Fogerty

"Got a beat up glove, a homemade bat, and brand new pair of shoes;
You know I think it's time to give this game a ride.
Put me in, Coach–I'm ready to play today.
Look at me, I can be Centerfield."

When Jimmy was barely old enough to walk, I took him outside with a small plastic bat and a wiffle ball. The first time he hit the ball he was hooked and from that moment on, he was always asking me if I could throw him some balls. Before long, Tucker joined in. When he grabbed the bat the first time in a left handed stance, Katie immediately brought it to his attention that he was holding the bat from the wrong side. I stopped her before she could stunt the growth of a natural hitter and told her it was OK if that was the side where he felt most comfortable. I explained to her that it was a real advantage to bat left handed because you're closer to first base and most pitchers are right handed so you see the ball better. She looked at me like I had three heads and said, "Really, Sean. He's only three years old. What difference could it make, now."

I gasped. Then I reminded her that Carl Yastrzemski batted left handed, and Ted Williams, and Roger Maris, and Lou Gehrig. I lost her after Ted Williams.

"The poor kid," she said. "He's doomed."

It was inevitable that my passion for baseball would be passed on to my boys–whether they liked it or not. Fortunately for me, they both loved it. As the years began to gather their carefree springs in the backyard, we graduated from plastic bats and balls to a wooden bat and a bag of tennis balls. I became the pitcher, the batting instructor, and the retriever–the one who got to chase the tennis balls all over the yard and, as the boys got older, into the neighbors' yards as well. Baseball in the Cassidy backyard was a daily activity that began the minute I got home from work.

When Jimmy turned nine, we signed him up for farm team in the Danville Little League system. Tucker wanted to play too, but because of his age, he was only allowed to play if I agreed to coach the team. For the next twelve years, I coached every team the boys were on through all the levels of baseball. There were many highs and lows, many triumphs and tough losses, many memorable experiences. I loved coaching. I loved working with young people teaching them the right and wrong way of doing things with the ultimate goal of making them better athletes and better citizens. At times, it was tough on our boys. It's never easy to coach your own kids without someone criticizing you for favoring them, or worse, for being too critical of their play. Fortunately, I was blessed with two kids who were well liked by their teammates and who were tolerant of their father's occasional irrational rant. Through it all, we had a great time. The various leagues and teams afforded us the opportunity of meeting a whole group of great people who became lifelong friends. The ultimate satisfaction was in the knowledge that I had made a difference in innumerable young men's lives, many of which went on to success in a host of different careers. The irreplaceable bonus was the time I got to spend with my boys and the bond we formed over the years because of it. To this day, the single most endearing salutation I can receive is when one of my former players addresses me with the very simple, but affectionate title of "Coach."

Chapter Fifty

Chasing a Ghost

> "What lies behind us and what lies before us are tiny matters compared to what lies within us."
>
> Walt Emerson

"Where the hell is Iraq?" Baxter asked when he stopped by at the house to play some basketball with the boys in the driveway. I never wasted a chance to impress someone with my knowledge of geography or of ancient history. It didn't seem that there were many people who much cared about life before the birth of Christ, certainly not many in Danville, and certainly not Baxter; but I nonetheless answered his question from an historical point of view.

"It used to be Babylonia, babe. In ancient times, it was a part of Mesopotamia. Babylon, the capital city, was known for its wealth and power and was famous for its hanging gardens that were considered one of the Seven Wonders of the World. Iraq is in the middle of the Middle East and is located between the Tigris and Euphrates rivers. It's bordered by Iran and Turkey."

"Well, I guess I asked the right person, but wasn't Babylonia that hot looking chick who was a U.S. figure skater?"

Of course Baxter was referring to Tai Babilonia who partnered with Randy Gardner on our Olympic team in 1980.

"Baxter, Baxter, Baxter. You always turn the conversation around so it includes a good-looking girl."

"Well, to be honest with you, I could care less about any hanging gardens that existed a million years ago. I just wanted to know where Iraq was?"

"And now you know. It's located between the Babilonia and Gardner rivers." We both laughed. It was obvious that the history lesson had fallen on deaf ears, but at least, he asked.

I welcomed Baxter's visit. Humorous moments were becoming rare and life's little joy ride was becoming bumpier by the day. Business was slowing down and I feared another recession. Certainly a war in a far off land would only serve to put more strain on a faltering economy. Basketball in the driveway was a temporary reprieve for my psyche, yet it didn't clear up the single biggest concern I was facing entering my third decade in the business–the continued influence on my mother by my brother-in-law.

The latest sign of impending trouble was my mother's request that Clinton analyze our financial statement to see if he could find any areas where we might concentrate on to counter the effects of a sluggish economy. I had made the mistake of telling her that business was off and it looked like we might be in for another drawn-out period of recessionary results. She innocently offered Clinton's services as a way of helping me out. I had never mentioned to her the incident several years ago when Clinton and Jack were poking around my office while I was away. It wouldn't have served any purpose other than Mom having to take sides. Even though I was her youngest, somehow I wasn't comfortable with her allegiance to me. She was a very generous and compassionate woman and Clinton had long been subliminally working on her generosity to achieve his goal of sharing in the success of the family business. I decided to accept his offer of constructive assistance. After all, it might just expose his true motives to my mother. I should have heeded my father's warning to: "Keep Clinton away from the dealership."

A week later, my mother called and said Clinton was ready with some constructive ideas. We set up a meeting for that afternoon. My mother arrived first and her opening statement was a portent of what was to come.

"I'm glad you let Clinton analyze the credit statement. He said English majors some time don't understand the trends indicated in these reports. He told me he would have some interesting things to say."

I was about to gag when Clinton walked in–like he owned the place.

"Thanks, Sean, for allowing me to look at your financial statement." He mentioned some insignificant trends a moron could identify. Then, expecting the unexpected, I was even stunned by his next remark.

"Mrs. C., do you realize how much money Sean made last year? It's no wonder the business is off."

I reacted like I almost always did when I was around Clinton. The man made my skin crawl.

"I'm sorry, this meeting is over. I allowed you the opportunity to provide us with some concrete ideas to help through this recession and you used this occasion to ambush me. Get out and stay out."

The volume of my voice had been heard in the showroom. Both John and Bob came to the door to see if everything was all right. Clinton looked at the size of these two and realized that he was about to be escorted out. He meekly left the statement behind, but I was sure he had made copies for his future schemes. My mother was astonished at what she had just witnessed. She looked at me almost apologetically and told me quietly to calm down. She said she had no idea he was going to criticize me for the way I ran the business. She then got up and left my office to go talk to Josette. When I cooled off several minutes later, I thanked John and Bob for their assistance and told them I was going for a ride to get my head straight. As I was pulling out of the driveway of the dealership, I turned the radio on and there was that song again with those familiar lyrics that had haunted me since my father's wake.

"Every breath you take, every move you make, I'll be watching you."

Chapter Fifty-One

Who Let the Bear Out?

"Work eight hours and sleep eight hours
And make sure they are not the same hours."
T. Boone Pickens

John "The Bear" Upton was an enigma. He was extremely humorous, gregarious and very likable, yet he was also bombastic, boisterous and easy to dislike. There wasn't much middle ground when it came to "The Bear." Because of his size, which was comparable to that of an interior lineman in the National Football League, many people were intimidated by his presence. I had known John since he transferred to our high school as a junior from West Virginia. He came out of nowhere, that mythical transfer that we all dreamed of having on our football team–the huge kid who looked like a mountain in a football uniform, was fast for a big guy, and mean enough to scare the garter out of a snake. He brought with him a zest for life, a penchant for raucous behavior, and a need to sing at the drop of a hat. The only thing he enjoyed more than squashing opponents on the football field was leading the songs that the team would sing on the bus to away games. He taught a bunch of northern boys–Yankees he would call us–songs we had never heard before, but were soon singing along with him. His favorite was *Cotton Fields*, written by a country singer that none of us were familiar with, Buck Owens. He said the song reminded him of his mother and the nurturing she gave him and his eleven siblings while little kids growing up in the hills of West Virginia.

Cotton Fields

When I was a little bitty baby
My Mama would rock me in my cradle.
Oh, when those cotton balls get rotten
You can't pick very much cotton.
In those old cotton fields back home.

Just as John had brought joy and a sense of fun to our football team many years ago, I envisioned him supplying the dealership with that same "joie de vivre." In many ways I wasn't disappointed. John was charming to the office staff, very accommodating to the customers and full of mischievous fun. You either loved him or disliked him immensely. Other than Bob, who viewed him as a distraction, John got along fairly well with his fellow workers. Benny, however, was scared to death of him, avoiding any disagreements at all costs. When Frankie returned to ask for his job back, the scene was set for some fireworks. It was without a doubt the most talented group of salesmen I ever had, but like all things positive in the car business, the situation was not without its problems. With too many alpha males loose in the same showroom, it was a recipe for disaster.

Bob's problem with "The Bear" was his friendship with me. He thought that John was using that friendship to exact favors from me. Looking back on those tumultuous times, I could see how he thought that. Bear re-introduced me to golf, a sport I had stopped playing when I was a teenager. He convinced me that golf was the perfect remedy for bad business. He convinced me that sitting in the showroom during a slow day was contributing to my angst and that whacking some golf balls would be good therapy. I was ready for a diversion and Bear was providing it. We would go off once or twice a week and play an afternoon of golf. He was right about golf being therapeutic, but we both overlooked the strain it was putting on Bob and the rest of the staff who stayed behind and worked while we were playing. It didn't help the situation when Bear and I would come back half in the bag after an extended trip to the nineteenth hole. When golf season turned into hibernation during the winter months, Bear would convince me to go to lunch at the Old Towne Pub where we would play some "serious pool" with a whole collection of local sharks. My long lunches took a toll on not only Bob's patience, but also on Katie's as she was getting tired of my new lifestyle. I was eating way too much at lunch and drinking too frequently in the afternoons. I had always been concerned with physical fitness and health, but now I was eating poorly and gaining weight. I was having fun with my old friend but at what cost?

I started to come to my senses when one day we decided to have lunch at a notorious club in Miller Falls called the Midway Hotel. We had heard that some good sticks hung around the pool table and that the hamburgers were terrific. We were disappointed when we first arrived because we were the only ones there. We sampled the hamburgers that more than lived up to the billing as the biggest around. After a couple of beers, we racked them up for one of our spirited games of nine-ball. We were trash talking as always and having a good time when we heard the roar of engines in the parking lot. The front door slammed open and in walked a group of dangerous looking motorcyclists wearing their gangs' colors on their vests. Their attention was immediately drawn to the Bear when he insisted on screaming out after one of his shots that he had the cue ball "dancing." It didn't seem to bother John that these guys were staring at us in our ties and sports jackets and making disparaging remarks about us being intruders. Ever vigilant and mindful of the ugly headlines that could be in tomorrow's papers, I furtively observed that several members of this group were quite scary looking with a couple as big as the Bear. The obvious leader, a tall muscle bound freak with long stringy blonde hair and tattoos covering every part of his exposed limbs, came to the end of the bar closest to the pool table to observe our game. He was silent but menacing as his attention was definitely on the two of us. As the gang became more rowdy, I thought to myself that we were in a serious predicament. I knew from past experiences to expect the worst if Bear removed his teeth and reached for an ashtray to use as a weapon. That was usually the signal that he was ready, in his words, to "stand up when he should shut up." Just when my apprehension was at its highest, suddenly Bear began to sing one of his favorite songs from his party days in Texas.

'Great,' I thought to myself, 'we're about to get our asses kicked by these ten huge bikers and my buddy decides he wants to sing.'

Out of the blue he blurts out, "It was all that I could do to keep from crying," and much to my sheer amazement and relief, the blonde leader of the gang joins in. Before long the whole gang began to sing.

You Never Even Call Me By My Name

It was all that I could do to keep from cryin'
Sometimes it seems so useless to remain
You don't have to call me darlin', darlin'
You never even call me by my name.
(Words and music by Steve Goodman and John Prine)

When we got back to the dealership, Bear was laughing and bragging about how he had charmed the pants off of this motorcycle gang. I counted my lucky stars and thanked my Guardian Angel for the good fortune that had kept us out of a beating and a possible stay in jail. Bob was noticeably disturbed by the chaos of another late luncheon return and the resultant disruption Bear's boisterous rendition of the incident had on the rest of the staff. I made up my mind that day to curtail my luncheon exploits and go back to being a responsible businessman. There's nothing wrong with living every day like it was your last as long as the liberties you're taking aren't affecting those around you. I had to get back to setting a good example to my employees. Bob and Bear would continue to maintain a frosty relationship, but as long as they both did their job, it didn't matter how they got along. Bob was the rock of the organization. It was time to reward his years of dedicated service. I decided that I was going to offer him the General Manager's job that he had asked about months before. To fill the empty Sales Manager's position, I promoted John with the caveat that there would be no more drinking at lunch. He smiled at me with his big old false teeth that fortunately for both of us stayed in his mouth at the Midway Hotel, and gave me his answer as only he could–by singing: "It was all I could do to keep from crying."

Chapter Fifty-Two

The Terminal Dilemma

> "Family quarrels are bitter things. They don't go according to any rules. They're not like aches or wounds; they're more like splits in the skin that won't heal . . ."
>
> F. Scott Fitzgerald

It was evident by our last meeting that the situation was hopeless between Clinton and me. His visits to my mother's house were becoming more frequent and often he would stay during the week and then return to his home in Vermont on the weekend to rejoin my sister. What she did all week while he was gone was anybody's guess. My sister Jaime was the brilliant one in our family and it seemed like she squandered her God-given talents while living her life vicariously through Clinton. She had been very successful in her academic accomplishments and later in her brief professional career, but the fruitless years of idleness was, to me, a huge waste of a superior intellect. Occasionally, they would both come down and spend several days with mom. They would take my mother places and keep her entertained, which was admirable as long as there were no ulterior motives involved. Whenever she was in town during the week, Jaime would visit the dealership with my mother. It was always good to see her because of her infectious sense of humor. They often acted like sisters, laughing at one of the salesman's jokes or giggling with the girls in the office. Jaime seemed to be appreciative of what we were doing at the dealership, often complimenting us on the way the showroom looked, on our treatment of the customers, or on the success of one of our promotions. Knowing that she had always been someone that supported me in my varied endeavors and celebrated my accomplishments on the athletic fields of my youth, it seemed incomprehensible that Clinton would be able to drive a wedge between us; it also became evident that he needed her allegiance to perpetrate whatever latest scheme he was dreaming up to share in what he would constantly refer to as "the family business."

My other sister, Pat, was cut from the same cloth that I was. She was fiercely independent, but extremely loyal to those who were lucky enough to call her friend. She inherited the role of mediator between my mother and me whenever either one of us was being unreasonable. The Clinton factor was wearing on me. It was quite apparent after our meeting in my office that his intentions were far from honorable and were not intended for constructive criticism. I wrongly took out my frustrations on my mother, creating an icy relationship between us that was limited to discussions about the business. My mother could be as stubborn as I was and when the two of us were not communicating, the impasse could go on for months. She would tell Josette that she was sorry for the strain in our relationship, but was at a lost as to how to fix it. Different people tried to intercede, including Jaime, but it was to no avail. Neither of us was going to admit we were being childish. Then one day after many weeks, Josette buzzed me that I had a visitor. I told her I was busy, but she insisted that I should take the time to see this person. I reluctantly agreed. As I wondered who was so important, I could hear a familiar voice say to one of our new salesman that she knew the way to my office.

"Hello, there. I bet you didn't expect it to be me."

It was Pat.

"Well, hello, yourself. How are you doing, Pat?"

Since her divorce several years ago, Pat had been on her own. She had lived for a couple of years out west, but had recently moved to Maine to help a friend start a business. We had kept in contact through the mail and occasionally by phone, but had only seen each other on holidays. Because there was only one year that separated the two of us in age, we basically shared our childhood years–the memories and the secrets. She remained one of my favorite people in the world. It was wonderful to see her–although I wondered what she was up to.

"What brings you back to the Quiet Corner of Connecticut?" I asked.

"Well, it was slow at work and I thought I'd come home to see Mom and my boys. I heard about your problems with Mom and quite frankly, I came in to see what sense I could drill into your thick skull."

Same old Pat, I thought to myself-never one to mince words.

"Sean, you do know that Mom is not getting any younger. Every day that your stubborn personality stands in the way of your reconciling, you're losing one more day with your mother. Think about it for a second. You always told me that you wished you had gone to see Dad five minutes earlier before he died. You regretted missing that moment you wanted to tell him you loved him. Well, what if something happens to Mom. You're going to regret it the rest of your life. Don't you think this little squabble can be put aside and resolved?

"Did she send you?"

"Yes. She would like to end this quarrel. Don't let anyone get between the two of you. It's not worth it."

"Pat, you know I can't say no to you. Tell Mom I'll call her later. By the way, can I take you to lunch?"

"I can't today, Sean. I have an appointment with Doctor Robinson. I've been having some pains in my stomach and I don't trust any of those doctors in Maine. I'll be here until tomorrow. Maybe I'll see you tonight over at Mom's house."

"It's great to see you, Pat. I can't believe you straightened out the great family crisis with just one visit. I thought June was the only one who could do that. You must be the heir apparent to June as the family referee. Good luck with that responsibility."

I hugged my sister goodbye and told her to take care of herself. I wasn't able to go to my mother's house that night, but I was sure I would see Pat soon. A week later, Mom called me with the news that the doctor's test results were back and Pat had been diagnosed with terminal Cancer. I cried myself to sleep that night.

Chapter Fifty-Three

Curve Balls and Sliders

"We cannot always build the future of our youth, but we can build our youth for the future."
Franklin D. Roosevelt

Jimmy Cassidy entered Danville High School in the fall of 1992. He got his way despite the strong opposition of his mother. It turns out her fears were misguided as he seemed to assimilate quite nicely into the local school. He was popular, a good athlete, and most importantly, a good student. At the end of the first semester, we got our first taste of how different a public school is from a private school. I came home one night for supper and Jimmy was in the den with three or four of his friends from the freshman basketball team. I said hi to all the kids, and then went into the kitchen to say hi to Katie. Jimmy followed me into the kitchen and began to whisper.

"Dad," he said very softly, "I have to tell you something."

My radar was beginning to work. "What's up, Jimmy. Why are we whispering?"

"Dad, I'm the top student in the class for the first semester."

"Jimmy, that's great." My voice began to rise.

"Dad, shhh! I don't want my friends to know."

Most people would be jumping for joy and shouting, but my son didn't want his friends to know what he had accomplished academically. Katie just shook her head and said to me, "I told you so." Jimmy went back to his friends.

"Katie, aren't you happy with what he accomplished? We know from the homework he's had and the test papers that he's brought home that he's getting a good education. His teachers in the honors program seemed to be top notch. What's the problem?"

"The problem is when he starts looking for a college, he may not get in where he wants to go because academics are a second thought at Danville."

"Katie, you went to a public school and so did I. Sometimes colleges like to admit public school students because they feel they're more well rounded . . . you know, they've been exposed to more. The honors program is all college preparatory courses. He's going to be just fine."

"Oh, I don't know. I just wish he was happier doing so well . . . so he could at least tell his friends."

I felt Katie's concerns were baseless. Some recent graduates from Danville had gotten into some high profile schools, including some Ivy League colleges. I believed that Jimmy's academic accomplishments, combined with his athletic ability in basketball and baseball, would appeal to almost any college he wanted to apply to. I also thought we were jumping the gun a bit. He was only beginning the second half of his freshman year. It would be our job to keep him on track for the next four years.

Baseball season started and although only a freshman, Jimmy made the Junior Varsity team as a pitcher. He was small in stature but had some nasty stuff including a lively fastball, a sharp breaking curve and a filthy changeup. The JV coach, Mr. Brakeman, was a delightful character who combined a strong knowledge of the fundamentals of baseball with a humorous, sarcastic personality. He was literally the first person, other than me, to coach Jimmy. They had a great relationship and Jimmy loved playing for him. After a good season, the JV's were scheduled to finish their season with a game against Norwich Free Academy, the largest school in the state. Coach Brakeman picked Jimmy to pitch the game. NFA had a huge enrollment with a tradition of having very good baseball teams. Jimmy took to the mound and you could immediately hear some of the remarks from the other team about who was the midget who was pitching against them. As the game progressed, the jeers turned to compliments when with two outs in the last inning Jimmy had a no-hitter going. Danville was leading by only a run. The next batter swung and popped it up to left field. For some reason, the left fielder went to sleep on the play and the ball dropped for the first hit. Unfazed, Jimmy struck out the next batter to complete the one-hitter. Jimmy was fourteen years old pitching against fifteen and sixteen year olds. The NFA coach was very complimentary after the game as was Coach Brakeman. Introductory letters from several colleges arrived after his season was over. When he received a letter from Holy Cross, a college that Katie wanted him to look at, her whole attitude toward Danville High changed. We realized that there would be many challenges still ahead, but with one year under our belt, we were better prepared to deal with those tough teenage years.

Chapter Fifty-Four

Will-o-the-Wisp

> "The closing years of life are like the end of a masquerade party, when the masks are dropped."
>
> Arthur Schopenhauer

The late summer and early fall of 1993 were filled with raw emotions and false hope. Pat's diagnosis was a cloud that hung over our family. Ironically, her illness eased the tensions of the battling factions that had grown further apart, allowing a united effort to make her last days more tolerable. Pat was still in Maine, still harboring optimism that she would beat her fate. As a family, we attempted to support her as best we could and to make sure that she knew that she was loved. Two-day trips for Mom and me to Maine became part of our weekly schedule. Mom would help her with her daily routine, do her laundry, shop for groceries and cook her meals, providing enough extra leftovers to last until we would return the following week. I would try to keep Pat entertained as best as I could, by taking her to dinner, by driving her around town, and by relating stories from home of Katie and the kids. I would also include anecdotes of her friends from home who were constantly asking me how she was doing. During this stressful time, I marveled at the strength my mother displayed. She never let Pat see her discouraged or sad. She was always cheerful, helpful and positive. My mother had already lost one daughter to cancer, as well as both her sisters and her husband. I couldn't imagine the inner resolve she somehow summoned while her heart was breaking. She was truly a remarkable lady in so many ways. Pat's two boys and Chip joined us in Maine as much as their schedules would allow. In spite of Pat's love of Maine and her desire to stay there, it was becoming increasingly apparent that it would be more suitable for her back in Connecticut where we could all take better care of her.

As her condition worsened, Pat's concerns for money became an issue. She hadn't been able to work for some time and her savings were almost gone. I suggested to Mom that I had no problem with adding Pat to the Cassidy payroll and taking over the payments on the car she had financed through me a year ago. She was too proud to take what she called "charity," but I told her I expected to use her talents for consultation and I also expected her to send us some of her friends to look at cars. Under those conditions, she reluctantly accepted my offer. She stayed in Maine, living on her meager income, until she was too weak to take care of herself. She agreed to come back to Connecticut and stay at Mom's house but only if she could help with the bills. The independent streak that had long characterized her personality was in evidence when she said to my mother, "I don't want to be a bother to anyone."

Pat's son, Bill accompanied me to Maine to bring her back to Connecticut. Bill and I had a good cry on the trip up, but we both managed to hold it together once we got there. When we arrived back in Connecticut at my mother's home, Pat was too weak to walk into the house. Holding back my emotions as much as I could to keep from breaking down, I carried Pat into the house and placed her on my mother's couch. She would rest comfortably that night knowing that she was in the company of loved ones.

Pat's favorite holiday was Christmas. She returned to Connecticut in the beginning of December. Under the difficult circumstances, we all looked forward to making her holiday as memorable as possible. Christmas Day was special as Pat joined in our subdued celebration. Although she tired easily, she seemed to really enjoy the family interaction and the joy of the holiday season.

Four days later, on December 29th, Patricia Ann Cassidy passed away surrounded by her family. I think of her often, remembering her ready smile and her passion for life, her love for her boys, her great sense of humor and the tolerance and the unmitigated affection she had for her family and her impetuous little brother. Like a Will-o-the-Wisp, the flickering light of her indomitable spirit will live forever in the hearts of her many friends and loved ones.

Chapter Fifty-Five

A Welcomed Break

"The best way to keep loyalty in a man's heart is to keep money in his purse."

Irish proverb

No one could figure out where 1994 came from. The last six years had been difficult with the first four years economically mediocre under the presidency of George H. W. Bush, who waffled politically between parties attempting to appease the voting majority. At best, Bush the elder was described as a "pragmatic caretaker" whose attempts at balancing the budget and reducing the deficit proved fatal in his quest for a second term (Source: Wikipedia). His successor, Bill Clinton was elected in 1992 and brought a modicum of hope to the country. He was eloquent and dashing–two traits that unfortunately served to lead to his impeachment later in his presidency for perjury and sexual harassment of a White House intern. The 1994 congressional election left President Clinton with a Republican controlled Congress, which contributed to his abandoning the philosophies of the far left for a more centrist position. Somehow, through all the political turmoil, the economy took off in 1994. It was, however, more than a coincidence that the Internet/computing craze spurred the economic boom.

At Cassidy Motors, in the Quiet Corner of northeastern Connecticut, the sudden surge in business was a welcome relief. Two or three bad years in a row can drain a car dealership of its most valuable asset–cash. When a downturn continues, as this one did, beyond the fourth and fifth years, the situation becomes tenuous. Smiles returned to the faces of my most loyal employees who had stuck it out during a very slow period. The principals of business survival, which included controlling expenses and reducing costly inventory, had certainly been put to the test, but now we were ready to rebuild our war chest and look positively to the future. With the spirits of the staff at a high level, I held a meeting in my office to discuss our course of action. I started the meeting with a brief soliloquy.

"As most everyone here has undoubtedly noticed, business is on the rise. I want to thank all of you who have maintained your positive outlook and your good humor during this trying time. Some of you have even been in such a good mood lately that I have described to Josette that the atmosphere in the showroom is like being in the party room of the Titanic. For your loyalty, I commend you; for your patience, I salute you; and for your friendship, I shall be forever in your debt." Not exactly as powerfully spoken as the words of Shakespeare's Richard III but nonetheless effective in getting my point across.

The rest of the meeting was a repeat of complimentary statements back and forth. It had been a long time since there was this much enthusiasm in the showroom. Bob and I met after the meeting and his agenda was not a surprise.

"Sean, as you know I've been covering the finance department the last few months. I haven't complained but I think we're at a point now when we're going to need a fulltime F&I person (Finance and Insurance) to maximize our profit potential. Benny knows a guy who would be interested. He's from Norwich and they used to be in a band together. He's experienced and ready to work. Do you want to meet him?"

I surprised Bob with my reply. "Hire him. I'll consider it a referendum on the confidence I have in your judgment. Then if he doesn't work out, I'll have someone to blame. One thing though, we've got to be wary of any shady tactics in that office. It's easy to screw people in the finance department and quite frankly, I don't want my reputation tattered by some slick dude from the city who thinks he can take advantage of some poor country folks. Watch him closely, Bob, and give him just enough rope to hang himself. Hopefully, he'll be a man of integrity and there will be no problem. I don't have to tell you how easy it is to burn someone with a bad contract. I would rather make a little less money and keep people happy so we can build our repeat customer base."

Bob was in complete agreement, as I knew he would be. When it came to honesty and integrity, I didn't have to worry about Bob. He did, however, have another issue to talk to me about. He said our wholesalers in the past few years have been reluctant to step up and pay for the cars we had marked for wholesale. He said he met a guy at a horse show from Rhode Island, who was a bit of a character, but seemed legitimate in his desire to buy cars from us. He had taken the liberty to invite him to meet me. I thought to myself, 'what could it hurt?' I told Bob to have him come in and we'd see how it went.

The next morning our new F&I guy showed up and I was pleasantly surprised. It's funny how you form an image of someone in your mind and that person turns out totally different. I had imagined a long-haired, semi-hippy musician type with an earring and a vocabulary to match. What I got was a normal looking, sharply dressed, personable thirty something guy who had a genuine smile and a charming demeanor. I was impressed. He introduced himself as Dante Lauretto. His name had a certain lyrical sway to it, typical of his Italian heritage. We hit it off from the beginning as his boyish charm won me over immediately. In the days that followed, his knowledge of financing and insurance became evident, as did the increase in profits that were being generated from that office. I had a good feeling about this hire.

That same afternoon, I was startled by a rather loud speaking, x-rated individual who came into the showroom looking for Bob. Curiously, I came out of my office to see the person that fit the voice. To my great surprise, the voice belonged to a handsome, rugged, dark haired man, who was showing Frankie how to empty his stapler into his Popeye-sized forearms. Frankie was laughing hysterically, barely able to speak.

"Sean, this is Paulie Petrone. He says he's here to meet with you and Bob, but first he wanted to show me how to staple his forearm without showing pain." Frankie was slurping his words while he was talking through his laughter. "Paulie, this is Sean."

Paulie apologized for the little show he had just put on as he stuck out his meat hook of a hand to shake mine. I couldn't help but notice the staples in his arm. Our first meeting notwithstanding, as I got to know Paulie, you couldn't help but like the guy. His dialect was heavy Federal Hill in Providence and his expressions conjured up that "Godfather" music again, but I discovered that under his gruff exterior, there was a genuine personality. His colorful language was sometimes a little graphic, but somehow you got used to his greeting you with, "How the f--- are you?" Or his description of business associates who have yet to "f--- him up the ass!" To the conservative Connecticut Yankees that inhabited our little corner of the world, an Italian stud with a colorful Sicilian accent was someone to avoid, but Paulie won us over. His irreverence was the cloaking of an honorable man whose values were chiseled on the hard streets of a tough city. Still, he would remind us on occasion of where he came from by kidding that he was "duking" Bob with "dead Presidents" (slipping money) under his blotter in the General Managers office. Paulie was always good for an interesting story and his visits were always a welcomed break in our daily routine. The cast of characters in our ongoing Soap Opera was changing again, but Bob and I welcomed our two new Italian friends to our world.

Chapter Fifty-Six

Seven Deadly Sins

> "You take my life when you do take the means whereby I live."
>
> William Shakespeare

"I'm not looking forward to this meeting today. No good can come out of this."

Katie was well aware of the reservations I was feeling as I voiced my concerns about the requested meeting with Clinton's attorney and my mother. My wife and I had shared a couple glasses of wine the previous night and some raw emotions were unveiled. She shared my apprehension for the reasons for the meeting, knowing that Clinton had never stopped scheming to usurp my ownership in the dealership. His one avenue for success, unfortunately, involved my mother who was caught in the middle of a power struggle between an in-law and her son. I thought about the special relationship my mother and I had while I was growing up. It was a relationship of love and respect and it had seemed to grow to something special over the last twenty years. It didn't make any sense to me that my role in running the family business, a role defined by my late father, could be put in jeopardy by the underhanded manipulations of a relative by marriage. This wasn't going to be a spur of the moment meeting; this was going to be a meeting that was the result of his many years of attempting to convince my mother that the business should be part of her estate. As I would soon find out, it was also a meeting to announce that Clinton had been chosen as the executor of the estate.

As I drove the twenty miles to Windham to the offices of the attorney that Clinton had hired, I amused myself by recalling the Sunday sermon of our pastor that detailed the Seven Deadly Sins. Considering him to be evil, I wondered how many of the seven sins I could attribute to Clinton. GLUTTONY and SLOTH were eliminated right away. They didn't seem to fit his personality profile. LUST was also out. I had no idea whether he lusted or not. PRIDE was the first true fit for he had an unusually high opinion of himself. Some would describe it as a type of narcissism, but only God would know why he was happy at what he was looking at in the mirror. ANGER seemed to be appropriate because most of the time he acted like he was angry with me. Perhaps it was his show of disdain that he thought would sway my mother's opinion of me. ENVY seemed a perfect match for it was evident that he was envious of my position in the business; he was envious of our family's lifestyle; and he was envious of my stature in the community. GREED or Avarice was the most obvious trait for he would stop at nothing to insure that he would get what he considered his fair share out of the estate. He was like a vulture that was flying above the carcass of the business waiting for his turn to pick it clean. The exercise of portraying Clinton's personality flaws was good for a laugh while driving, but suddenly I realized the laughing was over. I was at my destination.

The lawyer was congenial as he greeted me with what I thought was a sympathetic look. My mother and Clinton were already there. The meeting started with the lawyer stating that Mrs. Cassidy had requested that he rewrite her will to better distribute the assets of her estate. In effect, the dealership would be part of the distribution. I would maintain total control of the daily operation of the business. Rather than argue my case without proper preparation, in a setting where the chips were stacked against me, I chose the option of fighting my battle on another day, on a friendlier playing field. To avoid upsetting my mother, my only choice was to temporarily accept the terms being presented to me in this charade. I did, however, make a personal vow that my acceptance would not be permanent. Pride, anger, envy, and greed–they all seemed to fit Clinton's profile perfectly. Imagining a dagger slipping slowly into my chest, I could see why they were called "Deadly Sins."

Chapter Fifty-Seven

Hurdles and Pitfalls

"Roads? Where we're going, we don't need roads."
Back to the Future

The last five years of the Twentieth Century were ablaze with excitement over the unprecedented growth of the stock market, the boom in real estate and banking, and the feeling that the good times would last forever. There was, however, a fear of the unknown, a haunting uneasiness of what was going to happen when the clock struck midnight on January 1, 2000. Would the world end? Would all the computers crash because of the programming nightmare of a century change? "Would the sun come out tomorrow?"

In Danville, our concerns with the change to 2000 came early. Even though the car business continued strong past 1994, Cassidy Motors was experiencing its own unique problems. Early in 1995, the state of Connecticut decided to expand Rte. 6 from Hartford to the Rhode Island line. At first, I was ecstatic with the news, because I thought a new wider highway in front of our dealership would bring increased traffic and higher visibility. When construction began in the latter part of the year, the only thing it brought to the dealership was three long years of a torn-up road, one lane of backed-up, frustrated drivers, and hours in the day when we had very few customers. Those customers that wanted to come to us had a difficult time negotiating the dump trucks and construction equipment that barely allowed access to our parking lot. Our sales figures tumbled in a market where other dealers were thriving. The timing couldn't have been worse. Chevrolet had initiated a movement called Project 2000 that was an attempt to eliminate smaller, underachieving dealers to allow bigger, more profitable dealers a wider, more lucrative market. In 1997, I received the first letter from Detroit listing us on a potential elimination list because of dwindling sales and poor profit performance. It was time to put together a case for our continuance in business into the next century. I started taking hundreds of pictures that were dated to show the chaos and nearly impassable conditions of Rte. 6. The dates spread out over a two-year period, providing graphic evidence of our impossible situation. Our factory rep was totally on our side. At my request, he arranged a meeting in the Boston Zone Office with our Chevrolet Zone Manager and the Regional Manager from New York. I invited my lawyer to accompany me to the meeting and together we put forth a compelling argument that there were mitigating circumstances for our poor performance the last two years. Our presentation was successful. Within two weeks, I received a letter from the Regional Manager that stated, "the good guys had won." He reaffirmed our position as a viable dealership and assured us that we would be removed from the Project 2000 list. It seemed that no matter which direction I headed, there were huge hurdles to overcome. Even with the success of our presentation, we were still facing an uncertain future due to the continued construction folly. Frustrated, I decided I needed a break. It was a beautiful day and the golf course was beckoning.

Paulie had come by earlier in the day to visit with Bob. For days, he had been bragging to me about his ability to hit a golf ball so hard he would knock it out of round. I decided to invite him to join me in a round at my favorite course, The Foster Country Club, in nearby Foster, Rhode Island. Paulie was familiar with the course and was anxious to play. To complete the foursome I told the Bear he could stop trying to act like he was busy and come play with us. He said, "Sh--! I thought you'd never ask." Dante was walking by when I asked the Bear and he said he was free to tag along. We had our foursome.

What a foursome this was–a frustrated Irishman, a large Southern redneck, and two Italian boys, one with a musical background and the other with a background of breaking noses. The Bear and I decided we would be partners. The match was memorable, not for the quality of golf, but for the strange and humorous incidents that happened during the round. I was anxious to find out if Paulie was bragging when he said he could dent his golf ball. Immediately I noticed that he swung harder than anyone I had ever seen. As long as the ball went a long way, he didn't care which direction it went. Dante, on the other hand, was a devious golfer who was quite adept at the "foot wedge", a subtle kick of the ball to get out of trouble, and the less than obvious "hole in your pants, drop a new ball in play" trick when it was obvious that the real ball was somewhere deep in the Rhode Island woods. The Bear, of course, was capable of his own shenanigans including finding his ball in the open in areas where the deer couldn't get through. His grand moment of the day was on the 10th hole, a tricky par four that ran along the road leading into the golf course. I reminded the Bear on the tee that he would have to keep the ball to the left of the road or he would be out of bounds. Through power of suggestion he immediately shanked his drive to the right, headed for the road. The ball hung up in the wind coming down perfectly into the open sunroof of a Ford Bronco that was driving in our direction. The driver was incensed that the ball had almost hit him while he was driving and got out of his vehicle to confront whoever hit the shot. When he got to the tee, flailing his arms in anger, he demanded to know who hit the ball. Dante and I stepped back and Paulie and The Bear stepped forward. The man's anger suddenly ceased when he saw these two huge guys with drivers in their hands. He apologized for bothering us and slithered off with his tail between his legs. We all had a good laugh and moved on. Bear claimed that the Bronco interfered with his draw, which was just starting to come back toward the fairway. He demanded a Mulligan. When he hit his second shot even further right, all he could say was, "Sh--!" On the fifteenth hole, a short par four, Paulie smacked a drive that almost made the green. When he got to his ball, he called me over and proudly showed me the flattened side of the ball. He had indeed knocked his golf ball out of round. We finished the day with a few beverages before we went back to work. It was a day of laughter, a day of relaxation, a day to get to know new acquaintances better. It was just the medicine I needed to tackle the endless problems of the car business.

Chapter Fifty-Eight

My Haven

"Women are the real architects of society."
Harriet Beecher Stowe

No businessman worth his salt would take credit for his success without including the contributions of the girls in the office. Through the many years of triumph and tragedy, of success and failure, the one constant for me was the support of Josette and her staff. Like a colorful carousel, the faces and the names changed, but the atmosphere of congeniality and camaraderie never wavered. Josette was of course the rock upon which we built our office staff. Her career at Cassidy Motors paralleled mine as we both joined the business in 1974. She was simply the most competent, elegant and fashionable lady I had ever met. In a business where honesty is a value that has to permeate all the departments, there was never a doubt about the character of Josette. She was meticulous, precise, and responsible. Her attention to detail was incredible. She once spent an entire afternoon looking for the five cents that was needed to balance her books. She took nothing for granted, gave no quarter to inappropriate behavior, while seeking perfection in her own position. She was a gem. As my business manager, she was also my confidante, and my friend. I couldn't even conceive of operating the dealership without her. So it was, when she started to talk about retiring in a couple of years, I started to envision the business without her. Next to Katie, she was the single most important woman in my life. It was going to be like losing another sister.

The girls that worked for Josette were cut from the same swatch. Josette demanded competence combined with compatibility. The girls had to know what they were doing, be pleasant with customers and staff, and be able to work amicably with others in a close office environment. Josette handpicked her staff and was very rarely wrong in her choices. Of course, when you hired young girls as assistants, there was a certain amount of attrition that went with the job. Some left to pursue other careers, some left to get married, some left because they were overwhelmed with the volume of work. With single girls, there was always the possibility of interaction with some of the single guys. That interaction, which was clearly discouraged, generally led to one, or the other, or both being dismissed. Clandestine romances were great in romantic novels, but in real life office situations, they made it tough on everyone.

The girls that stuck with the job became like part of my family. I truly thought of them as my daughters. I listened to the stories of their personal lives; I comforted them when they were down; I shared in the happiness of their triumphs. I watched many of them marry and congratulated them when they came to work pregnant and started their families. I knew their boyfriends and their husbands. I supported their good decisions and admonished them if they made poor ones.

Josette and I had our favorites over the years, most of whom had left for various reasons. Josette always had a tender spot in her heart for Lorraine, a beautiful girl who was among her first assistants. She was very competent and extremely shy, in spite of having the best set of legs on the East Coast. I think Josette saw in Lorraine a little of herself as a younger woman for it showed in the closeness of their relationship. Some of her other favorites were Tabitha and Molly, her first two assistants who came to work directly upon graduation from high school. Both blossomed under the tutelage of Josette, stayed for a few years, married and moved on.

One of my favorites was Sherry, who was the daughter of one of my good friends. She was gifted with an intelligence that belied her appearance because she looked like a Vegas showgirl. Her smile was constant as was her extremely short mini-skirts. As professional as she was at work, in her private life she was as wild as a feral cat. Her lifestyle eventually dictated a move south to Florida where she could better utilize her assets. There were many others, from the docile to the domineering, each girl bringing her special qualities to the job.

In the mid-90's, Josette and I were looking for someone that she could train to eventually take over her responsibilities when she retired. We looked long and hard to no avail. None of the candidates struck me as someone I would trust and depend on to the extent I did with Josette. We were getting frustrated with the process when one day Josette asked the young girl who was working as a service writer, Martine, to help her with some end of the year stuff in the main office. Josette was impressed with the job Martine did, and immediately asked me what I thought. I told her I thought she was very competent and if Martine was someone she thought she could work with, I would be willing to give it a try. The rest was history, as Martine and Josette worked together like a well-oiled machine.

I unknowingly relied on the support of my girls more than even I realized. They reminded me of forgotten appointments, birthdays and anniversaries; they ran interference for me when some idiot or malcontent was wandering around the showroom looking for someone to complain to; they laughed at one my many jokes stolen from Henny Youngman; they supported my family and treated my mother with respect. They were well aware of my moods and would mollify or console me depending on the wave of the moment. They wouldn't allow me to cross the line into egomania or transcend my limits of decency. But most of all, they tolerated me–a self-described incomplete human being. I knew I wasn't perfect and I encouraged them to remind me of that. They often did. For me, the most enjoyable part of my thirty-year experience in the automobile business was the working relationship I had with my girls in the office. They had provided me with a haven to escape the insufferable moments that were part of the everyday life of a car dealer.

Chapter Fifty-Nine

Graduation Day

"Though we leave in sorrow
All the joys we've known.
We must face tomorrow,
Knowing we'll never walk alone."
The Beach Boys

"Katie, is Tucker ready? We're going to be late for Jimmy's graduation."

I couldn't believe the years had flown by so quickly. The picture in the den of Jimmy as a one-year old sitting on my forearm as I looked into Tucker's carriage was still one of my favorites. Who could have imagined then the little red head with the crystal blue eyes and the ready smile in a cap and gown graduating from high school?

"Tucker, your father is waiting impatiently. We don't want to be late."

"I'm coming. I'm coming! Don't have a bird. It's better to be late. We won't have to listen to all the dumb speeches"

God I hated the age of sixteen–all those hormones cursing through the body and nothing going to the brain. We somehow managed to get through it with Jimmy and now we had to gear up for another run at independence and the irreverence that accompanies that run. Tucker was a little more daring than Jimmy, and definitely more prone to the persuasive influence of one of his mindless friends. These next two years promised to be a real rocky ride for all of us. Oh well, one monumental moment at a time. Today was Jimmy's graduation day. It was a proud day for the Cassidy family.

"Tucker, the only dumb speech you're going to hear is the one I'm about to give you. And don't raise your voice to your mother. You know someday you're going to realize that your parents weren't so bad–that we weren't as out of it as you think." God, I sounded like my father.

Tucker grudgingly consented to be on his best behavior for the evening. Being the parent of a teenager is a lot like being a recovering alcoholic. You take one day at a time and hope for the best.

"Dad, do I have to wear a tie?"

It was apparent that I hadn't quite won this battle yet.

The actual graduation was very nice with some wonderful speeches that I was sure even Tucker liked. Jimmy was honored with a couple of academic scholarships for ranking in the top five of his class. Our reservations concerning his educational opportunities at Danville High were long ago forgotten when he received his first college acceptance from Boston College no less. Other prestigious colleges followed, including Worcester Polytechnic, Williams College, and finally, Holy Cross; but, true to his beliefs that a public education was the equal of any, he decided to go to the University of Connecticut–with his friends. Initially, we were disappointed, but over the years as we met more of his classmates and spent more time on the UConn campus, we realized that he had made a good decision. His ability to network opened up many opportunities for him. After working in Boston for a couple of years following his college graduation, he returned to UConn for his MBA in finance and management. He had prepared himself well for a successful future and he had done it his own way.

Jimmy's graduation reminded me of my own, some thirty years earlier. When Jimmy and Tucker were a great deal younger and a captive audience in the back seat of my car, I used to play old songs from the 1950's and 1960's that we would harmonize to. The boys loved the old songs. The night of Jimmy's graduation, before he went off with his friends to celebrate, he asked that I play that special song that I liked so much by the Beach Boys. One last time, the three of us harmonized to "Graduation Day."

Graduation Day

"There's a time for joy
A time for tears
A time we'll treasure through the years
We'll remember always
Graduation Day.
(First sung by The Four Aces)

…………..

Tucker initially gave us a run for our money, but eventually settled down. When he wasn't playing baseball or basketball or otherwise getting into mischief, he would sit down and draw some incredible pictures. The walls of his bedroom were decorated with farcical caricatures from his fertile mind. In two years, he would also graduate from Danville High. He used his talents as an artist to gain acceptance at the exclusive Chamberlain School of Design at Mount Ida College in Newton, Massachusetts where he majored in graphic design. He would also meet his future wife there, a beautiful Southern girl from Dallas, Texas. After their graduation from college, they settled in Danville and Tucker came to work for me. Before long they presented Katie and me with a delightful baby boy. The natural progression of a family business seemed to be settling into place. Everyone at the dealership was calling Tucker the heir apparent.

Chapter Sixty

The Chapter Wasn't Long Enough

"Retirement at Sixty-Five is ridiculous. When I was Sixty-Five, I still had pimples."

George Burns

Most Mondays in the car world are filled with the hustle and bustle of following up on deals and leads from Saturday. Salesmen scurry around like chickens with their heads cut off. The busy finance department is inundated with applications. It's certainly not a bad thing, but when the commotion is interrupted by a phone call from an old friend, it's a welcome diversion.

"Sean, my good buddy. This is Pierre." It wasn't difficult to identify who was on the phone for Pierre always had a strong presence. His booming voice and the clarity of his words were unmistakable.

"I hear that the old Frenchman is finally hanging them up. We can't let this occasion go by without a big celebration. Have you planned anything yet?"

I marveled at how quickly the word of Francois' retirement had spread. He was so well known in the community and so well liked by his customers that it was inevitable that the news would leak out before we made an announcement. Since Pierre left the dealership many years before, we had all kept in touch with him. He had become a very successful businessman with his own advertising agency.

"It's good to hear from you, Pierre. Obviously, we all thought this day would never come. It certainly won't be the same around here without Francois."

"How old is he now?"

"He just turned seventy-five, but he still thinks he's irresistible to women and that every customer is his. That causes a problem with the salesman who sells a customer and Francois claims them after the deal is done. But, as you know, I've been living with that for many years."

Pierre chuckled. "God bless him! He's one of a kind. What are you planning for him?"

"We've rented the Elks hall for a month from Friday. By then we'll have the invitations squared away and the entertainment all set. It should be a great night."

"Well, you can count me in. There's nothing I wouldn't do for Francois. Hey, what about me as the master of ceremonies. I could tell some interesting stories about Francois that everyone would get a kick out of."

"Sounds like a great idea. I doubt if I would have gotten through the presentation without tearing. Try to remember, though, that his wife will be there and we don't want to embarrass her."

"Sounds good. Keep me informed of the rest of your plans and I'll be ready to roast the Frenchman on his big night. I can't wait."

I knew having Pierre involved was perfect for celebrating the career of Francois. I had the tickets printed and hired a band that included one of my nephews and a bunch of young guys who all knew Francois. They promised to mix in some military songs with their contemporary sounds. The tickets went rapidly as townspeople representing all levels of the economic spectrum–from doctors and lawyers, to plumbers and garbage collectors, to veterans of the car business–wanted to pay their respect to someone who had been part of the fabric of Danville for many, many years. We should have gotten a bigger hall.

Pierre, as promised, put on quite a show as the master of ceremony. He poked good- natured fun at Francois and managed not to divulge too many incidents that would have upset his wife. When he mentioned Francois' service in World War II, including being one of the first soldiers to reach shore at Omaha Beach, Francois began to sob. Many years had gone by since D-Day, but for Francois the horrible memories of that day were fresh in his mind. It was a grim reminder to all in attendance that this man had heroically served in our Armed Services in the most memorable battle of World War II. Pierre pointed out to the newer generations in the hall that we owed a debt of gratitude to people like Francois whose sacrifice and bravery provided us with the freedom that we so often took for granted. When the band, on cue, struck up the Star Spangled Banner, there wasn't a dry eye in the place. The night ended with some light bantering and some dancing before we gave Francois his retirement gift–a rocking chair. He was thrilled with all the attention.

For me, the evening was a reminder of the many years Francois and I had spent together. I had a tendency to break down my life into chapters in an imaginary book that I stored deep in the recesses of my mind. This chapter, in spite of its apparent length, was too short. I went home that night thankful for the many friends, employees and customers who had attended to honor Francois. I was sure the evening was a highlight in his life.

Going to work on Monday certainly seemed different. There was bound to be a huge void for I had never known any time in my automobile career where Francois wasn't around. Saddened, I walked into the showroom and to my surprise, was greeted with, "Bonjour." I looked up to see Francois sweeping the showroom floor. I guess the chapter that had Francois riding off into the sunset hadn't ended yet.

Chapter Sixty-One

Y2K

"The world is round and the place which may seem like the end may also be only the beginning."

Ivy Baker Priest

What event could be bigger in one's life than the turn of a new century? Certainly nothing so out of our control could be bridged with such anxiety and such fear of the unknown. Was God's calendar set to end in the year 2000? What cataclysmic event would be unleashed on humanity to welcome in the new millennium? Was Nostradamus correct in predicting the Armageddon? Or to a lesser degree, was our computer network going to universally crash when the date switched to the new century. All these concerns made the approach of the New Year less of a celebration and more of a climax of fear. When the clock struck twelve on 1/1/2000, the world breathed a collective sigh of relief. We were still here. The sky had not fallen. Fire and brimstone had not destroyed the planet. The computers still worked. A new century had begun. It was time to celebrate.

To me, the New Year marked more than the end of the Twentieth Century; it marked the end of business as usual. I had once declared that no one was irreplaceable. I was wrong. When Josette announced her official retirement, I felt like a Captain lost at sea without a navigator.

For over twenty-five years she had been my First Mate. Although she had spent several months training Martine as a replacement, I was still in denial that her official retirement would ever happen. I had no doubt that Martine could do the job; she was hand picked by Josette and had become very knowledgeable in the complicated Chevrolet accounting system. But, Josette was the personification of Cassidy Motors. She handled all the Chevrolet and GMAC representatives with great dexterity. Customers loved her. Her co-workers cherished her. Her boss thought the world of her. She would be sadly missed, not only for her business acumen, but also for her friendship and her loyalty. The advent of the new century would have to be managed without the council of one of the sharpest woman I have ever met. First Francois and now Josette. The old guard was passing the torch. It remained to be seen if the new guard would carry it as far or as well.

The rest of the year was an exercise in transition. Martine hired a young gal from sales to take over her old job. Jayne had grown tired of being the oddity in an all male sales team. She was a welcomed addition to the office staff that also included Penny whose job description included handling customers at the window, and creating a positive impression when answering the phone. Together they made a very compatible team, but I nevertheless felt like my haven no longer existed. I avoided spending a great deal of time in the office simply because I didn't feel as comfortable going in there. Josette and I were like brother and sister. We often came to the same conclusions and frequently finished each other's sentences. I could confide in her and know that she would be discreet. I never thought of her as an employee. She was more a part of the family. The new girls actually treated me like the boss. It was an odd dynamic that I would have to get used to.

Sales and service also saw a number of changes–some good and some bad. Frankie tired of the Bear and quit for the second time. The service manager quit. Two mechanics quit after an argument with Chip. The body shop lost its manager to a bigger chain. Bob Shanahan was growing noticeably irritable and was grumbling about his status. The Titanic was hitting some rough seas.

As the year progressed, the bad news just kept coming. Clinton succeeded in getting my mother to agree to the new corporation with the multiple dividend holders. His influence on my mother was becoming more and more astonishing. She was now in her mid-Eighties. As strong as her independence had once been, it was as if she gave up all semblance of self-reliance. Clinton became her spokesman, her agent, and her decision maker. To me, it was obvious that his motives were not all altruistic. The new corporation presented a unique set of problems that weren't going to be solved without a great deal of bloodletting. When I objected to my mother about the ramifications of such a move, her response was programmed: "Clinton said it was best. He's looking out for my interests. I'm lucky to have him around." We didn't share that sentiment.

In the fall, the suspected disenchantment of Bob Shanahan came to a boil and he resigned. His dedication to the business and his integrity would be almost impossible to replace. I realized that his leaving had a great deal to do with the pressure I was feeling from all the personnel changes and the family problems that had caused my grumpy attitude. I became critical of everyone, including Bob, and that ultimately led to his resignation. I always thought that I was capable of handling pressure, but sometimes it could become overwhelming. Pressure can boil over. The car business was not for the faint of heart.

In December, while sitting at my desk going over the bad end-of-the-year financial statements, I felt a strange burning sensation in my chest. I called in one of my salesmen, Jean-Paul, a former classmate of mine at Danville High who was an auxiliary policeman knowledgeable in emergency medical response. I told him I thought I might be having a heart attack. He called my doctor who directed me to go right to the emergency room. Katie was notified and she met us at the ER. Before I knew it, I was in the Intensive Care Unit where I would spend the night being probed and prodded like a side of beef. The next morning, I was sent by ambulance to UMass Medical Center in Worcester, Mass. I was rushed into surgery. The angiogram showed five major blockages in the arteries to my heart. During the next four hours, I nearly died on the table, but was given a reprieve by a very competent group of cardiologists and technicians. Stents were inserted in my arteries to aid in the flow of blood through damaged arterial walls. I would have to undergo several months of cardiac rehabilitation and a complete overhaul of what I ate. My cardiologist contributed some sage advice about my diet to aid in my recovery. He said with a laugh, "If it tastes good, spit it out."

My life certainly changed dramatically in the first year of the new millennium. For better or worse, I was looking at a future that no longer looked as rosy, with a heavy heart that no longer was one hundred percent healthy. I would have to call on my competitive spirit, that same spirit that served me so well as an athlete in my youth, to see me through this latest bump in the road of life.

Chapter Sixty-Two

A Cowardly Act

"With confidence in our armed forces–
With the unbounded determination of our people–
We will gain the inevitable triumph–so help us God."
Franklin D. Roosevelt

One of the best reasons to live on the East Coast of the United States is the glorious weather that accompanies the beginning of autumn. So it was on a spectacular early morning in September that my thoughts of restructuring Cassidy Motors were tempered by the most beautiful blue sky and the surrounding presence of crystal clean air. The temperature hovered around a delightful 70 degrees and the humidity was seasonably low. It couldn't have been a more perfect day. I took the long way to work that morning, giving myself time to gather my thoughts on what was going to be a critical reorganization of my remaining staff. It was the beginning of the fall foliage season, the annual festival of colors that covers the New England countryside with a pallet of dazzling shades of red and orange and yellow. The drive energized me. It had only been a few weeks since I finished my cardiac rehab, but I felt I was ready to tackle the myriad of problems that awaited me. My thoughts were interrupted by the brilliance of the September sky. God truly deserved a pat on the back for this magnificent day. As I reached the dealership and parked in my usual spot, Jack came out to greet me.

"Have you been listening to the radio, or watching the television?" he said nervously. When I told him no, he proceeded to tell me that a commercial jet had hit one of the towers of the World Trade Center in New York City.

"It's too early to tell, but we might be under attack."

The idea that the United States of America was under attack on our own soil seemed incredulous. I told Jack, it was probably just a horrible accident. We both went into the waiting area where most of my employees had gathered in front of the television to see what was going on. Moments later, another plane hit the second tower. It no longer appeared to be a coincidence. Some of the veterans that worked for me were noticeably angry and wanted instant revenge. But who was the enemy? Details were slowly coming to light. It appeared that two commercial jets had been hijacked in mid-air after taking off from Boston. Both planes were taken over by middle-eastern extremists who were trained to deliver a devastating blow to the U.S. through a series of suicide attacks. Later, another hijacked plane crashed into the Pentagon. It was reported that there were probably more planes in the air that were targeting specific sights. Our new president, George W. Bush, was being confronted with an unprovoked attack from an unidentified enemy. His task as Commander-In-Chief was to assure the people of our country that the government was still in place and that the tragedies of this day would not affect the resolve of our nation to withstand this cowardly attack and punish those that were responsible.

If the terrorists thought that bringing down the towers of the Trade Center would induce fear into the American people, they were mistaken. In the days that followed the attack, a wave of patriotism swept across the country, "from sea to shining sea." The American flag was everywhere, on people's houses, on businesses, and on almost every car in the country. The distinction between Democrats and Republicans was obscured and politics were put on hold, as suddenly the whole country was proud to be Americans. A tragedy of monumental proportions had triggered an explosion of nationalism. We mourned our losses and praised the many heroes of that fateful day, from the first responders–the police and fire departments of New York and Washington–to the heroes of United

Flight 93 who in a selfless display of courage, overwhelmed another group of terrorist hijackers and brought down a plane in the farm lands of Pennsylvania that seemingly was headed for the White House. The United States of America had already begun to defend our homeland. President Bush soon after declared war on terrorists.

My sense of history dictated that I talk Katie into visiting New York a few months after the attack. We took the train, like we always did, from New London and arrived at Penn Station. It was February. The weather was unseasonably warm allowing us the opportunity to walk around the city. Immediately we noticed a change in New Yorkers. They were pleasant and helpful, not like the rude and arrogant people we had been accustomed to dealing with on some of our other trips to the city. On the second day, we summoned the courage to head to Ground Zero to visit the sight of the 9/11 attack. When we first got off the subway a block from the sight, we recalled the images we had seen on the news of streets buried in dust and debris. We were amazed at how thoroughly clean the streets were. At Ground Zero, the rescue workers had constructed a temporary observation deck from which you could observe the devastation below. The observation deck became a busy tourist stop where people would solemnly ascend up the ramp to view the carnage and pay their respects. In order to control the crowds, visitors were given a number and when your number was called, you headed up the ramp. While Katie and I waited for our number to be called, we noticed the small chapel that sat unscathed adjacent to the site. We were told that this was St. Paul's Chapel a beautiful old example of contemporary baroque architecture that stood directly in front of the Trade Center. We meandered over to visit what had quickly become a shrine to the victims of the attack. It had miraculously survived, completely intact, without so much as a single window broken or damaged. It became a haven for rescuers, a place to go for a meal, some hot coffee, a change of clothes, or a nap. More importantly, it became a symbol to the American people that through the mayhem and the confusion of an unexplainable tragedy, we would survive–with the help of God and of our fellow citizens.

Our emotions were already on edge after our visit to St. Paul's when our number was called. Katie was quietly sobbing while I was biting my lip, trying to control myself. We got to the deck where the crowd was rather subdued. There was no pushing, cutting, or shoving while in line. Every one was courteous and respectful of their fellow citizens. The sight that lay before us was devastating. Even after five months, there was a small cloud of smoke rising from the ashes. On the far left corner of the lot where once stood two one hundred and ten foot towers was a burned cross formed from the steel girders of one of the buildings. The sight of the cross below was as close to a religious experience as anything I had ever observed. After a very emotional few minutes standing at the edge of the sight of one of history's most infamous attacks, we decided to leave. As we were descending the down ramp from the observation deck, I noticed two uniformed members of the New York Police, an older male and a younger woman, approaching from the opposite direction. I instinctively went over to them and asked them if we could take a picture with them. They graciously accepted and Katie took the picture of me and the two members of the police standing in front of the plaque that listed all of their fallen comrades from that day five months before. As I shook their hands and thanked them for their courage and bravery, I looked into the eyes of the younger policewoman and we both began to cry. I could never describe the rush of sadness that filled my heart as I looked into this brave young woman's eyes.

There were many horrific images associated with the destruction of the Twin Towers on that fateful day in September, but the one image that stayed with me is of the few poignant moments we shared with two members of the New York Police and the picture Katie snapped of the two dedicated officers and the appreciative tourist who couldn't thank them enough for their service and their bravery. The tears visible in the picture are a reminder of the powerful emotions we all felt in the aftermath of the tragedy that will forever be marked by the date of 9/11.

Chapter Sixty-Three

The Epiphany

> "I am always most religious upon a sunshiny day."
>
> Lord Byron

"Katie, do you know what I've done with my hammer? It's not where I put it."

"Sean, you never leave it in the same place. You somehow believe that your tools magically put themselves away. Did you try looking in your toolbox?"

Grumbling to myself I checked in my tool box and ...

"Sean, can you get the back door? Someone just rang the doorbell and I'm still in my pajamas."

"Yeah, I got it." I grabbed the hammer from the toolbox and ran up the basement stairs to the back door. It was Baxter.

"Baxter! Where have you been? You've been harder to get a hold of than Jimmy Hoffa in Giant Stadium. We were beginning to think you moved on to better friends."

"You know that could never happen. I've been busy with my new life of serving my Lord and Savior, Jesus Christ. I've rededicated my life to spreading the word of the Lord."

I looked at him skeptically for enough time, I thought, for him to break out laughing–but he never did. "Katie!" I yelled out up the stairs.

"You've got to come down here to hear this." This joke was too good for just one of us to be a part of.

"Did you find your hammer? Who was at the back door?"

Before I could answer, Katie came bouncing down the stairs. She was just as happy as I was to see Baxter for it had been over a year since he came over to visit.

"Baxter, it's good to see you. Sean and I wondered how you were doing. What have you been up to?"

"Carol and I joined a new church. I never realized how comforting the Bible really is. We spend most of our free time with members of the church discussing different passages in the Bible. We try to live our lives as Jesus would want us to."

"Then you're not kidding about this stuff," I said. "What happened to the guy who gave Quaaludes to the Prima Ballerina of the Boston Ballet, the guy who boffed every stripper at the Two O'clock Lounge. What happened to the guy who used to get our dogs stoned and who made marijuana brownies that my girlfriend mistakenly ate. Did he have an epiphany? Where did Baxter go, Katie, and who is this imposter?"

Finally, I got a smile out of Baxter. "Those were good times," he said, "but now I've seen the light of salvation. From now on, I'm going to follow the path set forth in the Bible by Jesus. I knew you guys would have a difficult time believing that I've changed, but I have. The old Baxter no longer exists."

"Well, if it makes you happy, Baxter, then we're happy for you." Katie was speaking for both of us because she realized I would have a difficult time speaking with my mouth stuck open. Baxter stayed for a while longer and we discussed our families and how I was doing with my heart condition. He said when he saw me lying in the hospital he realized that life is too short. If his change of life could be attributed to my heart episode then I suppose some good came out of it. With everything else that was going on in the world, maybe Baxter was on to something. We all decided to get together again soon and discuss his change of life further. It certainly is strange how things turn out. My blocked arteries led me to a complete change in lifestyle, including a moderation of diet, an increase in exercise and an enhanced appreciation of my family and my friends. For Baxter, it led to his vicariously deciding to change what was important to him and to pursue a more fulfilling life. Like so many incidents in our lives, we were both the beneficiaries of a single event. We had decided many years ago to share an adventure in the city of Boston. Through all the subsequent years we had maintained our friendship, even after we both had married and settled into separate lives. Some people have a more significant influence on your life than others. Regardless of Baxter's spotted past and his seemingly extreme metamorphosis into a God-fearing religious zealot, as a friend, his significance would never change.

Chapter Sixty-Four

The Exodus

> "Yesterday is gone. Tomorrow has not come. We have only today. Let us begin."
>
> Mother Teresa

The joke had long been that our sales department was like the party room of the Titanic. Revelry among impending tragedy engendered a certain amount of gallows humor that was relevant in the months following the terrorist attacks. Business was not good, but that was to be expected. Our central banking system had taken a major hit and Wall Street was teetering on the edge of total collapse. The state of the economy was alarming. A direct result of this climate of doom was a further exodus of personnel. Retaining employees had become a critical issue. As a dealer who had seen bad times on too many occasions over the last ten years, a sense of humor was necessary to get through each day. The "Bear" was always good at raising my spirits with one of his inane jokes or down-home stories, but he, too, was feeling the strain of a tightening financial belt. As a harbinger of things to come, "Bear" resigned as the sales manager to move to western Massachusetts to be closer to his future second wife. I would miss the "Bear" for his friendship and his loyalty and his ability to bring out the human side of me.

Then the parade to the door began. Chip retired early in his mid-fifties, although I continued to pay him. Benny was next, then Dante, and finally Jack, who had assumed the job of Service Director. Benny and Dante were itinerant employees, both superb at their jobs, but who were constantly on the look out for greener pastures. Jack was family, but my trust in him since the incident several years ago with Clinton had diminished to the point that I didn't have any faith in his allegiance or any confidence in his ulterior motives. It was a bittersweet ending to a relationship that had started as teacher and mentor many years ago. In my opinion, he was the prime example of someone in my family who turned on me when Clinton tempted him with a piece of the action when and if the estate of my mother came into play. The defections were complete and I was left with basically a clean house. I had no General Manager, no Sales Manager, no F&I Manager, and no Service Director. With a mountain of issues to tackle, I had become a one-man show. I needed to find some help.

Most people don't buy into the theory of Divine Intervention, but I had enough encounters with unexplainable happenings over the years, that I believed anything was possible. My faith in a higher power was renewed when I met Penny's boyfriend, Ryan, one day while he was visiting her in the office. I was immediately struck with the young man's demeanor and the strong handshake he presented when I first met him. Every reply was prefaced with a "Yes, Sir," or "No Sir." Needless to say, I knew right away that he wasn't from Danville. When Penny told me later he was from North Carolina, my interest was piqued. I asked her if he was employed and she said he was interviewing at several places. I told her to have him come in and see me.

Hiring Ryan was a no-brainer. He was a sharp, very polite Southern gentleman that easily won over anyone who met him. He rose quickly through the ranks in the next couple of years, going from salesman, to manager of F&I and then sales manager, to the ultimate position of general manager. Everyone liked Ryan. I thought to myself that he wasn't sent from heaven, but North Carolina would do.

To replace Benny and Jack, I hired two young men who had played baseball for me when they were kids, and a young man who had played basketball with Tucker in high school. To complete my staff, a very popular ex-athlete who was the eldest son of a friend of mine, came into the showroom from out of the blue and ended up with the sales manager's job. I always said former athletes made the best salesmen. My staff was complete. I had filled the vacant positions with youthful enthusiasm. The showroom was full of energy and fun again. Although I was now the old codger in the group, for the time being, at least, we seemed to have righted the ship. The Titanic had slipped by the iceberg.

Chapter Sixty-Five

A Mother's Gift

"Our death is not an end if we can live on in our children."

Albert Einstein

May 2003

The annual Saint James Tournament was scheduled for the last Wednesday of May. It was the culmination of months of work, of coordinating events, of accruing sponsors, of lining up golfers–every last detail was scrutinized to insure a smoothly run tournament that had taken on a reputation as one of the 'can't miss' sporting events of the year. As the prime organizer, my first responsibility was putting together a group of volunteers, headed by Katie, to assist in the myriad of duties that had to be perfect to provide our golfers and volunteers with a memorable day. My number one and only assistant was Paul, a retired state police investigator who had become a Deacon in the church. Together we made a great team. We only needed to have one meeting where we would divvy up repeat and potential sponsors to be contacted, and divide the ancillary tasks of securing signage and organizing competitions, trophies, presentations, raffles, etc. For three solid months, we worked countless hours putting the final touches on the tournament. It was like having a full-time second job. What made all our efforts worthwhile was the positive feedback we got from the golfers, and the knowledge that the church community was the beneficiary of a wonderful day while making a great deal of money for Saint James School. Our church pastor, Father John, was always delighted to have the opportunity to play scramble golf once a year with some dear friends. It was a big day for everyone associated with St. James. This year, however, was bound to be different.

In the late evening prior to the tournament, May 27, 2003, with Jaime, Chip, Clinton and me by her side, my mother, the matriarch of the Cassidy family, passed away quietly. We all hugged and for the briefest of time, we all got along. Ironically, in death, my mother had united the family. Going off for a moment by myself, I allowed my mind to wander back over the final months of my mother's life. In January, she had celebrated her eighty-ninth birthday. She appeared as sharp as always and in great spirits when she made her daily visits to the dealership. Martine loved to see her and the two became good friends. One day in March, Martine and I were talking to her when we noticed that Mom was repeating her stories. We looked at each other with concern but passed it off as a symptom of age. Days later she began to complain of headaches. A visit to her doctor led to tests, and subsequently to a diagnosis of an inoperable brain tumor. The days dragged on as she slowly regressed. When she was finally admitted to the hospital, it was discovered that she had contracted pneumonia as well. Her passing was not unexpected, but was still painful for each of us. You only get one mother, and we believed that we were all fortunate to have our mother bless our lives for eighty-nine years. I left the hospital in the early hours of the morning with a decision to make.

I rose early after a night of very little sleep with the heaviest of hearts. My thoughts were in disarray, as I had to make a choice whether to go on with the golf tournament. After discussing my options with Katie, Paul and Father John, I decided that I would go through with my role as tournament organizer and master of ceremonies at the awards banquet that followed the golf. I felt I had to put aside any personal feelings for one day and mask my emotions in an attempt to provide the golfers with another memorable golf tournament. It was my responsibility to create an atmosphere of revelry and good cheer. With those goals very much on my mind, I was determined to take part in the day's activities and the awards ceremony without announcing to the crowd that my mother had passed away the night before. I didn't think it was appropriate to cast a cloud over the tournament's proceedings.

My mother had been involved with Saint James Golf since the first year, five springs ago, when I asked her to be a sponsor. Her generosity in the community was well known and she established her role with the golf tournament early by becoming my first major sponsor. Her sponsorship included a team of golfers that was comprised of Jimmy and three of his friends. The Cassidys, as always, were well represented.

After a successful day on the course, I found myself sitting alone with my thoughts before the ceremony began. My inner grieving, which led to my sleep deprived night, was mitigated by the knowledge that my mother had lived a good life. She was well known for her effervescent personality and her devotion to her family. She was beloved by all who knew her. Although I struggled with the decision whether to partake in the tournament, I made the decision to do so because I knew she would have wanted me to. I just had to get through the banquet without losing control of my emotions.

Katie was concerned that I was taking on an impossible task. She knew how emotional I could become, yet she also knew how determined I was to put on a happy face. The ceremony went well until I had to announce the winners of the tournament. Ironically, Jimmy and his friends, playing in honor of my mother, won the first prize. When I presented them with first place money, they all hugged me and tears began to well up in my eyes. Jimmy took over the mike for a moment to allow me to compose myself. He had grown up to be a pretty special kid and I knew my mother was pleased and proud of the young man he had become. Recomposed, I thanked him for his words, which were selected carefully with regard for my wish for privacy. We were almost through the ceremony when Morton, a lawyer friend, who had been a sponsor from the beginning, asked to say a few words. As I sat down next to Katie and Father John, Morton began by thanking me for all my efforts in putting together this tournament every year. He then unveiled a plaque that he had personally brought before the Governor of Connecticut, John Rowland, declaring May 28th, 2003 as Sean Cassidy day in the State of Connecticut. Katie grabbed my hand knowing that such an honor would be difficult for me. The timing of the tribute was too much. I stood to accept the plaque with tears flowing down my eyes. I hugged Morton for his wonderful gesture then decided to make the announcement to the crowd that this award had special significance, particularly on this day, because my mother had passed away the night before. A hush came over the crowd. Everyone stood and gave me a standing ovation, a tribute I shared with my mother. Later on that evening, reflecting on the final moments of the banquet, it was clear to me that Mom was with me in spirit and that her presence would continue to be a blessing to all future Saint James golf tournaments.

Chapter Sixty-Six

The Thickening Plot

"Pride that dines on vanity, sups on contempt."
Benjamin Franklin

My mother's death brought a strange calm to the hostility that through the years had grown to a fever pitch between Clinton and me. I guess out of respect for the wishes of Jaime, he had acceded to the strong emotions that lingered throughout the family. Several weeks went by and out of the blue we received a bewildering invitation to join him and Jaime for dinner. The invitation caught Katie and me by surprise. We accepted, more out of curiosity than a desire to reestablish a relationship between us that had for so long been considered irreconcilable. My ever-positive wife imagined that the invitation was a gesture of good will, signifying their desire to patch up our differences and resurrect our family bond. My take on the invitation was less receptive and more prone to the image of the "spider and the fly." Whatever the motive, I convinced Katie that we should be cautious in our approach to this meeting.

The conversation remained light at dinner as most of the talk gravitated to anecdotes of the kids. Jaime had always been interested in the boys and, at times, she and Clinton travelled great distances to watch them play sports. They both were very encouraging about what the boys accomplished while being moderately supportive of their embattled coach. Somewhere along the way, a disconnection between the two families occurred. The innocuous dinner ended without any conversation about my mother's estate or the new corporation that had already begun to suck the blood out of the business. We left for home scratching our heads, wondering what was the purpose of this light-hearted dinner. Maybe, just maybe, they were laying the groundwork for a better relationship between our two families.

"You know, Katie, Clinton and I used to get along. He was a few years older, but we played a lot of tennis together. He was very competitive–like me–and sometimes our matches got a little too heated, but certainly nothing happened that could have been the cause of our feud. Do you remember when he used to do our taxes? He always seemed to have a need to know what we were making. Somewhere along the line, his interest in what we were doing became a crusade against me. In his view, I wasn't smart enough to be running a dealership. I wasn't good looking enough to be married to you. I wasn't a good enough athlete to be beating him at tennis. I was too cocky, too arrogant, and too successful. I don't know how it happened but I became the fall guy for whatever was wrong in his life. That was such a long time ago, but I guess his dislike for me grew into a vendetta."

"None of that showed up at dinner tonight. Maybe we should give them the benefit of the doubt. It would make everything a lot easier if we all got along."

"Katie, there's a place for you in the United Nations. Your world is all blue birds and lollipops. There's no room in your world for demons." With that final word about the gullibility of my wife, we arrived back home.

The following day, while Katie and I were eating lunch, the doorbell rang. It was an officer of the probate court with a subpoena to appear. Included in the paperwork was a lawsuit to recover funds from dealership accounts to enhance the shares of the petitioners of the estate, the dividend holders. Our brief honeymoon with Clinton and Jaime was over.

Chapter Sixty-Seven

Captain, We're Taking On Water

"Learn to live well . . . you played and loved, and ate, and drunk your fill; walk sober off; before a sprightlier age comes tittering on, and shoves you from the stage.
Alexander Pope

Like a Broadway play, the show must go on. In spite of the many subplots that had enveloped the future of the dealership, I owed it to my new enthusiastic staff to maintain a stiff upper lip and continue to operate without evidence of impending doom. Martine knew the severity of the problems we were confronting but I had confidence in her that such information would remain confidential. The screws of Clinton's master plan for the business were turning tighter and tighter, yet I was determined to continue to battle that which I had no control of. I was still in command of the ship, however that command was being undermined by a corporate squeeze. Profits or loss were no longer the main concern. Paying dividends, guaranteed by the new corporation, to fourteen shareholders on a monthly basis became the burden of necessity. As the months gathered and the total amount of the dividends increased, my one hope was a favorable outcome in probate court. It was a good thing for me that I somehow kept my sense of humor.

"Don't you wish you were my niece," I said to Martine as I entered her office to discuss the day's finances. "Just sit at home and make money every month without doing anything. It makes the last thirty years seem like a waste. I feel like a priest without a parish and no second collection to look forward to."

"I have to admit, Sean," Martine replied. "It must be great being a member of your family. Talk about the Golden Goose! I really don't think this is what your mother had in mind."

"Martine, I have to confide in you that the thought of selling and moving on to greener pastures, separated forever from the image of my family members with their hands out, is becoming more appealing. If it weren't for all the great people working here, including you, I would have bailed out long ago. Both boys are through with college and both our houses are paid for. Why am I killing myself to stuff the bank accounts of my relatives. You know I always use the Titanic as a reference for the troubles of the dealership. Well I think the reference is becoming more valid as I look at these bank statements. We're definitely taking on water. Whether we sink or not depends on the next few critical months. I've already convinced Katie that we're going to loan the business some of our personal money, but if the future continues to look bleak, I'm going to have to consider borrowing money. For thirty years, we've never had a mortgage on the building. Those days may be coming to an end."

"Sean, I'm sure your father would have wanted you to do whatever it took to keep the business going. Please don't worry about it. We don't need you back in intensive care."

"You're beginning to sound like Katie. It's reassuring that so many people are concerned with my health. The unfortunate thing is that none of those people are related to me. We'll do whatever is needed, Martine. Thanks for listening to my troubles. It always helps to know I'm not in this mess alone."

"We're with you, boss. All the way."

That afternoon, I heard a familiar voice out in the showroom. Paulie Petrone was visiting and he was in the middle of entertaining the new young guys with one his stories about his life in Providence. I had heard the story before, but I thought it was entertaining enough to listen to it again.

"So, I told my buddy, Dino, I wanted to feel what it was like to be shot. He got his shotgun, along with two fairly thick boards and the Providence phone book. I held the boards and the phone book against my chest and braced myself in front of Dino who was about two feet away. I told him to go ahead and shoot. The gun misfired. I relaxed, calling him every name in the book, when the gun suddenly went off. No longer bracing for the impact, the explosion knocked me across the room. Dino thought he had killed me, but other than a bunch of splinters and some buckshot imbedded in my chest, I was fine. We had a good laugh at that one."

The new guys were incredulous, not knowing whether to believe Paulie or not. I knew better because Dino had verified the story to me. Life in Providence was different than anything my guys had experienced growing up in Danville. Paulie's stories were always colorful, tainted with an Italian flavor and full of invectives. Nevertheless, he was always entertaining. He eventually came into my office, put his feet up on my desk and we began to chat.

"Sean, my good friend, I've got to tell you, the word on the street is your selling this place. What's happening? I heard something about a brother-in-law getting involved. What's really the story?"

"Paulie, you and I have become good friends over the years, so I'm not going to lie to you. Is there trouble in paradise? The answer is yes. Is there a solution to the trouble? That answer is still to be determined. We're still fighting the good fight. We'll see what the future brings."

"Sean, listen to me. I've got this friend. He's very persuasive. If you want I can talk to him. He's a big man, head like an anvil–he's great at negotiations, if you know what I mean. Maybe you'd like him to make a visit–you know, a social call to ..."

"Stop right there, Paulie. I appreciate your offer, but I'm afraid I'm going to have to refuse it. It's not my style, but keep his number handy in case I change my mind."

"Sean, give me a call anytime."

With that said, we shook hands and Paulie left. His visit reminded me of my father's riddled advice years before given by Polonius to Laertes in Shakespeare's Hamlet–"To thine own self be true." It also reminded me of all the various types of people I had gotten to know in the car business over the last thirty years. Some, like Paulie, were more colorful than others; a few, like the full mooners, were borderline crazy; some were dangerous; many were unforgettable; most were just good and honest folks who only wanted to be treated fairly. I decided that day that no matter what the outcome of the Probate, and the meetings with the lawyers, and the spats between family members, my commitment to this business and the thirty years spent in this building were all worth it. It had been a good ride.

Chapter Sixty-Eight

Sneak Attack

> "I have not observed men's honesty to increase with their riches."
>
> Thomas Jefferson

"Did you ever see the movie, *Twelve Angry Men?* It's an old black and white movie made back in the fifties about a group of jurors in a murder case. On the surface, the evidence seemed to dictate an easy verdict of guilty. The group consisted of twelve total strangers who were summoned together to decide the fate of this loser son who apparently had killed his father in a moment of rage. Although the evidence was strongly tilted against the accused, one member of the jury harbored some doubt and therefore blocked a unanimous guilty vote."

"Sean, we hardly have time for one of your movie reviews of old, forgotten movies. We're going to be late for the meeting."

"Hold on for a second, Katie. I'm getting to my point. The reluctant juror insisted that they go over the evidence again. In doing so, he convinced one, and then the others, that they might have made a rush to judgment. In the end, the most difficult juror to convince was the most irascible, a gentleman who obviously had some issues in his personal life that he had brought with him into the jury room. When he finally relented and provided the last vote for acquittal, the accused man was declared innocent of the crime. The point of the plot is that one man, demonstrating a voice of reason, can influence a whole group that are otherwise predisposed to a different outcome. Katie, tonight I plan to be that voice of reason. We're walking into an angry room. Clinton will have his followers fired up by promising them all kinds of rewards if they just go along with his leadership. It's like he's become the Reverend Jim Jones in the family and he's about to serve all of them the lethal mix of Kool-Aid."

"Sean, you can mix metaphors better than anyone I know. It's just a meeting. Don't get yourself all riled up over things that haven't even happened yet."

"Cool, calm and collected. That's me. Are the boys ready?"

"Yeah, we're cool, too, Dad," Jimmy answered. "We can't wait to see how calm and collected you remain."

The meeting was to be held in my lawyer's office. All fourteen of the beneficiaries of the estate were invited. To my knowledge, this would be the first time all parties would be informed of the terms of the Probate. The first order of the meeting was a question and answer period in which anyone could comment or question the executor. After a few moments, it became obvious that there had been previous secretive meetings between the beneficiaries outside my immediate family and Clinton. Seemingly, they had been schooled in carefully prepared responses. The tension immediately filled the room and my cool meter was rising to infuriated. When Katie asked a question, she was dismissed as uninformed by Clinton. Tucker's attempt at a question wasn't even considered worthy of an answer. It was becoming apparent that we were being ambushed. My lawyer, sensing the fury building in my quickly reddening face, called for a recess. During the break, while I was out of the room, Clinton came over to Katie and asked her if she understood everything. When I returned, she informed me of his condescending remark. When the meeting was called back into order, I stood up and outlined for Clinton and the rest of his flock, the credentials that my wife brought to the table. Not only was she a graduate of City of Boston School of Nursing, in Brighton, Massachusetts, but she also received her Bachelor of Science degree in Economics from Eastern Connecticut University where she graduated Magna Cum Laude. I stated that she was more than capable of understanding whatever dribble was put on the table by our executor with the two-year accounting degree. Katie saw how worked up I had become and reminded me of my promise to stay calm. My lawyer sensed an impasse in the meeting and called for an adjournment. My mother's estate had been in probate for more than two years. It was evident from this meeting that we were far from a suitable conclusion.

On the way home that night, I thought more seriously about selling the business. I didn't know to whom or even when, but I knew that the animus that had built up between Clinton and me would never subside and his intended interference in the business for personal gain would be a constant. I didn't mention my thoughts to Katie or the boys, but I knew I had their support. The days ahead would be full of reflection, indecision and remorse. My priorities had to change. I had always lived by the credo: God, family, business. My definition of family would now have to be modified to include: Katie, Jimmy, Tucker and their families. There was no need for me to question the love I had for my mother and father, but it was clear that my father's unfulfilled promise many years before to turn the business over to me, and my mother's reluctance to execute his wishes after his death, were the basis for the family discord on full display at the lawyer's office. Any decision to sell the business would be the result of those unrewarded assurances. I felt betrayed.

Chapter Sixty-Nine

Baxter's Advice

"The weak can never forgive. Forgiveness is the attribute of the strong."

Mahatma Gandhi

"Do you remember the bar on Commonwealth Avenue that had the pool inside? I loved it. It seemed like all the classy girls in Boston used to go there. The girls used to dress up to kill–short skirts, high heels and lots of makeup. And they all smelled great. What a place. Do you remember the name of that bar?"

Baxter had come over to visit. The boys were out and Katie and I were alone. We hoped that he wasn't there to convert us. Neither of us was ready for Baxter, the apostle. It appeared, however, that he had just come over to reminisce. We broke out the wine.

"That was *Flicks*, Bax. You were right. There were more gorgeous girls per square foot in that place than anywhere else in the city. I remember the night when a drunken guy made a pass at a girl and she bumped him into the pool. The bouncers had to double as lifeguards. It was a great club, but I always felt slightly out of place there. We weren't rich enough, cool enough or suave enough to make it in that place. But it was fun to people watch."

"Yeah, well we did pretty well in some of the other bars: *Ken's Pub, Bunratty's, The Point After, Brothers' Four.* We were legends in those places."

Katie decided to break in to our distorted look back on our good times in Boston.

"You guys were legends in your own mind. You should hear the two of you. You sound like Clark Gable talking to Cary Grant. Two old has-beens remembering who they thought they were in a world that no longer exists." She thankfully laughed at her own remark to save our bruised egos and then added: "You forget that I remember the two of you as you were. You were both adorable, and loveable, but you weren't movie stars. I'd rather have you guys just the way you are."

I turned to Baxter and said, "If I looked like Robert Redford, she'd be happy with that."

The three of us continued to drink and reminisce about life in Boston. We had shared many of the same memories and those memories were still vivid after all the many years away from the city. We talked about life at our apartment complex, Chandler Pond in Brighton, about our two canine roommates, Goldie and Sam, about our many friends in Boston and the numerous parties we hosted. Katie and I teased Baxter about his sordid past–his days as a bartender in some of the most notorious bars in the most dangerous sections of Boston, of his life on the edge, where everything and everyone seemed to be fair game. I kidded him about his busy social life that included a long relationship with a very sexy Italian stewardess, and many short-lived dalliances with a seemingly endless list of waitresses, strippers, and one really hot Boston ballerina. It was great to think back to those days when we had very little responsibility and a whole lot of fun. Baxter, after several glasses of wine, finally blurted out, "I wish I was in Boston again."

"Bax," I said, "I don't think Boston is ready for our return. It's much too exciting here where the average citizen is in bed by nine o'clock."

"That's what bothers me," he said. "I've become one of those average citizens. Life is going by too fast. What's next–babbling in a rocking chair?"

With that cheery thought, Katie said good night and went to bed.

"You know, Bax, you've made a remarkable turn-around in your life. You've gone from sinner to saint. I'm sure your father and mother would have been proud of that."

"Isn't it ironic, Sean. We spent so much time trying to get away from our parents and, now that they're gone, we miss them. I'd give anything to go ice fishing with my father again. And my poor mother put up with so much from me, and she never even knew the half of it."

"It's just as well our parents didn't know some of the things we did. It would have killed them at a much younger age. But, you're right, I miss my parents a great deal."

"What's going on with your mother's estate? Is it settled yet?"

"No. My relatives aren't finished picking my bones yet. Who would have thought that this mess would happen to my family?"

"What's going to happen next? Are you going to sell the dealership?"

"I think that's the only direction I can go. There will be too much outside interference by non-working family members to continue. With my heart condition and the headaches that come with the job, I think it's time to sell. The Golden Goose is going to take flight."

"How much do you hate your brother-in-law for causing this?"

"Hate's probably too strong a word, but I don't care for him much."

"Let me go out to my car and get my bible. There's a passage I want you to read."

"Baxter, Baxter, Baxter! You're not trying to convert me, I hope."

"Don't be silly. I just think you'll get a good feeling from reading this passage. I'll be right back."

I couldn't believe that with all we've been through together that I was turning to my born again little buddy for advice. One never knows from what direction comes the guidance we seek. With the help of many glasses of wine, I was, at least, willing to listen.

Baxter came back into the house and immediately opened the bible for me to read.

"Sean, read this passage from *Matthew 6.* Start with verse 14."

I read aloud the words of Matthew written centuries ago.

"For if you forgive other people when they sin against you, your heavenly Father will also forgive you. But if you do not forgive others their sins, your Father will not forgive your sins."

"This then, is how you should pray."

Our Father in heaven,
hallowed be your name,
your kingdom come,
your will be done,
on earth as it is in heaven.
Give us today our daily bread.
And forgive us our debts,
As we also have forgiven our debtors.
And lead us not into temptation,
But deliver us from the evil one.

I went to bed that evening with a weird buzz in my head; some of it I'm sure was the wine, but most was the realization that my path had been decided many centuries before. If I harbored any thoughts of revenge, I was giving in to the evil that caused those thoughts. To choose the path of forgiveness would be easy, knowing that my antagonist's fate would be in good hands. To seek revenge feeds the evil one; to forgive is divine. I received the message of forgiveness from the unlikeliest of messengers, my good friend, Baxter. Somehow, we had both survived our demons, our long list of indiscretions, and our propensity to enjoy the dark side. We had managed to find contentment in our lives. Baxter, of all people, had become the voice of reason that I had been seeking. There was great comfort in knowing that I had such a reliable friend as Baxter and so many blessings in my life. In spite of the family troubles of the past few years, I considered myself to be a most fortunate man, blessed with a good wife and great children and surrounded by the loyalty of a host of great friends. I slept soundly that night for the first time in many months.

Chapter Seventy

One Day at a Time

"Here's looking at you, kid."
Humphrey Bogart-*Casablanca*

2009

My quick trip to Miller Falls brought back some disturbing images of the last days of Cassidy Motors. It was in November of 2005 when Katie provided the final push in my decision to sell the dealership. Her emotional plea got my attention.

"Sean," she screamed in exasperation, "if you don't get out of this business, one of these days I'm going to find you dead at your desk. You're a bundle of raw nerves. With your medical history, it's just a matter of time before I'm a widow. Type A personalities usually don't last long when they're constantly put in stressful situations. I can't imagine being left behind to face all your relatives. It would be like a feeding frenzy and I would be the bait." She then laughed and said, "Is that dramatic enough? I hope you realize that life without you would be a circus. I need my warrior husband to fight these battles for me."

"Oh Katie, you know the funeral would be fun. All those fake expressions of sympathy would be quite a show. I'm sure everyone, especially Clinton, would be extremely comforting to you."

Katie realized the sarcasm that was dripping from my remarks and suggested we open a bottle of wine to calm her nerves. The wine was strong enough for Katie; I needed a glass of bourbon for this life-changing discussion. I was on my second glass when I said to her: "Another recession is coming; the value of the dealership will be plummeting; life as we know it will never be the same. I've been giving this a great deal of thought since the night of the meeting in our lawyer's office. I think our run is over. Now we have to suck it up, count our blessings and move on."

I raised my glass and proposed a toast. "Here's to my father, to my mother, and to the dealership. May the new ownership prosper, whomever that might be?" It was a solemn toast for we were drinking to the demise of our once proud family business.

The following morning I began the search process for a new dealer candidate. I sought out an aggressive buyer whose resources would be more than adequate for Chevrolet's strict financial requirements. After a surprisingly short period of time, I was fortunate to find a candidate who possessed impeccable credentials. The potential new buyer was a good deal younger than me and started out at a rival dealer when he was in his teens. He had already accomplished a great deal in his life, having acquired three other dealerships in the area. Because he had started with Chevrolet, he appeared to be infatuated with the idea of owning a Chevrolet dealership in a location close to his hometown. His solid financial backing resulted in a quick approval process, and made the transition from the old dealership to the new one, rapid and seamless. Chevrolet did require that I stay on for four months until the new owner was ready to begin his operation. I initially relished the time so I could say my goodbyes to our many friends and customers who had frequented our business over the years. The waiting period also allowed me time to ruminate about the thirty-five years I had spent in the building my father had built in 1974 with the goal of carrying on the Cassidy family business. I thought about the many people that I had employed over the years, and about the many episodes, good and bad, that I had shared with so many people. With each passing day, the countdown to the final moments of Cassidy Motors began to slow to a crawl. It was becoming very difficult to imagine the end.

Our years in the car business afforded Katie and I the chance to meet and befriend many wonderful people that would remain lifelong friends. It allowed us the opportunity to travel the world, enjoying our lifestyle while we nurtured our sons into wonderful young adults with goals and aspirations of their own. My one regret was that the boys would not have the opportunity, as I did, to operate the family business and keep the Cassidy name in perpetuity. But I took solace in the knowledge that God had a plan for each of us and by allowing our faith to supersede any feelings of disdain for those who contributed to the demise of the dealership, we would collectively continue on our way together with our love and respect for each other in tact.

As the final days approached, words from a Jimmy Durante song rang in my ears: "As the days dwindle down to a precious few." I realized that the final chapter of this story had been written and that a new story was about to begin. I would have to face uncertainty for the first time in thirty-five years, but I knew that with Katie by my side, we would go on–one day at a time. I knew it would be difficult to forget all the highlights and the lowlights that made our life so interesting. Our memories of the greatest times of our lives, when our very existence depended on the countless challenges and the decisions we often faced together, would live forever in our minds–memories too vivid to fade with the sale of the dealership. Indeed, there would be many times when I would drift off into thought and again imagine that I was back in the showroom.